Return to Calypso Station

Return to Calypso Station

Caenys Kerr

RED AVENTURINE PRESS

For my mother, Audrey Coombe, for her continued love and support
on my writing journey.

Acknowledgements

This story has come to light with the assistance of so many people, I fear I'll forget one or two. No matter whether you offered comments or simply listened to where the story was heading, thank you.

My friend, Carol, and her family who farm in central-western Victoria were quick to identify a problem easily fixed but would force a sudden pause to harvest in progress. My nephew, Jay, filled me in on what would happen to a low-slung vehicle travelling over a rutted track, and followed up with information about the weight of a fully grown eastern brown snake.

Comments from my reading team of Kathy, Alison, Jodi and Audrene confirmed that mateship within a military setting can, at times, turn toxic; that a small flock of Saxon sheep is feasible if husbanded well; and they offered a suggestion for a sex scene (it didn't happen.) The team warned me, too, that a damaged character like Nash would be confronting for some readers. I hope you'll see beyond his surface behavior to find the man he really is and understand why Danielle loves him.

Finally, I must thank my family. They celebrated with me when the story received wonderful feedback from competition judges; commiserated when rejections came from publishers and encouraged me to see the positives like presenting the opportunity to publish it myself. The uncompromising nature of their love and support is magnificent and I return it tenfold.

Contents

Chapter One

"Face your demons! Set them running like cowardly bullies!"

The words of his early army instructor chanted their mantra through Nash Broderick's head. Strange they should resurrect themselves now, here in the haunt of invincible enemies.

He loosened the death grip he held on the steering wheel, eased himself from the black convertible and stood, noting the changes time wrought on the place where he'd been born and raised.

It felt like home—the crackle of dry grass beneath his feet and the closeness of the atmosphere. He breathed in the air. It smelled like home—the fragrance wafting from sun on the gums and the tangy freshness of sheep not too far away.

He saw himself here in little things like the fence he'd built with his grandfather, and the pride he'd earned for a job well done. The main post listed now in a way that would horrify his perfectionist Granddad. He'd make sure to fix it before he left.

His heart swelled. He belonged here, where his forebears stood before him. They'd named the place 'Calypso Station' commemorating the ship that gave them safe passage to make a fresh start in Australia.

Growing up, he'd loved every corner of this piece of heaven. He'd loved the people, his parents, his grandparents, his sister Cassie—and Danielle.

Danielle Dawn... In his mind's eye, he saw a skinny girl with an amazing grin and long, light brown hair darting towards him from the corner of the house.

She was the reason he hadn't come home, and she was the torment stopping him from taking up his father's legacy, from coming back permanently to run the place in the way his father and his grandfather did.

Shattered dreams of forever love tainted this corner of the world and he, sure as hellfire, wouldn't willingly revisit that place of humiliation. With luck, Danielle and the child she bore to another man were long gone from the area.

His heart clenched, and unexpected and unwanted tears stung behind his eyes. He blinked hard squishing them away.

Him and Danielle—even now her name conjured the dreams of his youth and the want and need of his body for hers. He'd loved her wholly, body and soul, and then...

Nash slammed the door of the car hard, closing off the wave of memories trying to escape their incarceration, hefted his duffle and tromped to a cream, Federation-style farmhouse with green roof and green-trimmed windows.

Gravel crunched under his feet and dust sprinkled over the brilliant sheen of his army dress shoes until he reached the five meters of grassy verge surrounding the building. He grabbed the railing, propelling himself up the few steps and onto the veranda.

The whump of a tail banging wooden planks drew his attention to an aging border collie resting under the love seat to his right. "Hey, Nell. Is that you?" Walking over, he scratched the scruff of the dog in the way she'd loved as a pup. He sat on the seat and Nell eased herself to her feet to rest her head on his knee. "It's good to see you, girl," he grasped the dog's ears and peered into her face. "Have you been looking after the place here? Yeah, of course, you have. A bit slower than you used to be, eh? You got an offsider to take up the slack? I guess I'll find out. Is Grandma home?"

The dog swiveled her head to the door of the house.

"Right, then. I'll go say hello."

He stood, patted the dog's head, straightened his jacket, and approached the screen door protecting the interior of the house. He hesitated. Should he knock since he'd been gone so long? The pause was brief. He banged twice on the door frame, swung open the screen and yelled, "Grandma?"

A short, rotund, grey-haired vision moved from the kitchen and across the hall towards him as if it wanted to bustle but couldn't quite work up the speed.

"Nash? Good grief man, are you trying to give me another heart attack?"

He didn't wait for her to finish. Instead, he dropped his bag and bent his considerable height to engulf her in a bear hug. "Ah, Grandma, I've missed you."

Anna Broderick pushed herself from his arms and looked up. Her soft blue-grey eyes misted as she whispered, "I've missed you too, child."

It was a long time since anyone called Captain Nash Broderick a child, and only this woman could survive referring to him as such.

They studied each other, assessing inevitable differences. Anna's face showed more wrinkles than when he'd left, but the twinkle in her eyes and the love radiating from her were the same.

Anna broke the silence. "I'll bet someone told you I was at death's door." She grimaced. "Well, I'm not. Don't go looking for imaginary troubles when there are enough real ones in the world. Come on in and I'll put the kettle on."

He grinned. *Nothing changes.* His sense of self had been born in this house and developed in the home a couple of hundred meters further west—in the place his parents built when he was little.

"Who was it?" His grandmother spoke over her shoulder. "Cassie or one of your aunts?"

"All of them. I couldn't keep up with the texts. I took Aunty Abby's message with a grain of salt but when Aunty Jenn and Aunty Siobhan both followed, I got worried." He carried his duffle through and dropped it next to the table.

"No Cassie?"

"Yep. She was the one who changed the scratching at the door to a full-on mortar assault. Cassie doesn't panic. If she was weighing in, something serious was going down. What happened, Grandma?"

"Ah, silly really. I wanted to wash the windows, but the universe nixed the idea by knocking me down when I hauled the big ladder from the shed."

"Why didn't you ask for help? You can pay someone to do windows. Don't you have a manager or a workman or someone on the property? Or Cassie? I called into the Children's Centre on the way through. She's fit and healthy."

"She is and she has her own work to do. Frank's still the workman, but I've always cleaned my windows. This time shouldn't have been any different. No point to ask someone else to do what I'm quite capable of handling. Don't you fret, dear. I learned my lesson. I'm hale and hearty now. Tell me about you. What are you doing these days? How long can you stay?" She spun to answer the demand of the whistling kettle and poured the water into a porcelain teapot.

Nash pulled out a seat at the table and lowered his long frame into it, buying time to sort through his answer to the questions. When he got the last text from his sister, Cassie, he'd applied for, and been granted, three months' leave from the Army. She said Grandma was doing better but the heart attack was serious. So, he'd come. If his grandmother truly was as well as she insisted, he might not need the whole period of leave and he should head back to Canberra. On the other hand, driving through town and in the farm gates exerted a pull on him he didn't anticipate.

He had three months. In a tactical situation, three months could be a lifetime or a flutter of eyelashes.

"I've been in Strategic Planning in Canberra for some time now. It's a great experience working with people from across the Australian Defence Forces."

"You were in Afghanistan a while ago, weren't you, when your grandfather died?"

He grimaced. "Yep. Two tours." He didn't want to talk about the war. It wasn't just the fighting, the heat of the desert, the death he'd dealt with in those days, but the personal war too. He volunteered both times from the belief if Danielle forgot him so easily, then everybody else would too. He wouldn't be missed. Dumb luck kept him alive.

"Did my letters arrive?" Nash asked.

"Mmm. They didn't say much, you must admit, but they let me know you were alive."

There was nothing for him to say.

"I figured your stint in the Army would be a short-term thing. I figured you for a country boy and you'd be home soon." Anna narrowed her eyes.

"You know why I didn't come home, Grandma." His face darkened, and he flicked his unfocused gaze to the opposite side of the room. "The Army's been good to me. But it wouldn't take much to turn me country again." Nash tilted one corner of his mouth.

"Good. If I die and you're still away, there would be no reason for Calypso's remaining trustees not to redistribute the land to actively farming Brodericks—your uncle and your cousins."

"Uncle Sean wouldn't let that happen." Fear curled in the pit of Nash's gut. This was his legacy. His home. No one had the right to deprive him of it. He recalled his father saying something along the lines of there always needing to be a Broderick on Calypso when he was much younger, but the likelihood of the caveat being actioned seemed remote then. His father and his grandfather would be here to look after things.

"Times have been tough," Anna said. "We're keeping our heads above water here and so are your cousins. For now, they're happy to let things ride. I'm here and we're still working the land. Sean and the boys come and help us with harvest and shearing and we go over and help them, but a financial boost from the extra land on Calypso would help them tremendously. You'd get your severance package, of course—the same as your sister and your aunts—but you'd have no further claim on the land and neither would your children."

Nash raked a hand through his hair while his mind absorbed the implications of what his grandmother said. It could be the end of everything he'd looked forward to, everything he'd planned with Danielle.

"Enough of that. We're doing okay for now," Anna said, dismissing the topic. "Tell me, is there anyone special in your life?"

"Nope. Just friends." Even now, Danielle crossed his mind. Best not to open that door. Danielle made her choice years ago and there was a child to show for it. Besides, she meant nothing to him now. He'd convince himself of the fact, even if it killed him.

~ * ~

Anna recognized sadness and loneliness in Nash's dark blue eyes—a giveaway to those who knew him as she did, but easily overlooked if a person looked no further than the tough military bearing Nash conveyed to everyone else. There'd been fear there too, when she reminded him of the lien over the land that her husband's grandfather had laid down generations ago.

Her heart wept for the boy who'd been full of laughter and mischief as a young man and prepared to take on the world for his Danielle Dawn.

He was the son of her son and so much in love with the girl.

"What you need is some fresh air! Come, take a walk with me. I love to wander about at this time of the day, but the family worries if I'm not within coo-ee of the phone. Ever since the heart attack, they have conniptions if I don't pick up within the first three rings and I hate using the mobile phone Robbie gave me. But Cassie knows you're here." She chuckled.

She grabbed a wide-brimmed straw hat from the bench at the back door and negotiated the steps with one hand on the railing. Old Nell wandered across to join her. Nash bent to scratch the dog's head when she nudged his leg. Nash was always the dog's favourite.

"We've made some changes in the years since Gordon died," Anna plonked her hat atop her head. "Even when he wasn't well, your grandfather kept control of the farm. With him gone, we've learned and re-learned a lot to keep the place manageable and productive."

"You still have your chooks." Nash strolled with her in the direction of the large, fenced run where a dozen Australorp chickens stopped pecking at the ground to observe the intruders.

"Oh, I couldn't do without them. I give them the kitchen scraps and a bit of feed and, in return, they give me up to eight eggs a day—enough to keep us going." She scanned the area. A big smile bloomed on her face. She passed a hand along his forearm.

"Do you remember the time when the big rooster got out? He chased you around the paddock for ages. You were such a wee thing, five years old, and the rooster was huge."

"I remember." Nash's smile broadened to match Anna's. "Bertram! He terrified me for weeks afterward." He draped an arm around her shoulders.

She dug her elbow into his ribs. "It didn't stop you. You collected the eggs every morning carrying a big bit of cardboard to ward off the beast. I was proud of you. You didn't let him beat you." She tilted her head against his chest.

"Didn't a fox get Bertram soon after?"

"Yep. Bertram was always escaping the run. He strutted around, lord of all he surveyed, until the night the fox came. Ah well. You found the new rooster much more friendly." She chuckled.

She kept up a stream of conversation as they wandered across the most accessible sections of the property. Nash prompted with a question here and there. Anna didn't find it difficult to infer the love of farming burned strongly within him.

What she did find difficult was reconciling this with his long period of self-imposed absence. Denying responsibility for Dee's child was one thing, but hiding away from it, didn't seem like the thing he would do. He'd always been Dee's protector and loved her to the end of the earth.

Once he went to Canberra, things changed. She didn't know why. He wouldn't allow Dee's name to be mentioned. He shut down a conversation, no matter who was speaking, if anyone alluded to her. People learned not to refer to her in any way.

Country people had a way of letting things be. If Nash didn't want to talk about her, that was his business. They wouldn't push. It remained so for more than six years long years.

For Nash to act as though Danielle or her son didn't exist? Things didn't add up.

A billow of dust heralded the arrival of a large vehicle on the dirt verge of the main road bordering the property.

"Oh, Lordy. Is that the time already? Quick! I have to meet the children!" Anna scurried towards the house.

They arrived at the back gate as a tousled dark-haired boy banged his way out the back door with a miniature of himself in tow.

"Anna Nana? Where are you?"

"Hold your hair on Brodie. I'm showing Nash around the place. He hasn't been home for a long time."

"We were worried." The boy stopped dead, eyeing the stranger suspiciously. "Who's he?"

"Nash is my grandson, Aunty Cassie's brother."

"Aunty Cassie said her brother would be here. I expected a kid." The boy glowered at the man.

"He's all grown up, now. Because he's Aunty Cassie's brother, you can call him Uncle Nash." Anna's heart contracted as she issued the directive knowing the true relationship between the two.

"Okaaay, Anna Nana. Jacob hurt his arm on the door of the bus. I think you should look."

Anna smiled inside. This youngster was a protector. He behaved like he was much older than his nearly six chronological years.

"Who is Brodie?" Nash asked.

"Brodie? He's Dee's boy."

Nash tensed. "Danielle is in Hamlet Brae?"

"Oh yes. She lives here on Calypso. She's the manager. I put her in your parents' place."

"And this one?" He pointed to Jacob. "Is this her second?"

"Jacob is Cassie's. Haven't you kept up to date with anything?"

Nash frowned at her. "I knew Cassie had a child. I'm not a totally insensitive older brother. These two are identical."

"Yep. Blood will out," she shrugged.

Chapter Two

Danielle Tillson flexed her tired shoulders. She'd been late to bed last night making sure her lessons were well-planned for the day. Then, she had Bill Henderson's funeral thrown into the mix—a funeral in the middle of a school day during a critical stage in her final placement.

The principal of a city school might have questioned her commitment to teaching when she asked for a two-hour lunch break to continue her funeral celebrant role to see off one of the town's most prominent citizens, but not Margaret Ranley. She intimated Dee might need to do an extra day at the end of the placement to make up the time, but she gave her blessing for Dee to undertake the community task. An extra day at school was no punishment for Dee. She loved the whole experience of being in the classroom.

Mourners ambled from the town's scrappy-looking cemetery where tilted old headstones surrounded by straggly long, brown grass, contrasted with the newer, clean lines of graves, with embedded plaques, created in the last ten years. Dee barely registered their departure.

Minutes before the ceremony started, she took a call from her best friend, Cassie. The news she imparted, of Nash's return, was a shock. Like death and taxes, the reality was alarming, no matter how well she'd prepared. She gathered her gear and climbed into her truck.

Nash had to come home sometime. His self-imposed exile would end eventually. He'd wanted the Broderick legacy, to rebuild 'Calypso

Station'. She and Nash planned to do it together. Instead, since his grandfather's death, Dee and Anna kept the farm going.

Dee worked hard on the property to ensure the property and the house both were in good order when Nash returned.

Oh, how she'd loved him.

Now he was here.

Driving into Anna's front yard, later in the day, she braced herself. Forewarned is forearmed, they say. She could treat him like any one of Anna's distant relatives travelling through. It didn't have to be personal.

She climbed the steps to the landing and in the front door.

The two boys were lying on their stomachs playing with a small train set Dee bought for Brodie last Christmas. At her entrance, they looked up and Brodie waved one hand. "Hi, Mum."

"Hey!"

Dee continued to the kitchen where Anna was preparing a meal.

"Hi, Anna. You okay here?"

"All good, Dee. How did the funeral go?"

"It was good. With Bill gone, I don't think Edith will be the doormat everyone thinks she is."

"You're right. She was a hellion back in the day. It'll be good to see her get her spirit back." Anna chuckled even as her hands continued with her task.

Dee propped a hip against the kitchen counter. "I'll grab Brodie and go home to prepare for tomorrow. I can take Jacob too if you like. They can look after each other while I work."

"Let's work the other way around, Honey. You leave Brodie here and Cassie can drop him over when she collects Jacob. The boys can eat with us and you can do what you need to do."

"Sounds like a plan. I'll tell Brodie." She went back to the lounge room.

"Hey Little Bit, Anna Nana will keep you here with Jacob until Aunty Cassie comes. Okay?"

"What are you doing?"

"The usual."

"Boring," Brodie sang. "I'll stay here."

Dee stuck her head back through the opening to the kitchen. "Thanks, Anna. I'll catch you tomorrow, then."

"Fine, child. Don't work all night!"

Dee laughed. "It'll take as long as it takes, won't it?" Dee recited a chant Anna often drummed into Cassie, Nash, and herself.

"Go on with you!" Anna admonished.

Dee laughed again and turned back to Brodie. "Got a kiss?"

The boy bounced up, gave her a quick hug and a kiss and was back at his place beside Jacob. "Love you, Mum," he called over his shoulder.

Dee's smile slipped. The hair stood up on the back of her neck. Nash was behind her. She closed her eyes to breathe him in. She rotated her body with care to find him filling the cavity leading to the bedrooms.

Oh, God! It really was him. A swarm of bees buzzed in her head and tears stung her eyes. *Come on, you knew he was here. Pull yourself together.*

Six and a half years of not seeing him and he stopped her heart. His face was all hard angles, and his heart-throb blue eyes were missing their trademark cheeky sparkle, but her body reacted to him as though their time apart didn't happen.

"Hello, Danielle." The rumble of his voice with those two words reignited all the memories she kept locked away. The vibration of his tones resonated with something deep inside her. She wanted to hold him—badly.

She hooked her thumbs on the waistband of her trousers behind her back. "Nash. You're looking well." The words forced themselves past a boulder in her throat.

Brodie sprang up again and ranged himself beside his mother, drawing the man's attention. She hugged her son close with one arm.

"This is your boy?" His body was a study in leashed power.

Dee lifted her chin. "Yes, he's mine."

"You okay, Mum?" Brodie's concerned face turned to his mother.

She ruffled Brodie's hair. "Sure am. Have you met Nash?"

"Yeah." Brodie's tone was dry as he flicked a warning sideways glance at the man.

Dee swallowed. "Well, I'll be off. Things to do. You be good for Anna Nana, Little Bit. Bye, Nash." She gave Brodie's shoulders a squeeze and fled the house. Her heart was pounding. She felt like a nervous schoolgirl with the big bad wolf on her tail. And, hellfire, wasn't that the truth...

~ * ~

Nash found himself at the front door, following the path Danielle took. *Fuck! She's still got me on a string.* He took two strides across to the love seat on the veranda and sat down, watching her stride to her vehicle. His jaw clenched—hard.

As she did earlier, Nell eased her body from beneath the furniture and rested her chin on his knee. His fingers tangled in the dog's black and white coat as his gaze tracked the retreat of Danielle's ute.

She was here—on Calypso. Nash's heart sank. There would be no escaping her—the source of his heartbreak and humiliation.

Six years or more, and she was as beautiful as ever. Her body was rounded in all the right places. Freckles dotted her nose the same as always, like she hadn't aged a day since he left.

She was his life, his inspiration, his reason to go make his mark and come home again.

"Except it didn't happen that way, did it, girl?" He drew his hand the length of Nell's spine. "She found someone new in no time flat. A fly-by-nighter who left her up the creek and up the duff." A heavy sigh escaped him. "I'd only been gone a month."

He cried like a baby when he learned she was carrying another man's child and wanted nothing more to do with Nash. He couldn't eat, couldn't sleep—he was a total wreck. And she'd sent her Dear John as a fucking message through someone he'd only known a few weeks.

Nell turned her face to him as though acknowledging his pain. "Yeah. You can't believe it either, can you, girl? Then she had the gall to change her mind about the truckie and claim the baby was mine." He'd never have believed her to be a liar until that day—the day she played on his love for her to whitewash her betrayal. She left him shattered.

Emotion was not something expected of a fresh Army officer cadet. It cost his friends a shitload of effort to drag him from the mire and back into training. Thank God. He gritted his teeth. If they weren't there for him, he'd have nothing. He couldn't come home and there was nowhere else to go. He'd learned his lesson. Danielle wasn't to be trusted. "History, eh girl?" He smoothed one hand over the dog's head.

Brodie dashed through the door carrying a soccer ball and leaped down the steps. Nash's gaze sharpened on the child. He was unwilling to process the sensations whizzing through him—a longing the child should have been his, rejection of the boy for the perfidy he embodied, the wrench of dreams misplaced, even dismay at the kid's easy dismissal of him.

The boy's features were familiar. He looked so much like Jacob, they must be related. Who was his father? There was a mystery here and he would get to the bottom of it. He spent his working life unearthing and unravelling secrets, he'd do it here, too.

Chapter Three

Late on Friday afternoon, Dee made her way to Cassie's home. Robbie pulled into the driveway at the same time.

"How's my favourite unrecognized sister-in-law?"

Dee gave him a hug. "With Nash back in town, you'd better keep such comments under your hat."

"Have you talked to him about Brodie?"

"Nope. No intention of doing so."

Robbie widened his eyes. "Are you sure that's wise?"

"Brodie is mine," she said. "Nash opted not to be part of the parenting thing."

They walked together into the home's entryway. Dee stopped with the boys and Robbie moved further into the house.

"Hey Little Bit, time to go. Get your gear ready. I'll say hello to Aunty Cassie."

"Aw Mum! Jacob and I are doing something."

"Then get it finished quickly."

Dee strolled to find Cassie where she was bustling around the kitchen.

"Robbie's gone to the back fridge to get some wine. You've seen him?" Cassie asked.

"Your lovely husband? Of course. We came into the house together," Dee grinned.

"Not him! Nash. Did you introduce Brodie?"

Dee's mouth twisted to one side. "Anna did already."

"It's funny. He seems to be angry with you. Shouldn't it be the other way around? After all these years, I can't understand why he walked away from you. Are you sure he was aware you were pregnant?"

"Yes," Dee sighed. "When I couldn't get hold of him on his mobile, I rang the barracks number and left a message with one of his fellow officer cadets, a Canadian, she sounded like. She was lovely and said she would get a message to him where he was training. When I rang the next day, she said she'd told him, and he'd told her to tell me not to phone again. So, yes, he knew!"

"She might not have been telling the truth."

"Cassie, you were with me when I tried again later, remember?"

Cassie was chewing her lip. "Uh huh, I remember. I couldn't believe what he said about the baby not being his."

"And he wasn't available to be a convenient daddy for my bastard? Me either. I tried again a couple of days later, on his mobile, and I got, 'This number is disconnected.'"

"He would never let me talk about you. It was awful. We were all close till he went into the army. You and Nash, me and Robbie—we were a team." She drew her brows into a distressed frown.

"Enough of Nash. How was your day?"

"Usual, no dramas. You? One more week on your placement to go." She grinned. "In a couple of months, you'll be a fully qualified teacher!"

"You're a teacher too."

"I have a husband who made sure I had everything I needed along the way."

"And I've got a best friend and her husband!" Dee laughed as Robbie came into the kitchen holding a bottle of local white wine.

"Drink?" he asked waggling the bottle.

"I'll take a rain check. Can we do it tomorrow after I finish?"

"I'll hold you to it." He reached into a cupboard for glasses.

"You're working on the property tomorrow?" Cassie asked.

"Yep. There's plenty to do."

"Would you like to drop Brodie here? He's no trouble and the boys look after each other," Cassie said.

"He's been with you all afternoon. I can't ask you to keep doing that." Dee frowned.

"Because Brodie's been here, there's not been a peep out of Jacob. He's usually whining around my legs by this hour of day. Such a day tomorrow would be lovely."

"Okay, if you're sure. It'll be early though," Dee warned.

"No problem. Leave him in his PJs and I'll get him dressed with Jacob after breakfast. Can you drop this prescription into Grandma on your way home?" Cassie handed over a white paper bag with the local pharmacist's logo on it.

"No problem. Catch you tomorrow. Ready, Little Bit?"

~ * ~

Driving into Anna's place Dee was on tenterhooks lest Nash should be around. There was no sign of his car in the driveway and she heaved a sigh of relief.

She sat with Anna sat over a quiet cup of tea until they heard a car pull into the area at the front of the house and heavy footsteps passing through the house and down the hall towards the bedrooms. The women looked at each other in silence, each in an attitude of having an ear cocked to hear what was going on.

Clearly Nash didn't want to be sociable. That suited Dee.

Brodie burst into the kitchen startling both women into giving a slight jump where they sat.

"Anna Nana, will you help me with my costume for Jacob's and my birthday party? I want to be a pirate."

"I surely will."

"Great." The boy leaned an elbow on her thigh. "Mum tries hard, but her costumes are never as good as yours."

"Let me have a think about it," Anna said. Apparently satisfied, the boy retreated to the lounge room.

Anna cocked her head again, this time in her thinking pose. "I've got an idea for Brodie's costume. Could you pop down to my room and find my old kilt pin? Not the MacGregor one, the other one. It's plain—a straight sword, sort of thing."

"In your jewelry case?"

"I'm not sure. It might be in the jewelry roll in my knickers drawer."

"I'll have a look." Dee moved her chair back from the table and stood.

"If you can't find it, give me a yell and I'll come and help."

Dee padded down the hall, past the closed door to Nash's old room. She scrabbled for a few minutes through the mess of bracelets and necklaces tangled together with earring shanks in Anna's jewelry box. *I must help her tidy this one day.*

Finding neither kilt pin, she moved to the drawer Anna suggested. Locating the beautifully embroidered jewelry roll, she drew it out and lay it on top of the dresser to unfurl it. It had a large single pocket at the back, three smaller zipped compartments and a finger thickness roll for storing rings. Dee looked first in the zippered compartments without success and moved on to the larger pocket. Here she found most of Anna's prized brooches. She smiled at the memories these evoked of the occasions when Anna deemed an occasion was worthy of one of these precious items.

This was where Dee found both the MacGregor pin and the plainer one Anna asked for.

She set it aside, rolled the jewelry bag into its former shape and replaced it in the drawer. She took hold of the pin as a harsh voice spoke from the doorway.

"Find what you're looking for?"

"Nash! You startled me." The blood pounded through her veins at the sight of him.

"Guilty of something, Danielle Dawn?" Only Nash called her Danielle Dawn. It was something special between them. She was his Danielle Dawn. Now he used it as a sneer.

"Show me what you've got," he said.

"Why?" Her stomach dropped.

"It seems to me you have the run of the place here and you know how infrequently my grandmother visits her jewelry roll. What did you think, Danielle? A piece here and there would never be missed?"

Dee's body shook. This was the reaction she felt the night the police showed up to take her away from where she was living alone as a four-teen-year-old. A sense of getting into trouble for anything nauseated her ever since. Nash knew it.

In most other circumstances, she would fight back, but being made to feel she was in the wrong, somehow, always made her want to throw up.

"Show me!" He stepped into the room and filled the space. With her body against Anna's dresser, there was no retreat. He took her hand from her side and unfolded it to reveal the pin.

"Not the most expensive piece, Danielle Dawn. Clever. Let's see what my grandmother has to say. Come along."

Back in the kitchen, Anna held a child-sized black Akubra Dee recognized as being one of Cassie's. Anna looked up with a smile.

"Did you find it?"

Dee swallowed. "Nash has it."

Anna's eyes focused on Dee's white face. "Goodness, child. Whatever is the matter? You're white as a ghost."

Dee held back a spurt of tears. "I'll go out the back for a minute." She took herself outside and sat on the back step, out of sight of the occupants of the kitchen. She put her head in her shaking hands and swallowed convulsively. Did he really think she was a thief? That she could steal from Anna? Really?

From inside the house, she heard Anna exclaim. "What? Of course she has the run of the place. There's no one I trust more. Dee has never let me down, never, not since the very first night Bill Hamilton dropped her at our door." The low rumble of Nash's voice said something in reply she couldn't make out, then there was silence.

Anna always had her back. Dee breathed deeply to settle her nerves, stood, and walked into the kitchen. She resumed the seat she vacated when she went looking for Anna's pin. The tea was cold, but she sipped it anyway, focusing on Anna's hands where she was working with the hat and ignoring Nash's brooding presence. Anna turned up one side of the hat and fastened the pin to it. It looked like a black version of a slouch hat – with the kilt pin in place of the rising sun emblem of the Australian Army. She wondered if Nash saw the similarity.

"I'll be working down in the sheds tomorrow. I'm taking Brodie into Cassie's. I'll drop him off and be back bright and early," Dee said to Anna.

"Yay!" Brodie's voice came from the doorway. He edged past Nash and came to lean an elbow on the table beside her. Like a switch being triggered, Brodie's presence restored her sense of self. She smiled at him, a real smile. Nash left the room.

"Can I stay all day?"

"That's the plan, because we women have a farm to run." Dee dropped an arm on his shoulders.

"Can I take my togs?"

"May I... and yes you may, but it will be up to Aunty Cassie to decide whether it is warm enough for you to go for a swim."

A mischievous look shadowed across Brodie's face.

"What are you up to?" she asked, squinting her eyes at him.

The look was gone, and innocence replaced it. "Nothing, but Uncle Robbie likes to go for a swim even when it's freezing. I'll ask him instead of Aunty Cassie."

"Like someone else I know," Anna said, tilting her head in the general direction of where Nash was likely to be. "Always looking for the best strategy to get what they want."

"Yeah. Right," Dee said, her heart plummeting. Nash certainly got her when he wanted her. When the want was over, so was she. She wouldn't fall for it again, no matter how much her heart and body wanted him.

"I've set him straight, by the way," Anna said, setting the hat to one side. "It's going to take some time to get to the bottom of what's going on with him, I think. Just keep your cool, honey."

Easier said than done when head and heart pulled her in two different directions. "Are you ready to go, Little Bit?" Brodie nodded and bounded over to the older woman and gave her a hug and a kiss. "I love you, Anna Nana. Heaps!"

The beaming smile he turned on both women made Dee's heart melt. His face was endearingly reminiscent of the younger version of the man who'd stood there bristling with indignation. Her stomach clenched.

"Love you too. See you later, you two," Anna said.

Walking ahead of Brodie, Dee whistled for her dog, Meggs, a red kelpie, who came flying around the corner and into the tray of the ute and on into her travelling cage before Dee and Brodie made it to the truck.

Dee was grateful Nash had slunk off into some other part of the house. She'd likely want to punch him in the gut if she saw him again today.

Chapter Four

Brodie bounced into the kitchen on Saturday morning while Dee was pouring her coffee.

"Hey Mum. Mwah!" The kiss that landed on Dee's cheek was a happy start to the day and a restorative remedy for her sleepless night.

"What's got you pumping this morning? I usually have to drag you out of bed."

"Not on Saturday and not on a Saturday at Aunty Cassie's house."

"It's not six o'clock yet. Do you want to have a shower and get dressed here rather than at Cassie's?"

"Okay. What time are we going?"

"I don't want to arrive before six thirty. You have plenty of time. Have you decided what you want to take with you—games, snacks to share?"

"All sorted Mum, and I've packed my togs too." His grin was a little devilish and a lot like his father's.

"Would you like some breakfast before you go?"

"Uh-uh. Maybe a piece of toast. Aunty Cassie does an amazing breakfast on Saturdays. I don't want to spoil it. I'll go and have my shower."

"Cold tap first!" The habitual warning slipped out and garnered the equally habitual roll of Brodie's eyes as he bounded toward the bathroom.

He returned to the kitchen as the toaster popped its comforting load. "Jam, honey or vegemite?"

"Vegemite, please. What are you doing today?" Brodie asked, sliding onto a bar stool.

"Me? Frank and I will check the shearing shed and the holding pens."

"Will I be big enough to help next year?"

"At the rate you're growing, my boy, you might be big enough next month!" Dee ruffled his hair. "You ready to go?"

"Yep."

"Clean your teeth," she ordered, turning to load their plates into the dishwasher.

"Why? I'll eat again at Aunty Cassie's."

"So you have a nice fresh breath when you say good morning to everyone," Dee conjured.

"Can we go then?"

At Dee's nod, the boy jumped from the bar stool at the kitchen counter and fled down the hall. The teeth cleaning event must have lasted all of fifteen seconds because he was back in record time, backpack in hand and heading for the door.

Dee flicked her battered straw panama from the hat stand and folded the brim without conscious thought. She would have preferred an iconic Aussie Akubra but the panama would have to do for now. She whistled for Meggs, and followed Brodie to the car.

As they pulled into Cassie's driveway, Cassie herself came to the door. "Thank God, you're here at last. Jacob has been up since five-thirty wanting to know when you'd get here." Cassie grimaced.

"You should have texted me. We've been marking time. Brodie was up early too. He said he was hanging out for your usual Saturday brekky."

Cassie's laughed. "Brekky's under way. Join us?"

"No thanks, but I'll take time this arvo."

"Great. Thanks for bringing the babysitter! See ya."

Dee waved and climbed into the cab of the ute, smiling to herself with the knowledge Brodie was loved and wanted.

She drove to the back gate at Anna's, released Meggs from her travelling cage and allowed her to jump down to sniff around Anna's yard and dash off to find Old Nell.

Dee stomped up the four steps, dropped her hat on the bench seat on the back veranda and slipped into the kitchen.

Nash was sitting at the table reading something on a tablet. He looked up as she entered and frowned.

"Nash," she acknowledged briefly before turning to Anna. Surely, she'd soon get past this agonizing yo-yo of emotions every time he was near.

He opened his lips as if to speak, closed them again and returned to his tablet.

"Good morning, Dee," Anna's enthusiastic greeting did little to cut through the tension in the room. "Can I put an egg or two in the pan for you dear?"

"Yes please. I ate some toast with Brodie earlier but your breakfast smells too good to refuse."

"What have you got on today?"

"Unless you've noticed anything more pressing, Frank and I will spend the day on the shearing shed, the holding pens and the shearers' quarters. We've got most of the top level done and the holding pens under control, but there's more to do. If we get through that, then the fences on the main road require a bit of maintenance."

"Frank is working on Saturday?" Anna asked.

"Uh huh. He wanted time to go to Melbourne with his mum on Wednesday. We negotiated he'd work today instead. We've got to be ready for Jim's team."

"You're bringing in the shearers?"

"With the harvest coming up, the shearing has to be out of the way. Plus, we need the shed for Catherine's Naming Day."

"What?" Nash demanded.

"I haven't filled you in, dear. In the Broderick tradition, we will hold the celebration and party in the shearing shed. When we planned it, we hoped it would be before harvest and it seems like the fates have been kind and it will work." Anna stopped speaking, with a frown marring her forehead as she placed a heaping plate of bacon, sausage, eggs, tomato, and mushrooms in front of Nash and another with a couple of doorstop-sized slabs of toast.

"Caro sent you an invitation. Didn't you get it? You know Catherine is your cousin Connor's little daughter, yes?"

A flush colored Nash's face. "It didn't seem important," he dissembled.

Anna's lips firmed ever so slightly telegraphing her irritation. Nash would have missed it because his eyes were on his meal, but Dee saw, and her heart ached knowing how much Anna hoped Nash would have been at the family gathering. For him to dismiss it as unimportant would hurt.

"Will you be here?" Anna's question raised Nash's eyes from his plate. His eyes flicked between the women ranged on the opposite side of the table.

Dee identified the moment Nash recognized he'd strayed into perilous waters. He straightened his back as if coming to a decision. "Unless I'm called back to Canberra, I'll be here."

The tension leached from Anna's shoulders and Dee reached to rub her back. "Good. I was looking forward to having the whole family here and now it will be complete." Anna sniffed quietly and turned to fill Dee's breakfast plate.

"Not too much for me, please, Anna. I have to be able to bend over without popping my buttons."

"With everything you have to do today, there's not much chance of that. You'll use up all of this goodness and then some, child."

"I'll come with you," Nash asserted as Anna put both Dee's plate and her own on the table.

Dee's head whipped around to face him, her heart thumping. Nash in close proximity during a working day?

Now who was in perilous waters? Nash was Anna's grandson. He'd been raised on this land and this was his home, whether or not he fully appreciated it.

"Not today. There's too much to do and I can't be looking out for a rookie. I don't need dead weight when I'm working." And, sure as hellfire, she couldn't cope with the distraction of his body.

Nash's skin flushed. He was not pleased. Tough. She did her best to ignore him, speared a piece of sausage and brought it to her mouth.

"I'm no rookie."

"I'm not prepared to take the risk." She went on with her meal.

Nash returned to his plate too, and she hoped the discussion was done.

The trio continued in silence for several minutes save for the scrape of a knife on toast or the rattle of cutlery on flatware.

As Dee placed her knife and fork together on her plate, Nash did the same. His voice forestalled her move away from the table.

"I was a rookie in the shed when I was seven, Danielle Dawn, a long time ago."

"You've also been gone a long time. Potentially deskilled. A safety hazard. I can't afford the risk of a worker being injured on site. The workplace safety people would shut us down while they investigate. Our schedule is tight."

She stood to signal the end of the discussion.

"I'm a shareholder not an employee. I have the right to inspect the property and assess how it's being run."

Dee raised one brow towards her forehead and deliberately lifted the corner of her mouth. "Then you need to give me two weeks' notice in writing," she bluffed.

His gaze flicked to Anna's composed features.

"She's right." Anna fudged. "It's in the agreement. It's to stop any-one thinking they can ride roughshod over the manager. There can be one boss and she's it!"

Bless you, Anna.

Dee gathered her cutlery and flatware and carried them to the kitchen sink. She rinsed them before depositing them into the dish-washer.

She hugged Anna around the shoulders. "Thanks for breakfast. It was excellent!" Turning to Nash, she said, "You can bring out the smoko to save Anna the trip. Around ten?" She offered the suggestion as an olive branch, leaving it up to him, the arrogant clod, to accept or not. She wouldn't be backing down.

Nash's gaze pierced her soul. "Fine. What vehicle do I use?"

Dee allowed the smirk on her face to edge out again. "You're right. The phallic symbol parked out front isn't much use, is it? Take the ute." She winkled the keys from the tight front pocket of her jeans, placing them on the table. "I'll drive the quad. Bring Meggs out then too. Come out back. I'll introduce you."

She gave Anna a quick grin and headed back out the door, collected her hat and moved down the steps whistling for the dog.

Meggs loped over, sniffed around Nash's legs, gave a short bark, and dropped at Nash's feet, looking up at him adoringly. Traitorous dog. She could have at least growled at the interloper. Nash always had the same effect with animals—a mutual respect thing.

"She's called Meggs. She's one of your Uncle Sean's pups. Connor helped me to train her and we're doing okay in the local sheep trials. It doesn't look like you'll have any trouble with her. Make sure you put her into the travelling cage." She bent to ruffle the dog's ears.

"See you at ten." Dee strode to Anna's garage, collected the four-wheel all-terrain farm bike and helmet, and set off down the track to the shearing shed with the eerie sense of Nash tracking her every move.

Chapter Five

Dee parked the quad bike next to a formerly black ute which rivalled her own for battered-ness. She pulled off her helmet and dropped it onto the seat of the bike and retrieved her panama from the cargo unit.

"Hey Frank! Have you looked around on this level? What do you think?" she asked.

"It's in pretty good nick, Dee. The tables need a wash and the floor swept, but I think it'll be fine. After we clean it, I'll have a squiz for loose nails and stuff. The quarters need some attention." He tipped his hat back and scratched his forehead. "I hear Nash is home?"

"Yeah. I told him to bring down smoko. He might or he might not."

"Yeah?" Frank's wizened features lit up like he'd won the lottery. "It'll be great to see him."

Dee laughed at his enthusiasm. "He's not my favorite person, Frank."

"Ah, forget the shenanigans. A boy has to sow his oats."

"And consequences?"

"Not a bloke's problem. Most girls know how to look after that sort of thing."

Dee was taken aback. Was that the way men saw the situation of a child being created when two people—TWO people— engaged in sex? Was it the way Nash saw the situation?

"I'll start with the sweeping if you can check all the electricals are working here and above." She refused to discuss her private life any further, and she didn't want to get into an argument with Frank at the start of a day's work.

They worked in a steady rhythm until the thrum of Dee's ute engine drew her out of the shed, hoping it was Anna who'd brought the refreshments. Nash uncurled himself from the vehicle and her body tensed as though someone had yanked hard on the belt of her jeans.

"Frank? Smoko's here," she called over her shoulder.

Frank rushed past her. "Nash! Good to see ya, fella!" He hauled the younger man into a fierce man hug. "Ah geez. You look good. You gunna give us a hand here?"

"I'm available, but Danielle's not sure whether I'm up to the task." He slid her a sideways glance.

"Bullshi-i-it!" Frank turned to Dee. "I taught this kid to wield a hammer when he was Brodie's age, Dee. You know he'll do okay."

"Let's have our morning tea and I'll think about it. What have you got for us, Nash?"

"Great!" Frank said, his tone reflecting his assumption the decision had been made.

Nash grabbed the basket of Anna's goodies from the passenger side of the truck and dropped it on the bottom step of the shed before hauling out a large thermos. "There are scones fresh from the oven and some egg and lettuce sandwiches."

"I'm starved, even after the huge breakfast Anna fed me," Dee said.

"Yeah. Grandma figured. Have some coffee." He poured then passed her a mug of steaming brew. His fingers brushed hers and the mug toppled. Nash caught it before the scalding liquid could do any damage. Dee's eyes ricocheted from the mug to his face. His sultry glance made her heart somersault. He lifted one corner of his mouth before turning to Frank.

"What have you been up to, Nash?" Frank asked.

Dee tried to tune out as the men's conversation floated on the air. She leaned against the wall of the shed and closed her eyes.

"Army stuff, mostly, Frank."

"Gimme more than that, mate."

"Hmm, I spent some time in Afghanistan..." Dee's heart froze. He'd been into a war zone? When? Why didn't anyone tell her?

"And you walked away? Geez! Was it as bad as they say?" Frank's coffee mug seemed to be forgotten in his hand.

"Pretty much, but when they didn't get me the first time, I went back again. I reckoned I wouldn't be missed."

Dee's eyes flashed open and clashed with Nash's gaze. What did he mean no one would miss him? What about Anna, Cassie? What about the child they created? What about her?

"The second tour didn't work either. I came back and went to the Solomon Islands." His mouth twisted to one side as he held her gaze.

She closed her eyes to block out his face, but it didn't silence the conversation.

"Lordy. Is Afghanistan what gave Anna her heart attack? Knowing you were there?"

"Nope. It was years ago, and it's been years since I was in Honiara, too. These days, I run a nice little desk in Canberra."

"I'll bet Anna's pleased," Frank said.

Nash's grunt was non-committal.

Dee stood and picked up another of Anna's sandwiches and wandered away from the men to the far corner of the shed. Her pulse was racing.

Why would he think she wouldn't miss him? Did he believe he meant as little to her as she apparently meant to him? He'd been to war without her knowing. She swallowed a sob. She looked down at the food in her hand and mechanically took a bite and then another.

She stiffened her backbone and walked back to the men. "Thanks for bringing down the smoko, Nash. We have to get back to work."

"We'd go quicker if Nash gave me a hand in the pens," Frank suggested.

Dee glanced at Nash. His face remained impassive. After his revelations over coffee, she was too heart-sore to argue.

"Do what you like. I'm heading to the quarters." She strode towards the quad bike. Nash's hand on her arm stopped her. The zing in her body at the physical contact was nothing new, but she hadn't felt it for years. She flinched away and studied his face. His beautiful eyes nearly made hers fill with tears.

"It would go faster with an extra pair of hands, but you're the boss," he offered. Dee accepted he was giving her a chance to save face. She cleared the lump in her throat.

"Okay, work with Frank. He seems to think the sun shines out of you. Don't do anything stupid and get hurt. And it's your job to go to the house to pick up lunch. Anna will have it ready around one."

"Yes, ma'am," he smiled.

Dee scowled at him, exchanged her panama for the helmet and rode away.

~ * ~

The shearers' quarters were in fair order but in need of a good scrub. She got straight to it.

Thoughts of Nash and war, and Nash and Brodie rattled her brain as she worked and her head had about gotten to the point where she reckoned it would explode when the oven timer sounded a reminder to break for lunch. The mop in her hand stopped mid-swish. The difference in the place was noticeable. It was clean and homely, though she had little memory of doing it. After lunch she'd tackle the sleeping areas.

She arrived at the sheds at the same time as Nash pulled Anna's basket from the ute. Ambling to where Frank was sitting, she unclipped her helmet and dropped onto a step. Nash handed her a cold drink and a baking-paper wrapped sandwich—a huge bread roll filled with ham and salad. The idea of eating it was almost fatiguing in itself.

Setting the sandwich on the step next to her helmet, she cracked the can of drink and nursed it between her knees.

"You've been busy," she said. The men had finished the holding pens and the area she started this morning.

"We're rolling along," Frank offered laconically.

"And you're exhausted," Nash said, his voice a growl of concern.

'Don't pretend you care.' Her heart jumped in her chest, and she flicked a glance at him. When she spoke, her words focused on the job at hand.

"What do you reckon, Frank? Can we be ready if I ask Jim to bring the shearing team in Monday week?"

"Yep."

"Have the sheep been dagged?" Nash asked.

"Yep." Frank bit into his sandwich and spoke around it. "Jim sent one of his young blokes. She's learning the trade. Jim figured crutching would be a good place to get her some experience."

"Jim's young bloke is a she?" Nash checked.

"Yep. Good country girl. Good to work with. She'll be here with the team, but she'll be an assistant on the main job."

"Worried about women taking over the world, Nash?" The notion perked Dee's energy enough for her to finish her sandwich.

"Frank, before I forget, I'd like you to bring in some hay bales during the week to use as outdoor seating for the shearers, please. Right. I'll head back to the quarters. You guys take a while longer."

"Take the ute. You're too tired to handle the quad." Nash's tone was shaded with concern—almost like the boy-man she used to know.

"You can't ride the quad without a helmet," Dee said.

Nash leaned across to take the helmet from her hands. He loosened the sizing strap inside and plonked the helmet on his head. "I have one."

"Whatever!" Dee flapped her hand at him and made her way to the ute. "Thank you for helping out today, Nash."

"That didn't hurt now, did it?" He followed her retreat and closed the door of the cab after her with both hands on the frame. Dee frowned at him. His traitorous, beautiful face was way too close. The sweat of the morning's work lingered on his body. If she leant her head just there, it would be like he never went away.

She jerked back against the seat and turned her head to call out the opposite window. "Later, Frank."

"Yep."

She started the engine without looking at Nash again. She was grateful the support of a full-sized vehicle was around her. Nash was right, darn it. She was too tired to be on the quad. A sleepless night over him and then a hard, physical day took its toll.

With the sleeping quarters cleaned this afternoon, she could make the beds next weekend, and the quarters would be ticked off her list.

Around four in the afternoon, she headed back to the sheds as Frank was packing away his gear before calling it a day. "All done, Dee?" he asked.

"It's clean, I just need to make the beds."

Beyond them, Nash worked his way down the traces. Dee braced herself to walk over to him out of hearing distance of Frank.

"You didn't have to spend all afternoon working with Frank. You'd done enough this morning, but you've saved me a load of work. Thank you."

"Couldn't you have done a lot of this stuff ahead of time?"

Dee narrowed her eyes at him. He'd touched a sore spot. She pushed her thumbs into the front pockets of her jeans.

"If you think you can do better, then come home and do it. Thanks for your help. The quad you're riding is Anna's. It goes back to her place."

~ * ~

Nash shook his head as Dee moved away. He didn't blame her for being prickly. He'd been a bastard since he came home.

He had a right to be here. It was his home. She was the hired help—same as Frank, manager or not. What were his grandparents thinking installing her in his family home? They must know what she did to him. You can't hide a baby and Nash was long gone when Brodie appeared on the scene.

Every time he saw her, he was on the verge of breaking down like a needy teenager and demanding she told him why she'd done it.

Meggs pushed her muzzle against his knee. She'd been trailing him all day. His mother told him years ago that dogs had empathy for people in distress. It was interesting the kelpie determined Nash required her attention rather than Danielle. "Forgot you, did she, girl? It's okay. You can come with me."

Frank hailed him. "Come have a beer, mate."

"A beer? Man, you're prepared." Nash accepted the proffered stubby and sat on the steps of the shearing shed.

"Yep. Gotta be or you miss out."

"Thanks. This will go down easy."

"Nothing better at the end of the day than a coldie, whatever time of year. Right now, when the work's done, well, it's my own quiet time before I head home. Ah mate! It's good to see you back. You haven't forgotten anything. Always did have your head screwed on straight."

"Not everyone agrees with you." Nash swigged his beer.

"Don't worry about Dee. I told her a man's gotta sow his oats. She's a trouper. Brodie's a great kid. You'd be proud of him. He gets in and does stuff and he's all of five years old." Frank wagged his head from side to side and downed his beer.

Nash finished his own drink, holding the empty container loosely in one hand, resting the other on Meggs' head.

Frank shuffled to his feet. "I'd better get a move on or Betsy will wonder what's happened to me. She'll have Bill Hamilton out looking for me."

"Bill Hamilton hasn't moved on?"

"Only cop in Hamlet Brae for years. He's a sergeant now. Finished? I'll take your bottle. Betsy takes 'em to this recycling place. It's her private nest egg. She won't get rich on ten cents a throw, but that's women for ya." He gathered both bottles, replaced them in his Esky and narrowed his gaze on the younger man.

"You comin' back Mond'y?"

"Sure, if you've got stuff I can work on."

"Yeah. Yeah. It'll be good. See ya, mate." Frank's open welcome was a balm on the sting of Danielle's wariness.

Nash stood, gathered the helmet, checked for anything out of place, and climbed onto the quad. He stretched his spine, easing a few kinks. Meggs jumped into the cargo hold and together, they headed to the house.

A hot shower would relieve the aching muscles in his back. If only it would wash away his insatiable craving for Danielle...

Chapter Six

As soon as Anna ended her call on Monday morning, she phoned Dee. "They've summoned me back to the hospital. I need help to think things through."

"Hey! Hey!" Concern flowed from Dee's voice. "We'll come right away. Let me put Brodie's school lunch together and we'll be over. Put the kettle on."

Within minutes, Dee and Brodie were there, right there, in Anna's kitchen. Somehow the worry lifted from Anna's shoulders.

"Would you like something to eat, Brodie?" she asked when the pair came into the kitchen.

"No, thank you. I'll go play with the dogs if that's okay?"

"Sure is, kiddo!"

Anna turned from the boy and placed two steaming mugs of tea on the table along with a side plate of hot buttered fruit toast. She sat down wrapping her hands around the mug in front of her.

"Okay. Tell me what's happened," Dee invited as she helped herself to the toast.

Anna stared into the mug. The tannin-black liquid offered no answers, so she focused on her young friend.

"They say it's routine. They want to check the stents for my heart and make sure I'm doing all right, but I shouldn't need to be admitted, should I? I mean, they should be able to stick a stethoscope on my chest or something and I can come home again."

"Anna, you're getting older. I know you don't always realize that, but even your late sixties means you're no spring chicken!" She chuckled.

Anna loved Dee's laugh. It always made things feel right.

"But I'm not ninety either and don't you forget it."

Dee laughed again.

"What they'll probably need to do is some stress tests. One when you get there and one after a night's sleep. I don't know—I'm guessing here. The staff won't work you to death. They'll want to check everything is working as it should. When do you go?"

"Wednesday."

"They don't give you much time to worry then. Just overnight?"

"Uh-huh." Anna's brows knitted. "Dee, what if they find something wrong?"

"Then they'll fix it, and we'll deal with it. Don't buy trouble. That's not what you do. There were no concerns coming out of your last lot of surgery and you've had no trouble since then – unless you haven't told me?"

"No, no. It's all been good, but I hate hospitals."

"They serve their purpose, love."

"Hospitals don't hold any good memories for me. I've watched so many people I've loved die in hospitals."

"You won't be one of them! At least not yet." Anna watched the dimple appear in Dee's cheek and knew some mischief was coming. "We still have to find that dress for you to wear to the baby's naming."

"Danielle Tillson, you will not get me into a dress."

"But Caroline wants the day to be cocktail dress. I thought a nice calf-length frock with a string of pearls and a fancy hat would be just the thing for you."

"Humph. It's never going to happen. It's a baby naming not the Melbourne Cup. If they don't like me in my usual clobber, they can send me home. I don't do skirts. Never have, when I've had the choice, and never will! I know what you're doing. You're trying to distract me. Don't you give me that innocent look, young lady. I know you too well. I'm a bush broad, no fancy pants lady."

"Some of your pants are pretty fancy." Dee chuckled again. "Okay. Then let's be serious for a moment. Your experience in hospital last time was a good one. They treated you with respect. You had the surgery and wonderful care before and after. Why freak out now?"

"I'm not freaking, exactly. Yes, the care was good—smotheringly so. There's no privacy. And trying to have a shower—yuck. They have those fussy rainforest shower heads or whatever they call them, that spray water from the top. They're absolutely no use for an old girl like me. I need the ones with the flexible hose where I can bring the water down to where I need it. Men designed rainforest heads, I reckon. And the food. It tastes well enough, but I always end up constipated. Then I get *haemorrhoids*. Last time, it felt like I had a pair of horse's cojones between my butt cheeks."

"Anna!"

"You wait, girl. You'll see what I mean. I don't want to go."

"Well, since I need you to be around for a while longer, you'll have to suck it up sister, go to the hospital, get checked out and come home and eat laxatives—the chocolate ones so you think you're having a treat!" Dee reached out, took another slice of toast, and nibbled at it.

Anna's laugh rocked out. "You always say the right thing, darling girl. All right. You can take me up to the hospital on Wednesday and I'll put you down as my next of kin again."

"What's going on?"

Anna jumped as Nash's voice boomed through the kitchen. Dee choked on her toast and set off a fit of coughing.

Nash stood immobile.

"This person is not your next of kin, Grandma. If you need someone to drive you anywhere or to nominate a next of kin, that will be Cassie or me. Not some outsider."

Dee's coughing came under control with a large gulp of tea and she glanced at Nash. As the tension thickened in the room, Anna waited for the explosion. It didn't come. It shouldn't have surprised her. Dee possessed a well of patience. What did surprise her was the glistening of tears in Dee's eyes and the slightest quiver of her chin. Nash's 'outsider' barb hit home.

"You've done enough here, Danielle Dawn." Nash's dismissal was clear.

Dee pushed back her chair and stood.

Anna's eyes swiveled from her beloved grandson to her dear friend. If only…

"Dee always takes me where I need to go, Nash."

Anna caught Dee's slight shake of the head as she came towards her. Dee hugged her around the shoulders. "If you need anything, love," Dee began.

"She won't," Nash averred.

Dee's jaw clenched, but she kept silent. Anna felt Dee's hand flex on her shoulder, then Dee brushed past Nash and headed into the back yard to find her son.

"What was all that about, Nash? Dee has been the one to take me to the doctors and hospitals, dentists and hairdressers for years."

"Well, I'm here now and you're my responsibility."

"I'm not sure I'm ready to be anyone's responsibility, except my own. Dee helps me out because it's what we do for each other. It's called friendship. We're mates. So, don't you go upsetting her or you'll answer to me. She was here when no one else was."

"I wasn't here because no one damned well told me you were sick."

"Don't you raise your voice at me, young man. No one told you because you didn't need telling. Everything was under control. You'd made it clear that coming home was not top of your priority list."

"You know why I didn't come home."

"No, I don't. All your family is here, but you've chosen to stay away for nearly seven years. Seven years, Nash!"

"It's not just family who live here, Grandma." His eyes shot in the direction Dee had taken.

"Dee? You put her through the wringer. Not being here when she needed you. You left her abandoned like everybody else in her life."

Nash's face hardened.

"Not then, not now. I won't be a convenience for her or her kid."

"Yeah!" Anna grunted. "We all know that and yet you preach to me about responsibility."

"I'm not responsible for her."

Anna's anger grew—that this boy whom she had loved and nurtured should react in this way was beyond comprehension for her.

She opened her mouth to tell him just where his responsibilities lay when their embodiment came back into the room.

"Anna Nana, Mum says you've started my costume for Jacob's and my birthday party already!" His eyes were wide. "That's amazing! Can I see it?"

"Mmm. Not yet. I want to try a few things first and then you can tell me what needs fixing."

"Oh wow! Thank you. Thank you. I love you, Anna Nana."

Anna swept him into a hug at her side. "And I love you so much, Little Bit. I'll see you tomorrow, eh?"

Brodie kissed her hard on the cheek, delivered a withering scowl in Nash's direction and led the way out of the house.

Dee flashed Anna a grin, ignored Nash, and followed her son.

"You shouldn't get too attached to the kid, Grandma. He's nothing to you and she'll be like her parents and take off on a whim."

"Ignatius Broderick. You really do not know that girl or her son. Brodie is family. One of my great grandsons. He always will be. Get over it. Would you like me to pull lamb or chicken from the freezer for dinner?"

She shook her head as he paid no heed to her question, turned on his heel and marched down the hall.

"Lamb it is, then," she muttered to herself, heaving herself out of the chair to clear away the tea things.

Chapter Seven

"Blast it! Darn it! Hello Hellfire! Oh, for goodness' sake!" Dee finally ran out of her favourite polite epithets as she looked down at the expensive phone lying shattered on the kitchen tiles. With her teeth clenched and her lips pressed firmly together, she gathered the pieces.

That's what you get for letting yourself brood about Nash Broderick instead of concentrating on the job at hand, my girl.

Stowing the bits into a zippered plastic bag, she deposited the whole into her handbag.

"Brodie. Come on. We're late already."

Brodie slouched onto the kitchen stool. *Nearly six going on sixteen,* his mother mused.

"What's on at school? Anything special you need?" She took his shrug to be a negative response and went on. "What would you like in your lunch box?"

"Chocolate, please."

She looked at him for a moment, biting her tongue. He forestalled her comments as he looked up from his bowl of cereal. "Yes. I know. Only at lunch time and only after I've eaten the real food," he chanted.

She smiled wryly and shook her head. While he ate, Dee made a dash to her bedroom to locate her old phone. Stashing it in her tote, she turned back to Brodie.

"Finished your breakfast? Clean your teeth. We've got to get going."

Brodie shrugged off the chair and headed to the bathroom. He'd been gone a moment or two when he called, "Mum! Billy's back," Brodie's voice reverberated through the house.

Dee raced into the bathroom where Brodie stood with toothbrush in one hand and paste in the other, frowning into the back yard.

Sure enough, just visible if you knew what to look for, coiled in the bark debris from the gum trees was a brown snake.

Dee's heart dropped to her stomach.

She lay a hand on Brodie's shoulder. "No playing outside then till I have the chance to take him back to the dam. He will have to wait. Let's go."

She retreated to the kitchen while Brodie cleaned his teeth and checked her snake-gathering equipment was where it needed to be.

Billy had been part of life since Anna had offered Dee the Broderick house to live in when Brodie was a baby. At first, Dee called the snake-catcher to come and remove him. On the third call-out, Clancy had carefully stepped Dee through the procedure of how to lift the snake from about twenty centimeters or so behind its head and wrangle it into a hessian sack for transport. Instead of charging her for the call-out fee, he sold her the snake hook, the sturdy sack with a metal sprung neck and a pair of welder's gloves in case she ever needed to touch the reptile.

The first time she had to remove Billy the Brown Snake on her own, it terrified her. Having done it once, she became far more confident. Now it was routine.

With Brodie beside her, she headed to her battered ute.

A sharp whistle brought Meggs off the front porch and onto the tray of the vehicle and into her travelling cage. With Billy around, Meggs would go to Anna's place. Yes, time was at a premium, but leaving Meggs to play with Billy wasn't an option.

Anna bustled out with a concerned frown as the car rumbled through the gate.

"Everything okay?"

"Yep, but Billy's back."

Anna nodded her understanding.

Dee whistled for the dog who needed no further invitation. She bounded down and ambled over to Anna, gave a huge yawn, stretched her back legs as far as she could, gathered herself up again and flopped at Anna's feet.

Dee chuckled. "I'll be at school all day," she said, "but I'll call by this afternoon. Is there anything you need in town?"

"Thank you, Darlin'. No. I'm fine. And Nash is here if I need to run around."

It seemed the mere mention of his name was enough to conjure the glowering army captain. He stood inside the screen door leading out onto Anna's verandah.

Dee's chest tightened, and she swallowed before she could get any more words out.

"I'll see you later, then. Have a good day," she said.

Dee scampered back to the ute and slammed the door. With a quick wave from the window, she spun the car around and headed out the gate. Would she ever get over the darned nuisance of a man?

Chapter Eight

That afternoon, Nash heard the screen door bang and Danielle's voice. "Is it okay if I leave Brodie with you for an hour, Anna? Billy's waiting for me."

"Sure Darlin'. Say hello from me. Enjoy the ride." His grandmother chuckled.

The screen door banged again, and a vehicle engine started up.

The thought of Dee with another man brought the taste of bile into Nash's throat. He should be past it by now. Every time he saw her, his heart beat faster than it should. He didn't want to spend any more time with her than necessary. It was dangerous to his equilibrium. But if she thought she could meet up with some dipstick called Billy and leave her brat here for his aging grandmother to look after, he couldn't let it ride.

He grabbed his keys and headed for the door, nearly tripping over the kid who was pulling an electronic tablet from his school backpack.

The males scowled at each other for several moments until Brodie went on with what he was doing.

Nash's teeth clenched in the same way as they did every time he encountered this living, breathing evidence of Dee's treachery.

"I'm going out, Grandma!"

"Okay, Nash. You take care." Anna called from the kitchen without coming to the doorway.

Nash slammed the door of his car as he climbed in, gunned the motor, and pointed the car toward his childhood home. A spectacular bump in the track forced him to slow the low-slung car. He needed the car in one piece and not with the sump being torn apart, the radiator base being bashed in or the steering arms destroyed. Any of them was possible on this rough track. It would be ironic if he had to ask for Danielle's help.

He slowed to a crawl. When he'd bought the car, he hadn't planned on driving it in this terrain.

The vehicle edged towards the house but there was no sign of the battered blue ute. He flung himself from the car and stomped around to the back of the house. The ute was there and close by Dee stood in heavy work boots and gloves holding out a long stick with a hessian bag attached in one hand. In the other hand was another long stick with what looked like...

He stood stock still. His gut registered the danger before his brain identified it. He watched Dee expertly drop the reptile into the hessian bag and give the bag a circular flick to close the neck securely. Nash was sure the eastern brown snake would have measured longer than even his one hundred and ninety-five centimeters.

"What are you doing?"

Dee spun at the sound of his voice.

"Shit, Nash! Don't sneak up on a person like that."

"You swear now?"

"There are some things in life that prompt it—like when someone shouts at me when I'm trying to deal with the second most venomous reptile in the world."

She hefted the bag onto the tray of the ute.

"What are you going to do with it?"

"Same as I always do. Billy and I will go for a ride out to the dam."

"Who's Billy?"

Danielle tipped her head toward the ute, headed to the driver's side door and climbed in.

Nash strode to the truck and peered through the passenger side. "There's no one here."

"Of course, there's no one else here! Just me and Billy. If I needed anyone else here, I would have asked for help."

"Billy's the snake?"

"Yep. Who did you think? Now, if you don't mind taking your head out of my window, I'll get on my way."

Nash withdrew his head but wrenched open the door and slid into the cab before Danielle had a chance to turn the key in the ignition.

"What are you doing?" she demanded.

"I'm coming with you. Drive."

He stared her down for several seconds until she shook her head, looked to the front, and drove.

Nash eventually broke the tortured silence filling the cab. He needed something, anything, to distract him from the nearness of Danielle. "What did you mean, 'same as I always do'?"

Danielle jumped. Nash assumed it was at the sound of his voice, but it could as easily have been another jolt from the landscape. Her voice was calm enough.

"Billy has been part of my life since I moved into your place. He might even have been around when you lived there, but maybe not. He probably hatched around the time you went to Canberra. Eastern browns live for seven years or more and he's still not fully grown.

"When he shows up, I take him out to the dam. During winter, it can be months before he comes back. In summer, it can be as little as a couple of weeks. You would have had snakes around when you were growing up?"

"My dad always said to live and let live as far as they were concerned," he said.

"I'm sure your mother would not have tolerated them being too close when you were little. I have an inquisitive nearly six-year-old and a valuable red kelpie sheep dog—neither of which I want to fall victim to an accidental snake bite. There's no way I'll willingly have an eastern brown underfoot," Dee said.

The mention of the kid set Nash's whole body on alert. He swung his eyes out to the paddock of canola and away from anywhere his vision could glimpse the driver, but the fragrance of her taunted him in the enclosed space.

Frustrated, he turned back. "Why didn't you deal with the snake earlier in the day?"

She swung her head towards him. "Don't you bloody well shout at me. You lost that right, if you ever had it, a hell of a long time ago."

Nash inhaled deeply. Big mistake. Her essence filled his nostrils. She wore a different fragrance from the one he remembered. That had been an old rose scent that his grandmother preferred. They'd all used it, even his grandfather. This was something new—like lemon and jasmine, sharp and innocent but seductive at the same time.

He hauled his mind back and struggled to calm his voice. "Why didn't you deal with the snake earlier in the day?"

"Better, but you still have no authority to be checking my whereabouts." She paused, and Nash thought she wasn't going to answer. Hell's teeth, this woman got under his skin. She'd done it as a skinny fourteen-year-old and she was still doing it more than a decade later.

Her voice broke into his thoughts. "I was at school today. I'm in the last week of my work experience requirement."

"Work experience? For what?"

"For my teaching degree."

"You—a teacher? Don't they have a vetting process for teachers?"

"What are you saying exactly, Nash Broderick?"

Now it came to the crunch, he didn't know if he wanted to put it into words. He clenched his jaw a moment. "A woman of loose morals." He growled.

The car skidded to a halt on the slope of the dam, throwing him towards the dashboard. He barely got a hand out in time to stop himself from hitting the windscreen. *Should have put my seat belt on.*

"How the hell would you know what sort of woman I am. You scurried out of town as soon as you had what you wanted from me and you left without a backward glance. Don't be such a bloody hypocrite. You were the one who 'loosened my morals'!"

Danielle slammed from the car to pull the bag from the tray of the ute.

Nash swung down from the cab. "I'll take that."

"Not on your bloody life. Get your hand away from the sack. There's no telling where his head is."

Nash snatched his hand back as Danielle snapped out her orders. She lowered the gate on the tray and grabbed the heavy gloves she'd left there. Putting them on, she took hold of the long handle to which the sack was attached and dragged it out. Holding it well away from her body, she carried the sack to the shade of a eucalypt and lowered it to the ground to tip out the contents.

The snake landed in a confused heap, straightening itself out and shooting into the nearby scrub. Laid out like that, Nash was sure it was well into the two-meter range and Danielle handled it like a pro.

"Whoa. The trip out must have heated him up. He made a super-fast getaway," she said.

She turned to Nash with a huge grin on her face which fell immediately her gaze landed on his face. Returning to the ute, she dumped the equipment in the tray, moved to the front of the car, got in and banged the door closed.

"Put your seatbelt on this time so I'm not tempted to do a few more sudden stops," she warned.

Nash did as he was told. His mind was wholly on her grin. It was the same grin on the same impish face he had fallen in love with. He wanted it back. He wanted her back.

No, he didn't. That was weakness. There might not have been another man today, but there had been at least one and the kid was proof of that. Nope, no way, he wasn't buying into Danielle again.

He didn't break the silence in the cab for the whole five kilometres to the house. Neither did she.

~ * ~

Dee dropped Nash by his car at the house and continued through the gate and onto the main road to pick up Brodie and Meggs. She glanced back to where Nash stood beside his flashy, impractical vehicle, with a look of consternation on his face.

As she pulled into Anna's driveway for the second time that afternoon, Nash's car was on her tail.

"Do you always go back onto the highway to come over here?" he demanded when he came level with her.

"Unless I'm riding the quad bike, yes. The track is way too brutal for the ute. You'd really need a four-wheel drive to be comfortable. Which way did you go? Oh! You used the track? In that thing." Dee gave a small derisory laugh and trod towards the house.

Serves him right if he smashed his steering arms.

"Why did you come over, anyway?" She swung back to him.

"I wanted to meet Billy."

"You wanted to meet a snake?"

"I didn't know Billy was a goddamned snake,"

"You didn't know…. What? You surmised I had a pre-arranged assignation and you what…? You wanted to catch me in the act so you could ramble on about loose morals? Or you wanted a piece of the action?"

Nash glanced away and then back at her. "Did the university shove a whole dictionary down your throat?"

"Fuck you, Ignatius Broderick!"

She winged her way into the house, stomped down the hallway and found Brodie shelling peas with Anna.

"Why the black scowl, honey?"

"It doesn't matter, Anna. Thanks for looking after Brodie. Billy's out of the way again so I'll get Brodie home. He's had a long day. Hey Little Bit, could you gather up your gear, please?"

"Do you have something for dinner, dear?"

"We're all set. Lasagna and salad with yoghurt and berries to follow." If she hadn't been able to come up with a menu for the evening meal, Anna would have insisted on them staying. She'd pull the lasagna and the berries out of the freezer as soon as she got home. At least the salad would be fresh. She'd had enough of Nash's proximity for one afternoon.

Chapter Nine

It had been longer than he could remember since Nash had driven through the village of Buninyong and he noted the new array of shops and restaurants nestled alongside the old. At the roundabout, he had the choice of going straight ahead past the golf course and on through Sebastapol or turning right, past Federation University, through Mount Clear and on through the main part of the historic city of Ballarat. At this time of day, he figured the traffic near the schools and university would be thick, so he opted for the former route.

The golf course and clubhouse had been spruced up. The tiny former gold mining village of Sebastapol now had a major supermarket, and a host of interesting enterprises amongst the pubs and clubs.

In the last month of spring, the weather in Ballarat was cool. Summer heat would hit briefly in January and February, spiking occasionally into the mid-thirties, but mostly it was like this—cool to cold.

He'd arranged for an early check-in at an apartment hotel close to the hospital and he drove there now. His grandmother had been quiet for the whole trip, resisting his attempts to draw her out.

As he turned into the driveway of the accommodation, she broke her silence. "What are we doing here? We're going to the hospital, not to the girls' school."

"It hasn't been a school for a long time now, Grandma. They've turned it into serviced apartments. I thought you might like to freshen up before we go up to Admissions."

"Well, fancy that. I wonder if the old nuns are spinning in their graves. I would like to freshen up. You never know what chemicals they use on the facilities in the hospital."

You could say the same of hotels, but he forbore from offering that information.

The room was pleasant and spacious, with the windows set high on the wall. They allowed light to enter freely but prevented easy access to seeing what was going on in the outside world. Nash wondered if this room had been part of the convent or part of the school.

"It's lovely, isn't it?" she enthused.

She couldn't discuss the weather while they were driving, Nash mused, but she was excited about the transformation of her former school? Women!

"Yes. Would you like a cup of tea?"

"I'd love one, but I can't have caffeine before I do the tests, apparently."

"Are you all right? How are you feeling, Grandma?"

"Apprehensive! Dee says I shouldn't be, that it's all routine. I wish she was here." Anna chewed her bottom lip.

Nash's first reaction was to stiffen at the mention of Danielle, but what did he know? Maybe it was easier for a woman to discuss her health with another woman.

"She went to school today, remember?"

"She would have worked around that, if you hadn't shut her out."

"Grandma, I'm your next of kin when Uncle Sean, Aunty Siobhan or Aibreann are not around. Then you have your sisters, a whole slew of grandchildren, including Cassie, and even great grandchildren before you consider an outsider for the role."

"Dee understands me. She was there when I was at my lowest. I wouldn't have made it without her. She's not an outsider, no matter what you say, Nash, but I won't argue about that now. I'm due at the hospital by ten."

Nash carried her overnight bag through the corridors and up to level four of the hospital.

A nurse greeted Anna as she stepped out of the elevator and onto the ward. "Anna, how lovely to see you again. You look wonderful. This is your room. Boy, do we have some fun in store for you today." The nurse's badge proclaimed her to be Melanie.

"That's what worries me, dear!"

Nash stowed Anna's bag on the visitor's chair.

"Dr Jack is on his way up. Ah, here he is now." Melanie beamed at the youngish medico before she turned and left the room.

"How's my favourite Anzac biscuit baker?"

Anna chuckled. "I've got some in my bag for you." Her voice lowered, "You'll get them at the end of the day if I'm still alive."

"You'll be more than alive. You'll be bouncing around. Is Dee with you?" The doctor seemed way too eager about Danielle from Nash's point of view.

"Not today. She's doing her teaching practice."

"That's a pity. She always tells me what you don't want me to know."

"She'll be here later this afternoon, if she can. Pesky child," Anna chuckled. "I'll have to have words with her about being a dibber-dobber. This is my grandson, Captain Nash Broderick."

Nash found himself being sized up by the medico before a hand was extended to him.

"Pleased to meet you, Nash. There's no need for you to hang around. We'll be moving from one set of tests to another with a break for Anna to have some lunch and catch her breath. She'll be back in her room about four."

"Is she free to go then?"

"If she were younger and local, I'd say yes. These activities are strenuous, and I want to have her monitored overnight in case there are repercussions. If she pulls up okay in the morning, she can be ready to go after I do my rounds. Is that okay with you Anna?"

"Whatever you say, young man, so long as you don't drive me to death," she said with a wry smile.

"Where can I get a decent coffee?" Nash asked the doctor.

"Ballarat has lots of excellent coffee shops if you don't want to go to the hospital cafeteria. There's one nearby in Errard Street and some good ones in the two hundred and three hundred blocks."

It took Nash a moment to remember this was how people in Ballarat gave direction – referring to the position numbers in the city's main thoroughfare, Sturt Street. The lower end, where the Mechanics Institute Library was located, was the one hundred block, Town Hall was in the two hundred block, the major department store was in the three hundred block and so on.

Nash nodded. "Thanks. Would you like me to come back over lunch, Grandma?"

Before his grandmother could respond, the doctor intervened. "We have a strict 'no visitors' rest period between one and two thirty, and Anna will need to rest. She should be right by four o'clock though."

Irritation shivered through Nash. Who did this jackass think he was? He narrowed his eyelids, holding himself in check. He didn't want to create any more tension for his grandmother than she was already feeling.

"I'll see you later then, Grandma." He bent down and kissed her cheek. "I'll be back by four."

"Thank you, darling boy. Could you give Iris a call and tell her what room I'm in, please? She'll pop up tonight."

Nash stood by his car and dialed Anna's sister's number. There was no answer, so Nash left the information on voicemail and hung up.

He drove back into the heart of the city, found a parking spot outside the art gallery and briefly took in the nineteenth century architecture that kept tourists flocking to the town, before finding a café nearby.

Nursing a long black, he remembered the first time Danielle had come with his family to Ballarat. It had been soon after his grandparents sort of adopted her. Danielle had been Cassie's friend at school for a long time but even Cassie hadn't known Danielle was living without an adult.

Looking back, Nash recognized he'd loved her then in an immature but real sense. The family had gone to Sovereign Hill, Ballarat's iconic outdoor museum set up as a gold mining town of the 1850s, complete with gold panning, bakery, lolly shop and costumed constabulary. Danielle had freaked out when Nash was 'arrested' for some infringement the 'constables' had invented on the spot. Her tirade had the actors stepping back and apologizing for their error. She'd held his hand for the rest of the visit, whether to protect him or for her own security, he didn't know, but he, sure as hellfire, would not let go.

His coffee done, Nash stood and walked out of the café to where the sign for the Art Gallery caught his attention. The family had all gone to the art gallery as well that day, despite the protestations of the teenagers it would be boring. It hadn't been. The variety of works had been fascinating.

He had time to kill now that he didn't always have to visit galleries in the nation's capital where he lived. The gallery here in Ballarat was the first such built outside a capital city in Australia and renowned for its collection. The automatic entry doors opened as he hesitated, luring him inside.

Nash wandered through the collection until he found the painting that captured Danielle's attention that day. She'd strolled past masterpieces by Tom Roberts, Russell Drysdale, and others, but halted suddenly to sit and contemplate a piece by Elijah Walton titled, "In the Woods".

Staring at it now, Nash could see why some critics panned the painting as overly sentimental in comparison with Walton's later mountainscapes, but equally he could see what would have attracted a fourteen-year-old girl craving a loving family.

Time passed as he lost himself in the piece until he realized he'd let himself stray back to a time when he thought the world revolved around Danielle Tillson. Hadn't his mate Mitch warned him not to let it happen again? What a fool he'd been. The soft and warm feelings the painting evoked, coalesced into a rock-hard ball of bitterness in his gut.

He strode out of the side gallery and down one arm of the elegant Y-shaped staircase and into the street. He climbed into his car and headed back to his accommodation.

It was just before three, so he hung his fresh clothes in the wardrobe and arranged his toiletries in the bathroom. He sat and untied his shoelaces before removing his shoes and placed them neatly at the foot of the bed. Stretching out on the soft mattress, he must have dozed because the phone startled him into wakefulness.

His Great-Aunty Iris shouted at him as she always did, and he held the phone away from his ear. Anyone would think he was the one who was nearly deaf rather than she. "Nash, dear, how lovely to hear from you. You can tell Anna that I'll pop up after I've had an early tea, so about five-thirty. I'll see you then. Bye!" Well, Nash thought, not giving anyone else a chance to have a say in the discussion, means you don't have to worry about hearing them.

He walked the five hundred meters back to the hospital and arrived on the ward as his watch marked the hour.

Anna was drinking a cup of tea. "Hello, dear. It's so nice to have my first cuppa of the day."

"How did the tests go, Grandma?" Nash snagged the visitor's chair from beside one of the unoccupied beds.

"They were awful, you know. They push and push until you think you'll keel over. My heart was pounding, I was puffing like a draught horse and all Dr Jack said was 'keep going'!" Anna cackled merrily. "He still didn't kill me, so I reckon I'm good."

"Excellent. Aunty Iris rang. She said she'll be up around five-thirty."

"How did she sound? She's been unwell lately."

"If the strength of her voice is anything to go by, she's hale and hearty."

Anna chuckled again. "It's as well there's no one else sharing this room. I'll be able to close the door to keep the volume down. Hello, Dee dear. What's up? You look worried."

Nash swung around as Danielle entered the room.

"How are you Anna? Did the tests go okay? Were they as bad as you feared?"

"I'm fine. The tests were worse than I thought and I'm not dead. Now tell me why you're worrying your bottom lip."

Anna's comment drew Nash's gaze to Danielle's mouth and his lower abdomen clenched. Her lips were rosy red and slightly swollen, probably from her gnawing at them, but they looked freshly kissed. He had to change position in his seat to relieve some of the discomfort.

"I drove my car ..."

"Oh no, you didn't!" Anna said.

"Yes."

"And?"

"There's white smoke or steam or something coming from under the bonnet."

"Oh dear. I warned you not to drive it out of town. You should have brought my car," Anna said.

"I've had no trouble with it lately, so I thought it would be fine."

"It sounds like you're overheating the radiator. Let me look at it," Nash offered.

"Um, okay. I brought these for you, Anna."

"You got me chocolate-coated caramels?" Childish glee burst onto his grandmother's face as she spied the bag with the name of the chocolatier they had driven past this morning. "Oh, goody!"

The comment wrangled a simultaneous laugh from him and Danielle.

"Don't overdo it," Danielle warned backing towards the door. Nash followed.

"Did you look under the bonnet?" he asked as they walked to the elevators.

Danielle shook her head. "Too hot. Plus, I feared if it was fire, it might erupt in the parking garage."

"I doubt it will be fire." Nash edged into the elevator after Danielle and was locked in place beside her by a young woman with a baby stroller, creating a weird yearning to have been with Danielle when she'd had her baby, even though he wasn't the father.

On the ground floor, Danielle led the way to the second floor of the parking garage where her battered ute sat.

Nash tapped the bonnet with the palm of his hand. "It's still warm. Release the bonnet. Do you have something in the car I can wrap around my hands?"

Danielle pulled the tab to unlock the bonnet and grabbed the welders' gloves she used for snake wrangling. "These do?"

Nash took them without speaking, put them on as best he could and raised the bonnet. "You've got no fan belt! It'll be a wonder if you haven't totally snarled your engine. It has to cool before we can do anything, check you haven't killed it and then, I might be able to do a quick fix for you."

"I need to get home. I have school in the morning."

"You won't be going anywhere tonight. Even if I can get something jury-rigged to get the car moving, you can't drive home in the dark in case it fails en route. Do you have friends in town you can stay with?"

"Usually, I would, but they're all out on placement like me." She gnawed her bottom lip again and Nash's body reacted right on cue.

"We'll figure something out."

They made their way back up to Anna. The medico Nash met that morning was talking with her.

"Dee!" The doctor's eyes lit up. Nash wanted to punch him.

"Hey Jack. How did our patient go today?"

"She's fine. You can take her home tomorrow."

"How early can we get away?" Nash asked.

"What time you want to go, Anna?" the doctor asked.

"First light."

"That might be a bit extreme. I do my rounds at seven, so the earliest you could get away would be seven-thirty. How does that sound?"

"It'll do."

"It means I'll miss out on time with Dee, but I can always call you back again."

Nash felt his body tense like it used to before he went on a mission in the desert.

"Don't you even think about it, young man. I hate hospitals!"

"Good. You'll have an incentive to look after yourself. I'll see you in the morning. Dee, do you have a minute?" He put his hand on the small of Danielle's back to lead her out. Nash's jaw clenched. The doctor's head bent close to Danielle's and she smiled up at him. Nash turned his head away and met his grandmother's knowing eyes.

"Darlin', you could fix it, you know. If you climbed down off your high horse."

"It was all a long time ago, Grandma. There's no way back now." Nash hoped his grandmother didn't hear the wistfulness he detected in his own voice. Best if he kept his mouth shut so only he would know how much jealousy roiled inside him from Danielle's casual closeness with the young doctor.

"How does the car look?" Anna asked after a long period of quiet.

"No fan belt. I won't be able to tell if there's major damage until it's cool."

"You two should have a meal while you wait. What do you think, Dee?" she asked as Danielle reappeared in the doorway.

"Hmm?"

"Dinner with Nash while you wait for the car engine to cool. You know the eateries around here."

"Umm." Danielle's gaze flew to Nash's face, looking like she'd received an unwanted challenge. She swallowed. "What sort of food do you like? There's quite a bit of choice within walking distance—pizza, pub, Indian, fish 'n' chips, Thai?"

"Pub."

"Okay. Enjoy your meal, Anna. We'll be back soon," Dee said.

"You gunna tell me what your mate, Dr Jack, said?" Anna wheedled.

Nash watched as Danielle screwed up her face in response to his grandmother's query. "Maybe. I'll think about it. See ya."

"Hmph."

"We won't be long, Grandma."

"Take your time. Iris will be on her way by now."

Nash caught up with Danielle at the elevators, wondering if it were a blessing or a problem for them to have time alone without his grandmother as a buffer. It might be the only chance he got to get the answers that could release him from seven years in an emotional wilderness.

Chapter Ten

Danielle walked past the carpark and continued to Mair Street, turning west in the direction of the lake. They kept their silence until Danielle said, "Here's the pub. I'm going a block further on to Lake Wendouree for a few minutes."

Nash glanced at her and kept walking too. Danielle got to the corner, crossed Wendouree Parade and made her way down to the water's edge, dodging cyclists, and dog-walkers as she went.

"It's beautiful, isn't it? Peaceful. It's hard to believe a few years ago the lake was empty because of the drought."

Nash didn't reply, content to watch the play of emotions across her face.

"What did the doctor say?" he asked when some time had passed. Danielle snapped her head towards him. "When he took you for a quiet word."

"Nothing much. Basically, he said that there's still a bit of irregularity in Anna's heart but there's nothing to worry about unless she wants to run a marathon."

"He couldn't say that in front of Grandma and me?"

Danielle shrugged and turned her gaze back to the water.

A few minutes later, she heaved a heavy sigh as if to release residual tension and stood.

"We'd better go if we want to have a meal, check on the car and see Anna again before visiting hours are over."

She moved onto the path and Nash grabbed her arm to haul her out of the way of a cyclist she hadn't seen. He felt a shock of awareness pass through him. *Steady, boy. You're falling into the same old trap.* Still, he didn't want to let her go.

She jerked her arm from his grasp and stomped towards the footpath on the opposite side of the street.

They stepped into the surprisingly quiet restaurant area of the pub, given the number of people already seated and those enjoying a drink at the bar. A young woman greeted them and showed them to a table, handed them menus, took their drinks order, and left. She was gone less than five minutes and returned with their drinks and to take their meal orders. Anna chose barramundi and Nash ordered a steak, rare.

"So, you're going to be a teacher?" He should at least try to make social conversation.

"Unless something untoward happens," Dee said.

"Will you stay in Hamlet Brae?"

"I'd prefer that, but I'll go where I can get a job."

"You're not committed to staying to watch over my grandmother, repaying her kindness and faith in you?"

Her expression blazed through his soul.

"Nash, we can sit quietly and avoid indigestion while we have a meal, or we can have an all-out brawl to entertain the other patrons."

"Just asking a question," he defended himself.

"It's not one you have a right to ask nor to expect an answer."

"Who's looking after the kid?"

"Cassie is caring for Brodie."

"Why isn't it you looking after the kids and Cassie coming to her grandmother?"

"Cassie has a full-time job she can't leave until after five. She would get here in time only to head straight back. She also has a husband who expects to enjoy her company. She looks after Brodie so I can help with

Anna, plus, the boys entertain each other so she can leave them alone while she has a drink with Robbie. It works for her and for me. It is not for you to question. You opted out of parenthood and family life, remember?"

Nash felt her accusation like a punch to the gut. "I'm not someone you can use as a convenience, ma'am."

"Like you used me? You made that clear." She stopped as the waitress arrived with their meals and Danielle smiled at her.

Even as his chest tightened in rejection of the hurt Danielle had done him, his heart softened with that smile.

"Bon appétit," she saluted before lifting her cutlery to attack her meal. "What do you think happened to the fan belt? How long do you think it's been missing?"

He recognized her tactic in redirecting the conversation.

"Did you have any warning noise like tires screeching on a concrete floor?" he asked. Danielle took a mouthful of her fish as her frown puckered.

She swallowed. "I did hear something as I started off from the lights to turn into Drummond Street. I thought it was the car next to me because it roared off."

"How far did you drive after you heard the noise?"

"It's about two kilometers from there to the hospital. It's straight through until you turn into Mair Street for the carpark."

"You were lucky, then. Driving without a fan belt can have your engine dead in very little time at all. Until I check it, I can't say you haven't already damaged it beyond repair."

Danielle's shoulders slumped.

"Don't go buying trouble," Nash advised unconsciously echoing one of his grandmother's mantras. "Deal with the problem when you know there's one there. Eat your meal."

They ate their food in silence, and both declined anything further.

Danielle reached into her handbag and pulled out her purse.

"It's my shout."

"I don't want to owe you anything," she frowned at him.

"Danielle Dawn, for God's sake, be gracious for once, so we can get out of here without a scene."

Her lips tightened, but she offered no further argument.

They covered the distance to the hospital and went to check on Anna. They heard her sister before they opened the door.

"Hello, Aunty Iris."

"Nash!" she said heartily, spewing wine-soaked breath at him when he bent to kiss her cheek. As he straightened, her eyes rounded, and her jaw dropped dramatically. "With Danielle!"

"Hello, Mrs. Tate. It's good to see you looking so well," Danielle said. Iris Tate's goggle eyes swung between the two of them before turning to her sister.

Anna smiled and asked about the ute.

"We'll check on that shortly. We wanted to make sure you're okay first."

"I'm fine, dear. You heard the doctor say I could be out of here early in the morning. What say you come up about seven and we blow this joint as soon as poss? You two deal with Dee's car and I'll see you tomorrow. Iris is keeping me entertained."

Grateful for the reprieve from spending too much time with his great-aunt, Nash conceded. "Okay. Seven it is." He leaned over and kissed her cheek and repeated the process with his great-aunt. "Bye, Aunty Iris." Her glance still darted between him and Danielle and she didn't respond.

He waited while Danielle farewelled his grandmother and led her from the room.

Back at the car, Nash lifted the bonnet. The engine was cold.

"You don't happen to carry a spare fan belt under the seat, do you?" He knew it was unlikely, but he couldn't resist baiting her. "Okay, we'll have to improvise."

He looked Danielle up and down, taking in the demure knee-length skirt.

"Are you wearing pantyhose?"

"Stockings," she said.

His heart tripped. Why on earth had he asked the question? The thought of running his hand up those long legs to the naked flesh high on her thigh was immobilizing.

"Take them off."

"What?"

"Take them off. We don't have all night."

"Why would I do that?" she demanded.

"Because you need a fan belt."

"And stockings will do that?"

"At a pinch."

Her eyes scanned his face. "All right." She moved to the passenger side of the car and, using the door as cover, shucked off her pumps and removed the first stocking. Although he couldn't see what was happening, Nash's imagination ran wild. He struggled to retain an impassive face.

"Do you want them both?" she asked as she handed over the hosiery still warm from her body.

"May as well, in case one isn't long enough." His voice strangled in his throat.

She went through the same wriggling and wiggling process again while he drew the stocking he held through a closed hand. His breath hitched.

"Here you go," she said, handing the second one to him. She stood, sliding her feet back into her shoes, smoothing her skirt and coming to stand next to him to peer into the engine block.

"What do we do now?" *Was she totally unaware of the effect she was having on him or was she a darn good actor?*

He cleared his throat. "Do you have any tools?"

"There are some behind the seat with the jack." She maneuvered the bench seat forward to access a leather-wrapped package of tools.

Nash took one of the stockings and stretched it from the pulley to the drive to test its length and used his thumb to mark where he should tie it off. "That'll work." He rotated the pulley wheels to check that the bearings were rotating as they should, and then went back to the tools. He unwrapped the roll and chose a spanner. Latching it onto the tensioning device he levered the spanner downward to release tension from where the fan belt should have been.

He tied a knot to join the ends of the stocking and threaded it around the pulley and the drive and checked the tension, took it off, and retied it to shorten the loop. He threaded it around again, tested it and levered the spanner back up to reset the tension. The stocking stretched tightly to fit neatly in the tracks intended for the fan belt.

He was conscious of Danielle watching every move he made. "Is there a knife amongst the tools?"

"Will a pocket-knife do?"

He nodded, took it, and sliced the protruding ends of hosiery. "Start the car. Let's see if this will hold."

The engine turned over. No damage he could see or hear, and the drive was turning to cool the motor.

"Right. Turn it off."

Danielle exited the car and came to stand next to him again. "There's no telling how long this will last so you can't drive it home tonight. Have you thought about where you can stay?"

"I'm okay. Thanks for your help and for your ingenious solution. I'll be fine now."

Nash didn't budge. The reprieve of walking away from her battled with his need to make sure she was okay.

"Danielle Dawn, where will you sleep tonight? You are not to drive this car in the dark."

She pulled herself up to her full height which was still many centimeters short of his. "You've already told me that. I wouldn't be so foolish. I'll stay here tonight and head off at first light."

"Here? You must be kidding me!"

"They patrol the car park all through the night. I'll be safe."

"No!" Something akin to fear and panic rushed through him. "If you've got nowhere else to stay, share my room."

"Not a good idea."

"It's not, but it's the final option that doesn't involve you driving anywhere in the dark on your own. If Reception is still open, you can check to see if they have a spare room, otherwise, you'll be with me. I'll drive so I can check whether things are holding. Get in."

It looked for several moments like she would defy him, but with him behind the wheel, she had no choice unless she wanted to sleep on the concrete floor of the parking garage.

"I have to pay for the parking." She strode away toward the pay station and returned minutes later, handing him the paid card.

The sign at the front of the hotel was starkly lit with NO vacancy. The question was answered before it was asked.

"Do you have any gear?"

"I planned to pop up and head straight back, so I have nothing—not even a toothbrush. Could I borrow your phone? I must give Cassie a call to let her know I won't be back tonight."

"You drove to Ballarat without a phone?"

"Well, I have one. It's an old one I can use for emergency calls. I smashed my usual one the other day."

Nash shook his head and handed over the instrument. He gave her space to make her call. Hearing only one side of the conversation was enough for him to know his sister was no more pleased that Danielle was spending the night with him, than he or Danielle were.

"All okay?"

"Mmm. I told her I'll try to be back early morning to pick up Brodie. Then we'll have to get home to get fresh clothes and pick up my work plan for school tomorrow. Does the couch fold out, do you think?"

"It doesn't."

"Oh."

"You can't sleep there, Danielle Dawn. It's too short. You'll have to share with me." Nash ran a hand through his hair. "I've got a t-shirt I was going to wear to bed. It'll be better if you have it."

Her hand brushed his as she took it from him. She had tears in her eyes. "Thank you." Her voice was a whisper. She turned and shuffled towards the bathroom. Minutes later she returned, her face pinkened by the hot water of the shower but looking no happier. She hung her towel on the back of a dining chair and smoothed her dress on another.

His t-shirt was long on her but not long enough to hide the glory of her well-toned legs, nor thick enough to disguise her lack of a bra.

"I'll go to bed and get out of your way," she muttered. "Good night."

Nash dropped onto the couch and put his head in his hands. There was no point denying anything to himself. No matter how many things he wanted to fault her for, he still loved her.

Grandma insisted she trusted Danielle. Why shouldn't he?

He could accept she'd had a fling with someone else out of despair. Hadn't he done the same? But to turn around and tell him the baby was his, after admitting there was another guy, he wouldn't – couldn't – accept that. He wasn't a total fool for her.

He made his way to the bathroom and saw she'd made use of one of the complimentary dental kits and a comb.

She was either asleep or acting very well when Nash entered the bedroom half an hour after her exit. She stirred slightly as he climbed into one side of the king-sized bed but didn't wake. He lay watching her sleep for a long time. His body got hard looking at her. As a teenaged lover, she'd been giggly and giving. What would she be like now as a woman? He wanted badly to reach over and find out. *If only things could have been how they ought to have been...*

"No use wishing for the moon," his grandfather would have said. He rolled away and turned out the remaining light.

Chapter Eleven

Dee woke surprisingly refreshed. She must have moved in her sleep because it felt like her back was against a wall. She stretched to remove the kinks in her body, when the wall moved and the log across her waist curled around her.

She opened her eyes, taking a moment to orient herself. She whipped her head to the left to see Nash still sound asleep. She closed her eyes to take in the sense of being in his arms. She'd slept soundly knowing he was near, and she was safe.

He'd been so caring in an offhand way last night, her heart was ready to break all over again.

It was almost a tragedy she had to climb out of the bed and walk back into the real world where she had only herself to rely on in the last resort. Leave she must—to nurse her car down the highway, pick up her son and organize herself for a day at school.

She eased herself from under his arm and out of the bed without disturbing him and hustled into the dining area. Grabbing the towel and her dress from the chairs, she retreated to the bathroom. A quick shower, teeth brushed, dressed in yesterday's clothes, Nash's t-shirt hung on the tiny towel rail and she was ready to go.

Dee strode towards the dining area to collect her keys and handbag and barreled straight into Nash's naked chest, her forehead thumping against the hard plane of his shoulder. His hands came to her waist to steady her and she let her head rest where it had landed while she breathed him in and listened to the ker-thump of his heart.

It might have been moments or minutes, but, eventually, she dropped a feather-light kiss on his chest and stepped back. He wouldn't have felt it, but it was a minor victory for her.

"I thought you'd gone," his voice rumbled over her, sounding sad.

"I'm about to." She tried to imbue her voice with sunshine and well-being. "I slept really well. Thank you for everything, Nash."

"Danielle, I..." He said nothing more but gathered her wholly against him. The weight of his head rested on her crown and her hands smoothed his torso as they reached to join at his back. A shudder passed through him and his arms banded more tightly around her. The stretch of his chest as he breathed in, forced her hands apart and she dropped them to her sides.

Her glance took in his closed eyes and his lowered chin. He snapped to attention.

"Right..." He jerked around as if looking for anything to break the tension exploding between them.

"Would you like some breakfast before you go? They have these continental box thingoes with cereal and fruit and stuff." Dee eyed the collection of food, her mind on their amazing embrace, a benediction, a forgiveness but who was forgiving whom was a question left unanswered.

"You need to get moving, but you've got to eat, too," he said.

"I'll take the muesli bar if you can spare it, then I can eat it along the way." She tucked it into the pocket of her frock. "I've got water with me." Gathering her handbag she willed her legs not to give way and her heart not to fall at his feet.

"Don't push the car, Danielle Dawn. The jury-rig might not hold. And you don't have a phone to call me."

He sounded so much like the boy who loved her. Her heart melted, and she rested one hand on his chest. His muscles jumped under her palm.

"Umm. I'll head home the way I came—down Drummond Street and then out through Sebastapol and Buninyong. If the car conks out, you'll find me on the side of the road, okay? You'll be about ninety minutes behind me. But I'd trust one of your jury-rigs to get me out of trouble any day. Thanks again, Nash." She ran her hand down his forearm.

She left him standing, puzzlement shadowing his face.

~ * ~

The trip to Hamlet Brae was a cautious one for Dee, not wanting to stretch the makeshift fan belt beyond its limits. She had the second stocking in the glove box of the car, and she *thought* she could reconstruct it the way Nash had, but she didn't want to try.

Getting home was Plan A, repairing it herself along the way was Plan B and Plan C, well... she did not want to consider Plan C—standing on the side of the road waiting for Nash and Anna.

Her shoulders were tense as she drove through Ballarat towards Sebastapol. They eased a little when she got to Buninyong and, forty kilometers further on, she relaxed. It took her an extra fifteen minutes compared with her usual travel time to get to Cassie's place, but at least she made it.

Her friend hurried out of the house to meet her. "You spent the night with Nash? Tell me! Tell me. I came out here so the boys and Robbie wouldn't hear."

"Your eyes are as big as saucers. Calm down. It wasn't like that. Let me show you why your brother had to rescue me."

She pulled the knob to release the catch, went around to the front of the vehicle, depressed the secondary lock arm, and raised the bonnet. "Look!"

"What am I looking at?"

"The fan belt."

"Where's the fan belt?"

Dee groaned. "Cassie, you're such a girl!"

Cassie batted her eyelashes. "That's the way Robbie likes me, strangely enough. Explain the fan belt."

"Do you see this here?"

"The bit that looks like it's a stretched stocking or something?"

"Yes. It is a stretched stocking or something. There was no fan belt when I got to the hospital. It was after hours by the time it cooled and no mechanic available. So, Nash used one of my stockings to fix it."

"How did he get said stocking? Did he roll it down your leg with his teeth?" Cassie's eyes drooped, and her jaw went slack as if to imitate her version of a porn star.

Dee laughed but the image that Cassie presented made her shiver. She couldn't bring herself to acknowledge it might be a quiver of pleasurable anticipation if only she'd had the courage to move forward on the hug he gave her.

"No. I removed it myself."

"Ah, you did the Mata Hari striptease?" She waggled her shoulders.

"I hid behind the car door."

"Geez Dee. You're no fun. But then you slept with him, right?"

"We shared a bed. A big bed. Him on one side and me on the other."

"With a bank of pillows down the middle?"

"Not necessary. I don't think either of us was interested in repeating past mistakes."

"Then you made it all the way home with a stocking for a fan belt?"

Robbie came to join them, and Cassie turned to him. "Did you know you could use a stocking to replace a fan belt?"

"Not recommended but it'll do in a pinch. Good elasticity going on but then it holds its shape around the pulleys. Why?"

" 'Cos that's what got Dee here."

Robbie peered into the engine well. "Good job, but it won't go much further. Can you see where it's worn on the tracks?"

"It doesn't have to go far—home, changed and back to school. I can get Josh to take it from there."

Robbie scratched his forehead. "Nup. Best take my car to go home, or Cassie's. Then come back here and drive it to the garage. It'll probably make it that far but not out to your place and back. Judging by the wear, it will snap any minute. There's an extra jolt of tension when you start the car so it could break then."

Dee gnawed her lip. "I'd be testing my luck?"

"Definitely."

She turned to Cassie. "Do you trust me with your precious little Piggie?"

"I'm sure she can handle it. You'd better move. It's nearly eight. I'll get Brodie and the keys."

"So how was the night with the big, bad army captain?"

"Tense but I would have been in a pickle without him. I was going to sleep in the car in the parking garage at the hospital. He insisted on taking me back to his hotel. No vacancy there, so we had to share. I went straight out to it. I have no idea when he came to bed. He did for me what you would have done, my friend, and that's saying a lot."

"You've forgiven him everything?"

"That might be pushing things a little too far, but he was there when I needed him this time. Though he did check I had no other options before he extended his invitation."

Cassie hustled back with Brodie in tow. "If I've gone by the time you get back, take the keys with you and I'll get them at lunchtime."

"Okay and thanks." She hugged Brodie to her side and rattled the keys in her hand.

"Come on, Little Bit." She kissed his head.

What bliss it was to drive a car with decent shock absorbers. "Did you have a shower at Cassie's?"

"Uh huh. Why didn't you come home last night?"

"Car broke down, Nash had to use a stocking to fix it. Robbie reckons it wouldn't hold to get us home and back so we're using Cassie's car.

When we get home, we need a record turnaround time. Feed the dogs and the chooks. I can't make your lunch, so you'll have to use the canteen today. You cool with that?"

"Can I get whatever I want?"

"May I... within reason. What were you thinking?"

"Pie and chips."

Dee frowned and then relented. "Since it's an emergency, I guess you can."

"Cool. Emergencies are fun." He grinned.

"Don't even whisper that. We don't want the Universe thinking it's free to send more trouble our way."

"Hehe."

"Here we are. You feed Meggs while I gather my school gear. Ten minutes in and out, then to Nana's for the eggs and feed the chooks and Old Nell. We might make it back so Cassie can take her own car to work."

Brodie's chatter calmed Dee's nerves as they drove the distance back into town. It was normal, something to focus on that left no room for worry about a slew of other issues.

They pulled into the driveway at Cassie's place as she emerged with her bag and Jacob dragging behind. "Perfect timing. I'll take Brodie with me so you're free to drop your ute at Josh's."

"Thanks for everything, Cass. Right, Little Bit, if you need me during the day, you know where to find me. Love you, have a great day."

"Love you too, Mum. Mwah! See ya."

Dee drove onto the forecourt of the garage, through the drive-through, where the pumps were located, to park in front of the service bays. Josh Gibson was rolling up the aluminum door to make a start on the day.

"G'day, Dee. What's up?'

"Fan belt problems, Josh."

"Let's take a look. Sheesh, would you look at that. You do this?"

"No. Nash rigged it for me to drive home from Ballarat."

"You drove all the way from Ballarat with pantyhose for a drive belt? Man! You were lucky. It's badly worn. In fact, if I touch it..." He did. "It'll snap." It did. He shook his head.

"Five-minute job. Want me to fix it for you now?"

"Sometime today, Josh. I have to be at school–like three minutes ago–so I'll leave you to it and call back at lunch time, if that's okay?'

"Sure thing, Dee. It'll give me a chance to check on the rest of it."

"Don't get too carried away, Josh. I can't afford it." Dee laughed to downplay the seriousness of her comment. "I'll see you at one."

"Good to know Nash is still good with his hands," he said with a grin, waved one permanently grease-stained paw and his face disappeared into the engine well.

Warmth flooded Dee's face. She spun on her heel and strode the length of the street attempting to outpace the memories Josh's off-hand comment brought to the surface. Nash had been good with his hands, but she was the one left to pay the price.

Chapter Twelve

On Friday morning, the last day of her scheduled placement, Dee grabbed the calico shopping bag with her planning documents and her handbag from the floor at Brodie's feet on the passenger's side of the ute and hurried into the school.

Hitching the heavy calico bag onto her shoulder, she pushed open the door. As she strode past the office, Amy Matheson, the long-time school secretary poked her head out the door. "Miss Tillson, Mrs. Ransley would like a word, if you don't mind."

"Now?"

"Yes, please."

"Mrs. Matheson, you can call me Dee. You've known me ever since I arrived in Hamlet Brae."

"Yes, dear, but that wouldn't be appropriate within the school grounds. What if the children should overhear us?" She looked pointedly at Brodie standing next to his mother.

Dee smiled to herself. *You can call me 'dear' and that's okay, but the children can't know my first name even though I went to school with a lot of their parents?*

Still, Dee recognized that Amy was the backbone of the school and had been sitting in her chair in the office for more than twenty years.

She knew everything about everybody but rarely passed on information without good cause.

Dee took Brodie in a hug. "In case I don't see much of you during the day, make sure you have a great one and have fun at the party this afternoon. I'll see you tomorrow, okay? Be good for Aunty Cassie."

"Yes, Mum." Brodie didn't have to roll his eyes, it resonated in his voice. "See ya!"

Dee wiggled her fingers at him as he scampered off and she turned to Amy.

"May I leave my bags with you, please?"

"Of course, you can, dear. Good luck!"

Good luck? What awaited her in the principal's office?

"Good morning, Danielle." Margaret Ranley sent her a beaming smile.

"Hello, Margaret. You wanted to see me?"

"Yes—about a couple of things, really. First, about the time you took off the other day for the funeral. We talked about you having to do an extra day at school next week to make that up. Correct? Well, Maria March and I have decided the extra work you've done more than compensates for the time you needed for the funeral. Plus, acting as the celebrant was a community activity which fits well with the engagement we expect of teachers in a country school. Let's not bother with having you come back in next week."

"Thank you!"

"Now, the other matter is your performance while you've been on this placement."

Dee tensed and waited for the principal to go on.

"Maria has given me her report to read before I sign off on it and return it to the university. I won't go into detail because Maria will do that with you. Suffice to say both of us believe you will be an outstanding teacher."

"Thank you again." Dee couldn't help the little bubble of pride swelling in her chest. This amazing educator thought she, Danielle Tillson, would be a good teacher.

"Which brings me to the last matter. It's something you might want to take time to think over." She paused a moment and a slight frown appeared on her face.

"I am aware that Nash Broderick has come home, that you two were involved some time ago and he is generally accepted as Brodie's father. Yes, I know it was before my time, but small towns…" She shrugged. "The reason I raise this, is because it might affect the way you respond to what I want to discuss with you."

The principal threw herself back into the depths of her high-backed chair and steepled her fingers under her chin.

"How long is Broderick going to be around and does his presence influence how long you are likely to want to remain in Hamlet Brae?"

"I really don't know how long Nash will be here. I have the impression he came home to check on Anna and wouldn't be here for more than a week. At this time though, he's not indicated when he will return to Canberra. Maybe Anna knows more. As far as I'm concerned, wherever he is in the world will not affect me unless he suddenly wants to act on Brodie's paternity and makes demands. He wasn't interested all that time ago, so I don't think it will change. On the other hand, being face to face with death in a combat situation and knowing he has a son who could be his legacy in the world might have altered his view."

"Do you intend to stay in Hamlet Brae?"

"Staying here would be ideal, but teaching positions here are not thick on the ground." Dee smiled, encouraging Margaret's agreement.

"As it happens, we do have a vacancy appearing at the end of term. Jason is taking a senior position in Bendigo. It's not public knowledge yet, so I'd ask you to keep it under your hat. What it means for us is we have a space we can offer as a Graduate Teacher position. I'd like to put your name forward to fill it."

Dee felt her reaction blossom on her face. Her eyes widened, and her jaw dropped. "Really?"

Margaret firmed her mouth. "There are no guarantees—a. we'll be allowed a graduate position or b. they'll let us have you, so don't get your hopes up. I didn't want to proceed down this path without you being on board. The other final year students have been good too, but I think they're both looking for city lights."

"It would be amazing for us. Brodie would have stability with what family he has around him and I could continue to watch out for Anna. I don't think you know how much it would mean to me. Why would you do that, Margaret? You know nothing about me."

The principal laughed. "I've got a fairly good idea. You'll soon find, as a teacher, nothing much that goes on in your community gets past you. Anna Broderick mostly raised you. On its own, it would be enough for me, but I've assessed you on your own merits too.

"What I see is a resilient young woman who has taken the lemons in her life and made lemonade, as they say. You've achieved so much. Your boy is lovely and confident. I doubt he sees you as anything other than Super Mum. If we can get this graduate teaching position across the line, I'd be more than proud to have you as a member of our teaching staff."

Margaret stood signaling the end of the discussion and held her hand out for Dee to shake. "If it doesn't happen, call on me for a reference for other positions. You're an excellent teacher, Dee, and don't you forget it."

The bubble of pride expanded in Dee's chest again, pushing away the bitter memories and past feelings of not being quite good enough.

"Thank you, Margaret. I really and truly appreciate your faith in me."

Dee walked out to the secretary's office to collect her bags. Amy Matheson sent her a worried look. Maybe it was because she had been in with Margaret for so long that the secretary thought something was amiss. Dee didn't know. She reached out and gave the older woman a hug and received a warm embrace in return.

"You have a good day, Amy," she said as the smile bloomed on her face and she continued her interrupted progress to the year four classroom.

Chapter Thirteen

It was close to five by the time the staff meeting finished and Dee had done a debrief with her practicum supervisor, Maria March. Maria had been glowing in the report she had prepared to send back to Dee's university professor.

"I hope we get to work together again, Dee," Maria had said as Dee packed her calico bag.

"It would be wonderful if we could. I still have a lot to learn and you've been a gracious mentor, Maria." Neither of them alluded to Jason's imminent departure, though Dee got the feeling that Maria knew more than she was saying. As a senior member of staff, Maria would be aware of what went on within the school.

Dee's heart had given a little bounce at the possibility of working at the school, but she tamped it down. Life had taught her to hope for the best but expect the worst. There were fewer disappointments that way.

She reached into her handbag to find the keys to the car and encountered the ziplock bag of broken phone. If it wasn't too late, she could see Robbie now. She crossed the street and entered the post office/general store/telecommunications outlet and business that Robbie shared with his parents.

The post office counter at the rear of the shop had a short queue of people wanting to chat with the affable Bob or to buy postal products. It was never clear which imperative was operating.

At the front of the shop, to the right of the door, was the telecommunications section where Robbie operated his business.

Dee gingerly withdrew the plastic bag from its hiding place and placed it on the counter. Robbie took one look at the bag and let out a crack of laughter loud enough to startle the customers down where Bob was holding court.

"How did this happen? Did you take to it with a cricket bat?" Rob asked gleefully.

"No, wiping down the kitchen bench." Dee smiled. "Rob, I need a phone, so what do I do?"

"Well," he mused. "I don't have any of this model in stock and it may take a few days for a new one to come in. Do you have another phone you can use?"

"Only the ancient one," she said, withdrawing it from the bag.

Taking the phone from her, he said, "These were really good in their day. One touch speed dial, good large numbers, fantastic microphones, excellent range, but they were only good for phone calls and text messages. Nothing flash like photos or calculators or playing music. I can set this up with a sim card with your phone number. It'll get you through in the meantime until the new phone comes in. We'll put it on to charge the battery while we do the paperwork."

"Thanks Rob."

"Geez Dee, if this happened with you tidying the kitchen, I'd hate to see what would happen if you meant to do some damage," he chuckled and gathered her into a one-armed hug.

Dee smiled up at him in thanks and waited while he configured the new sim and made sure it would fit in the older phone.

"We need to take the sim out of the broken phone too, so you don't lose your contacts and photos. I'll give you a folder to store it in." Their heads bent close together as they worked to extract the sim from the device.

Neither of them noticed Nash outside the window.

"Let's give it a go," Rob said. He finished settling the sim and putting the phone back together. "Who do you want to call?"

"Are the old contact numbers still in the phone?" Dee asked.

"They will be if you saved them to the phone's memory and not the sim. You used to be able to do both, remember. Try it out."

"What about speed dial?"

"We won't know till you give it a go," he replied.

Dee scrolled through the contact list. Some old names and numbers that hadn't transitioned to the new phone made her smile as she was treated to fleeting trips through old memories. There were friends from university she didn't see any more but whose features immediately sprang to mind and some former clients for funerals. Even Nash's number was there.

"Huh! This one's safe to try because they disconnected it when Nash went into the army. Let me see, his speed dial was number five because it was right in the center." Because he was the center of her world, she remembered sadly. She pressed the five and the large dial key.

She lifted the phone with a grin, quickly formulating an exit line if the number had been reallocated and someone answered it. She heard the burring sound in her ear at the same time as she heard a phone ringing nearby with the retro phone tone Nash used to use.

She laughed up at Rob. "It's ringing!" She turned to see who it was who might be receiving her call.

She saw Nash standing outside the window pulling a phone from his top pocket and watched his lips form a "hello" as she heard his voice through the instrument.

Dee felt the blood drain from her face. She heard Rob trying to get her attention, but she couldn't move. Her eyes remained locked on Nash as he looked through the window and caught her stare.

Something clicked in her brain. She spun away and gulped in air as Rob put an arm around her shoulders for support. Dee allowed herself to be held while she gathered her senses and looked up at Rob's worried face.

"It's okay," she assured him. "I'll be fine." She tried to smile. "Thanks Robbie. Let me fix you up for this. Do you need a deposit for the new phone?"

Taking Dee's lead, Rob let her reaction pass. "Nah," he said. "Leave it 'til it comes in. Who knows, the warranty and your insurance might cover some or all of the cost."

"Okay. I'll see you then and tell Cassie I'll talk to her tomorrow." She knew Rob would be on the phone to Cassie as soon as she had left the store. That's the way they were, looking out for each other.

She was almost out the door when she realized it was Nash's arm holding it open for her.

Her eyes blazed up at him, but she kept her voice low. Her family situation had provided way too much entertainment for the locals over the years and she'd tried hard to avoid any more fodder.

"You bastard!" she hissed. "You absolute bastard! Mongrel! Fucking mongrel! You have the same phone number. Get. Out. Of. My. Way!"

Nash reeled back with every word, looking confused about why his phone number should matter.

Dee took the opportunity to storm past him and reached her car before he recovered. She spun out of the parking space and drove past, ignoring Nash's hand ordering her to stop.

Chapter Fourteen

Dee steered the car around the first corner to head toward home, when her brain screamed, 'No! Not there'. No, too close, too accessible, too vulnerable. She needed time on her own with no interruptions.

She hung another left and travelled down behind the row of shops and then right onto the highway heading south. Once she got as far as the picnic grounds out of town, she pulled into the parking lot well off the road to calm herself.

She dropped her head in her hands. Her shoulders slumped, and her mind went blank. Eventually, her gaze focused on the small path leading to the creek where she had lain with Nash so long ago.

She heaved a deep breath and her stomach growled, reminding her it had been a long time since her hurried lunch. The basic grittiness of nature's demands forced her to smile wryly. Still, she wasn't ready to go home and if she went back into town, she risked running into Nash.

Continuing south seemed the best option.

As she drove, she mentally reviewed what she had to do this evening. Mercifully, her diary was blank until it was time to collect Brodie. Brodie! How could she have forgotten Brodie? She slammed on the brakes, thankful that there were no cars behind her.

She pulled over and prepared to do a U-turn when she remembered Brodie was staying with Cassie tonight to go to a birthday party. He wasn't expecting to see her until after she'd been to the hairdresser tomorrow. No one needed her at this moment. No one except herself. If anything changed, she had a working phone with her, so she was contactable.

Traveling on, she stopped at the truck stop south of town where she worked when she'd been pregnant, and where her mother worked before her. As she walked in, Emma, the wizened manager of the place greeted her with, "I hear Nash Broderick is home, ay?"

Whatever Dee's response, every one of Emma's customers for the rest of the day would hear it. Maybe they would for the next week unless there was something bigger to knock it off Emma's gossip list. Dee formed her face into a smile. "Yes, because of Anna's heart attack. He's grown up a lot," Dee offered.

"Weren't you and him an item back in the day?" Emma persisted in her gravelly voice.

Dee drew on her public persona skills to say with a dreamy expression, "Yes, we were. It was a long time ago. He's been married to the army for so long, I'm surprised he knew his way home to Hamlet Brae."

Emma's sharp gaze focused on Dee's face and she appeared ready to say more when the unmistakable sound of air brakes hissed as a B-double pulled into the truck parking lot.

"You'll be busy in a minute, Em. I'll have a sausage roll and a flat white please. A take-away cup will be fine. Oh, and a bottle of water, thanks."

Emma glanced beyond Dee's shoulder towards the driver emerging from his vehicle. "This one's always on yippee beans. He'll be dancin' a two-step if he's not served 'n' out of here in three minutes."

Dee paid and waited for Emma to pass her food. She sat at one of the four ancient and scratched Formica tables as Emma greeted the newcomer who delivered his requests in an over-excited spray of words.

Dee tuned him out. Alone with her thoughts, she pondered her next move. She could head home, lock the door, and pretend she wasn't there—but there was nowhere to stash the car.

'Keep driving!' the devil on her shoulder urged. 'No one will miss you. Take some time for yourself. Forget the world.'

The driver's voice intruded. *Definitely on stimulants.* Downing the last of her coffee and grabbing the bottle of water, she headed out. She wanted to get on the road ahead of the hyped-up driver, hopefully driving in the opposite direction.

His truck was pointed north, she'd keep heading south. Yes. That's what she'd do. Geelong was less than an hour away. Early evening on the beach would be a balm to her soul.

She hit some of the Friday afternoon traffic snarl as she entered the city's environs, but soon she reached the beach. Parking the car on the pier, she got out, grabbed her handbag, and wandered the length of the structure towards the restaurant at the far end.

There had been memorial services she'd conducted here for families scattering the ashes of their loved ones into the waters of Corio Bay.

Instead of going up the stairs into the food area, Dee moved around the side of the building to hang over the rails at the far end as she looked out over the bay and allowed random thoughts to scatter across her mind.

The stretch of water in front of her appeared endless. In reality, it was the tip of a nostril on the dragon's head forming the shape of the much larger Port Phillip Bay. The bay wore the city of Melbourne as its crown.

She breathed in a lungful of salt-laden air and let it out slowly. The sound of a barking dog disturbed her reverie. It took several seconds to register the noise was coming from her handbag and then another moment or two to remember she'd used to think the barking dog was a much trendier alert for her phone than the usual ringtones. The alert she had programmed on her new phone was far more discreet.

Plunging her hand into the bag, she withdrew the phone. Nash's name appeared on the screen. She clicked the button to reject the call and slipped the phone into her pocket. The barking resumed. She ignored it.

The intrusion of Nash into her conscious mind shattered the calm she had drifted in. The protective numbness of her emotional black hole was wearing off. Her damage heart softened toward him because of his care and concern on Wednesday night. Now, finding he still had the same 'disconnected' number from seven years ago scalded her sensibilities as another betrayal.

She began to feel microcosmic mood swings zinging through her soul: rage, sadness, more anger, action. She needed to find a private space to go to ground before she screamed out loud, burst into tears or ripped someone's bloody head off, metaphorically speaking.

She strode to her car and drove the few blocks to the hotel she used when she stayed in Geelong.

The receptionist recognized her as she walked through the sliding doors. His fingers rattled officiously over the keyboard in front of him. By the time Dee breasted the counter, he said, "I'm sorry, Ms. Tillson. We don't appear to have a reservation for you." Without looking up, his furrowed brow eased, and his expression changed to pleased surprise. "But we do have you as being eligible for a free standard room or a free upgrade to an executive suite," he beamed at her. "Both are available."

She returned the smile, albeit a false, saccharin version of her usual greeting, and thanked her lucky stars for her loyalty to this establishment and not needing to make explanations for her sudden appearance.

"Oh, how nice! I'll take the standard room, if I may."

"Of course! It's good to see you here Ms. Tillson. Here's your key card. If there is anything at all I can do to make your stay more pleasant, please let me know. Enjoy your stay."

"Thank you, Troy," Dee returned as she took a step back, thinking Troy would go far in the hospitality industry.

With key in her hand, she rode the lift to the fourth floor and let herself into the room. She dropped her handbag on the bed as the dog recommenced its infernal barking. She pulled the phone from her pocket ready to pepper Nash with a few pithy words when she noticed it was Cassie's name on the screen this time. She cut off the call and sent Cassie a quick text message, "Bzy. Talk l8r." She dropped the phone on the bed next to the handbag with a mental note to change the goddamned ringtone!

She trudged into the bathroom and splashed her face with cold water. Calmer now, she slumped onto the queen-sized bed and wondered what on earth she thought she was doing running away from home. It sure as heck didn't solve any problems.

She fell sideways onto the pillow and slowly dragged her legs up onto the quilt cover immediately falling into an exhausted sleep.

Her dreams were chaotic. Visions of Nash happy, angry, worried, loving, paraded across her mind. Nash and Brodie swapped features and identities. Then she opened a gate to be confronted by a dog, a small friendly looking animal that wouldn't stop barking at her.

The irritation of the persistent noise roused her from sleep, but the barking continued. Finally recognizing the sound, she lunged for her phone, and, seeing Cassie's name forced a smile into her voice.

"Hi!" she greeted her friend. Someone once told her people can hear the smile in your voice on the phone. Right now, she hoped it worked.

"Dee. Are you okay? Rob said you looked a bit sick in the shop today and I've had Nash in my ear demanding to know where you are."

"I'm fine," she said forcing a chuckle. "Since Brodie is with you tonight, I thought I'd treat myself to a night in town," she said, careful not to divulge which town.

"Where are you? Are you sure you're okay?"

"I'm fine," Dee repeated. "You can contact me if you need me. Is Brodie handy? I'll say a quick hello."

"Yes, he is." Cassie's voice didn't sound convinced about Dee's explanation but called Brodie to the phone. Years of knowing taught a person lots about her best friend.

"Hey Brodie," Dee said as her son said hello. "How was your day?" She listened intently as he enumerated the tribulations and triumphs of a day in the life of a nearly six-year-old child. As his list of information petered out, she said, "I've popped over to town tonight. If you need me, call and I can be there pretty quickly."

"Aw Mum, I won't need you. I've got Aunty Cassie and James' party and then there's Uncle Robbie!" *How does a mother take that sort of dismissal?*

"Okay then. Stay safe and remember I love you lots."

"Love you, Mum. Bye!" Brodie hung up straight away, saving Dee from another chat with Cassie.

Talking to her boy left her with a happy feeling in her soul. Feeling better, she rang housekeeping to order a firmer pillow and a dental kit. Then she called in-room dining and ordered the soup of the day, pasta of the day, green salad, and a small carafe of white wine. She didn't have the energy to consult the menu. She needed food and the chefs here had never let her down. No thinking and no conscious decision-making were required.

She showered while waiting for her requests to arrive and wrapped herself in one of the full-length oversized bathrobes she knew she would find in the wardrobe. She rinsed her knickers and left them on the hot towel rail to dry, as a knock sounded on her door.

She opened it to admit the waiter pushing the trolley with her meal. Hovering behind him was another attendant with her pillow and toothbrush. "I'm sorry I'm late Ms. Tillson. I knocked earlier. I don't think you heard me."

"Oh," Dee exclaimed. "I must have been in the shower." She relieved the maid of her load with a smile of thanks.

Once the waiter deployed the trolley into a table, explained that the hot food was in the hotbox below, and gone, Dee poured herself a glass of wine and walked onto the small balcony overlooking the bay. It was time for sunset, but she was facing east, so the sunset was more of a suggestion in the change of light rather than a golden glow on the horizon.

Still, it was a time for inner peace. She sat in the steel chair, swallowed a mouthful of wine and heaved a sigh. After several minutes, she moved back into the room to the table. She bent, moved aside the dish of what looked like fettucine Amatriciana and pulled the bowl of fragrant onion soup from the hotbox.

She reveled in the opportunity to enjoy her meal in absolute quiet—no television, no demands, no complaints—and the luxury to take time to savor the wonderful flavors.

The rest of the wine disappeared as she completed the meal. She collapsed the table before wheeling the trolley into the corridor for collection.

She wandered into the bathroom and cleaned her teeth. Warm and well-fed, she relaxed on the bed. Now she could let her mind try to make sense of what she had learned today.

In fact, she flipped back the pages of her memory to seven years ago—to the weeks before Nash marched in to officer training.

She, Cassie, and Nash would drive into town to Robbie's place, and then the four of them would take off down by the creek.

Nash's imminent departure loomed large for Dee and one afternoon, she hugged him hard and didn't want to let go. He'd gazed down at her and it seemed so natural for his lips to join hers. It was their first kiss, or at least the first time that their lips joined, and Dee felt a strange stirring throughout her body.

Things progressed rapidly after that. They found time together away from the other two and one afternoon in a secluded spot beside the creek, kissing and touching culminated in the ultimate intimacy. Dee was hooked. If this is what it meant to be one with the person you loved, she could do it forever. Who'd have thought that the rock-hard appendage between Nash's legs could give her so much gratification?

They made love as often as they could, storing up the memories against the drought to come when Nash left. Neither of them gave any thought to the natural consequences of such untrammeled pleasures.

Then Nash was gone, Dee found she was pregnant, and the rest ... well the happy ever after bit seemed to wander off and attach itself to someone else, because Dee was still waiting for it to find her. But she had

Brodie and he was her world now. Thankfully, it didn't appear Nash was going to be a threat after all.

Chapter Fifteen

Dee's sleep was disturbed during the night not only by her dreams of Nash and their days down by the creek, but also by the late arrival of a couple in the adjacent room. The music was low and there was the chink of glasses followed quickly by the distinctive sounds of intimacy with enthusiastic encouragements of "Ah! Yes! Yes!" An hour later the ritual was revisited. This time, the accompaniments were a more muted, "Oh, oh." More chinks of glass and quiet conversation.

Dee dropped off to sleep. When the activity resumed before six the next morning, it seemed that Dee wasn't the only one unimpressed. "Ah yes!" and "Oh, oh!" had become "Mmphh, mmphh!"

Dee rolled out of bed and headed for the shower. Enough was enough. Breakfast would be served downstairs in less than half an hour. She decided to eat and wander on 'the beach for a while.

Her stroll along the foreshore was quiet despite the number of joggers and walkers out and about. She noticed a couple of bollard people she didn't recall seeing previously. A local artist had painted the large wooden pylons to depict people at different points in history. There were about a hundred of them arranged along the shoreline and their varied facial expressions, alone, brought a grin to most people. Once Dee had found her favourite bollard, a lifesaver with a black eye, she retraced her steps to find her car and return to Hamlet Brae in time for her hair appointment.

Dee drove into the town, past the community hall and into the strip of shops that lined either side of the highway. She parked in front of the *Quiff and Curl*, a reinvigorated hairdressing business now run by Natalie Armstrong.

Natalie's predecessor was Donna, a motherly type, who was the only hairdresser in the town for forty years. Donna decided she should stop work and take time to travel. She and Bert wanted to do the Trek, to join the other hundreds of grey nomads on a caravan holiday around the continent—what the younger generations malevolently called the SAD tour—"See Australia and Die".

At home in Hamlet Brae, Donna remained one of Natalie's most steadfast clients and took delight in the modernizations already apparent.

Gone were the reliable, but noisy, cone-head hair driers, replaced by contraptions that looked like rotating doughnuts of ultraviolet light that Natalie called rolabords. The treatment stations were ergonomically designed so the hairdresser didn't bend too far to reach behind the client's head to ensure a good wash. The chairs positioned against the basins were more like electronically controlled leather massage lounges that effortlessly positioned the client to the most comfortable position for their hair treatments.

Everyone got the wash, condition, massage treatment whether they wanted it or not—from the school kids to the farmers. The complimentary treatment saved Natalie from trying to cut hair dirty with schoolyard sweat or those dust-encrusted manes so prevalent in the harvest season. It was also Natalie's way of making sure clients left the salon looking and feeling better about themselves and the world around them.

Dee opened the door to the salon and nearly crashed into Edith Henderson who was exiting. Dee halted in time to prevent a collision and held the door for her erstwhile client, closing it as Edith began to speak.

"Oh Dee, dear. Thank you. Listen, dear, you did a marvelous job of my Bill's funeral, you know. What you said about him... well you made him a lot more human than another person in your circumstances would have." She patted Dee's arm.

"My Bill was a good husband and a good father, but I, as much as anyone, knew that he wasn't always respectful to you. And he was worse after you got pregnant. Well!" Her eyes rolled dramatically. "You can imagine what he said about that. You shouldn't blame a child for her parents' wrongdoings. Your young love with poor Adam's boy was long term and lovely and it should never be heaped in the same basket as your mother's sordid affair with a passing truck driver."

"Edith, really, you don't have to explain. I know what people thought about me, but I hope those opinions have changed."

"Oh, they have dear. I made sure of that. You've grown into such a lovely young woman. Another person abandoned by her parents might have gone totally off the rails but you're strong, dear, so strong. Anna's done a great job with you, too. I won't deny she's been a good influence, even if her sponge cakes can never rival mine."

Dee's mind jolted at the non-sequitur. "Well, I won't keep you."

"You look lovely, Edith," Dee was compelled to say.

"Oh, thank you dear." Edith patted her newly coiffed head. "My daughter's coming up from Melbourne today to take me to the airport to fly to Sydney. I'm going on a cruise to the Pacific Islands."

"That's sudden, isn't it?"

"Well yes. But it's something I've had in the back of my mind for quite a while now and when Bill died, I went looking for the next cruise available. I need to get away." Dee smiled inwardly at the way Edith screwed up her nose and nodded her head at the same time.

The older woman leaned forward as if inviting Dee's confidence. "Bill left me quite well off, you know, because he never would spend penny without turning it over twice. So now, I can use the money by having some fun or waste it by leaving it in the bank till I die! Then someone else would get to play with it." Edith's rounded eyes communicated clearly that she thought that would be close to sacrilege.

"Is your daughter going with you?"

"Oh no, dear. She has work. I'm going as a leopard."

"A leopard?"

Edith's saucy look should have warned her, but Dee was unprepared for Edith saying, "Is that what they call them? Older women who pick up young studs? That's what I'm after. It's been a long time since I had decent sex."

Dee choked on her laughter. "I knew you were a devil in disguise, Edith." Dee's laughter rolled out. "I wish you luck. Your sense of humour will draw lots of young bucks, I'm sure. You'll be a highly successful cougar."

Edith's chest bobbed as she chuckled. "Cougar! Yes. I must remember. I knew it was some sort of sexy cat. Raow! Bye, dear!"

Edith rotated her shoulders and swayed her hips as she walked away.

Dee re-opened the door and stepped into the salon. The little bell over the door signaled her arrival. Natalie was hanging up the phone and adding something to her appointments book when she looked up to hail Dee.

"Dee, my BFF! How's it going?"

"Not too bad, Nat. I see business is booming."

"It's all a matter of rolling organization. I can finish doing Beryl's foils while Mannie washes your hair and then cut yours before Donna's color is ready to be rinsed. It works. Mannie, can you get Dee started please?"

Mannie led Dee over to a lounger by a wash basin, seated her and tilted the chair back. This was a little bit more 'me' time–when she didn't need to worry about Brodie, or anyone else, and definitely not Nash Broderick.

As she relaxed under the ministrations of Mannie, Natalie's apprentice, she reflected on how lucky the community was to have someone like Natalie who was keen to come to this outpost and develop her business. And she brought in more people like Mannie who might also learn to appreciate small town life and stay to build a home and family here.

Mannie's full name was Manjula Srivas……. something, maybe Srivastavanhana? The unfamiliar name from the Indian sub-continent was not easily pronounced in Australian English, thus not easily remembered either. The locals settled for referring to the coffee-skinned beauty with the big white smile, simply as Mannie Srivas. Her petite figure belied the strength of the survivor. Her eyes shone with humour and a passion for her work.

She chatted to Dee about the upcoming multicultural festival she was helping to organize. Her patter didn't require a response as Dee's hair was expertly shampooed, rinsed, shampooed, and rinsed. The chatter subsided while Mannie concentrated on adding conditioner to Dee's hair and massaging her head for a full five minutes until Dee's active mind finally gave way to bliss.

With a final rinse, Dee's seat was raised to the vertical, her hair was briskly towel-dried, and she was released to Natalie's cutting expertise.

The tensions of the morning had abated under Mannie's attentions, so Dee allowed her mind to remain blank as Natalie sized up the job and proceeded to subjugate Dee's hair to her will.

In the next chair, Beryl, another local more than thirty years Dee's senior, sat with her hair under foils, browsing idly through a gossip magazine. She commented now and then on the doings of various celebrities and just as dismissively said, "It's a pity that Rosie and John are on the skids too."

"Rosie and John?" Natalie demanded. "What do you mean?"

"Well," Beryl leaned over conspiratorially, "Rumor has it John's been having it away with the new girl in the Ballarat office." She sat back smugly.

"You're kidding! They've only been married a year."

"Mmm, I gather that John likes to play rough sometimes and so Rosie said no more sex till he grows up. And," she shrugged, "if a virile young man is not getting it at home, he's got to find it somewhere." She gave a wink that looked surreal coming from the face of a sixty-year-old matron.

Vaguely, Dee registered the tinkle of the bell over the door that heralded a newcomer entering the busy salon but took no notice. Neither, it seemed, did Natalie.

"What do you mean rough?" Nat sought clarification. "Does he hit her? I wouldn't have thought it, but if he does, she's better off gone!"

"No! No, just—I guess he wants it when she doesn't, you know? And I think she likes to pretend she's still a delicate virgin."

"Ah," agreed the knowledgeable Nat. "You've got to give a man some leeway. Sometimes they like to sleep with an ice-princess but just as often they like it hard and fast." She let out a cackle.

"Sweet and romantic or hard and fast? What's your preference, Dee?'

In her relaxed state and with her eyes half closed, Dee asked, "What is it with people and sex this morning? I listened to it all last night and even Edith was on about it."

"Well?" Nat demanded.

"It's been so long, I hardly remember!" She cut her quiet chuckle short as she cracked her eyes open and glanced into the mirror. Her gaze locked with Nash Broderick's quizzical expression.

Dee sat bolt upright, startling Nat, who also looked into the mirror to see what might have caused such a reaction in her unflappable client. Dee knew that Nat would only see about one hundred and ninety-five centimeters of gorgeous male, not the history that sat behind him. Mannie was hopping from one foot to the other, trying to get Nat's attention.

Mannie and Natalie were the only occupants of the salon who were not aware of the tension pulsing through the scene.

"Oops! Skirts down, ladies!" Natalie called as she focused on Dee's hair for a moment and then swiveled slowly on her heel to face the newcomer.

"Well, hello! How can we help you today?"

"A standard cut." Nash was succinct.

Natalie briefly consulted the clock on the wall and strolled over to glance at the appointments book. "We can fit you in now, if you like? I'll just be a minute here."

Nash nodded.

"Good. Mannie can you show...?"

"Nash," came the terse rejoinder.

"... Nash to the basin while I finish up with Dee? Thanks!" Nat turned back and waggled her eyebrows in the mirror at Dee who almost imperceptibly shook her head. Nat shrugged but lifted one brow. Her look said Dee wasn't getting off that easily, but it could wait.

"Skirts down? What's that?" Dee puzzled, so only Nat could hear.

Nat shrugged. "Haven't you ever heard me say that, after all this time? My Grandma used to say it. When women get together, they like to kick up their heels and their skirts are flying. If a man walks in, the women try to be more careful and make sure everything appears as it should. The boys have 'ducks on the pond' when a woman walks into their domain. Granny reckoned us women needed something similar, to warn of male trespassers." She grinned.

"Right..." *There must be logic there somewhere.*

"The hair looks great, Nat!" Dee forced a smile as the proximity of Nash Broderick stole into her thoughts. She spoke at normal volume to call Natalie's mind back to the job at hand.

Nat held the mirror to display the style from the rear. Dee wouldn't have cared if her hair were a bat's nest. Being in the same space as Nash Broderick with the avid audience of both Donna and Beryl waiting for fireworks was not her idea of fun. She needed to go.

She sprang from the chair and gathered up her belongings. After swiping her credit card across the touch screen reader, she hurried to the door, but couldn't avoid taking one quick glance in the direction of the subject of the 'skirts down' edict.

Nash was going through the same ritual that relaxed her such a short time ago.

She wasn't relaxed now! She stood on the footpath out of sight of the occupants of the salon and regathered her senses before returning to the ute and going to find Brodie.

Chapter Sixteen

Did he hear correctly? Did Danielle's response to the hairdresser's ribald query mean that there really was no man in her life? He hadn't seen evidence of one, but that would be a minor obstacle to overcome. Not that it mattered to him either way. She was history to him the moment he had found out that she was pregnant with another man's baby. So why did his chest always tighten with a weird, yearning, hopeless feeling when she was near?

Nash tuned out the rest of the salon as the assistant washed his hair and massaged his scalp. All this fancy-schmancy treatment was off-putting. If he had known it was part of the deal of having his hair cut at the only salon in town, he'd have waited till he returned to Ballarat.

Donna cut his hair when he used to live here. She didn't bother with washing someone's hair unless, she said, it was too stiff to get her scissors through. It had been a quick trip into the salon and out when Donna was in charge.

He noticed Donna herself sat in one of the customer chairs looking for all the world like she was enjoying the innovations the new hairdresser had brought to the town, or maybe it was the risqué discussion of the type he'd walked into.

His mind was floating on some plane of disconnected thoughts and images when the assistant slowly raised his chair to an upright position and plopped a towel on his head. She rubbed vigorously as if to reawaken Nash from the semi-somnolent state induced by the treatment.

"Where would you like Nash, Natalie?" the voice above his head asked.

"Over here, please Mannie." Nat directed him to the seat so recently vacated by Danielle. He sat, resting his hands where Danielle's had been. A wave of need and longing swept through him. It was a sense akin to trying to take a ghost into your arms, he thought.

Why, Danielle? Why betray me? His unguarded heart whispered the questions. He hadn't gone there for more than six years. He wouldn't go there now. He slammed the memories closed.

The hairdresser wrapped a protective black coat around him with the brand name reversed so it was read the right way around in the mirror. Passive advertising, he figured and gritted his teeth.

"Mannie, could you rinse Donna, please? Emulsify first and make sure you have all the color lifted from the scalp. Rinse, light shampoo, condition, and massage. Right?"

"Yep. Do you want to check after the first rinse?"

"Only if you're not sure. You're good at this. Call me over if you need the backup."

The young woman called Mannie responded with a huge smile and took the few steps over to Donna to help her from her chair and over to the washbasins.

Nash became aware Natalie's attention was now wholly on him. "Standard cut, eh? How do I interpret that? The same style shorter all over? Or something with a bit more flair? I could leave it longer here on top, so it sweeps across in the current style, then shorter down the back and taper the sides?"

He frowned at the woman. He didn't have to explain to a proper barber what he meant by a standard cut. "Just cut it!" he demanded.

"Okaaay. I'll cut it and if you want it shorter, you can tell me. I'll start with a heavy crop and fade and we'll see how we go from there." She ruffled her fingers through the thick wavy, black hair on top of Nash's head, using her nails to taper down to show where the hair would be shorter.

These fingers did nothing for Nash, but the thought of Danielle doing the same thing had his body stirring in places he'd thought were dead. Not going there, he reminded himself.

"So…" the hairdresser began. "Are you new in town? I don't think I've seen you around before."

"No." Nash's tone was terse. She could take that as the answer to both the question and the implied one, Nash thought.

"Nash was born and raised here," Beryl volunteered from the seat beside him. She had a rotating doughnut above her head.

Nash grieved for Donna's old cone hair dryers which made such a racket, a person would not have been able to hear a thing.

"Like Dee?" Natalie asked.

"No. Dee came here when she was near the end of primary school. She and Nash were sweethearts before Nash went into the army." Beryl's stream of information didn't look like it would abate. Nash wished himself anywhere else but here.

Natalie's hand lifted from his head, and she stared hard at him in the mirror. "You're not the bastard who got her pregnant and went swanning off, are you?"

"What Ms. Tillson did after I went into the army is not my affair. If you want to know her story, ask her. I'm here for a haircut, not to oil the cogs of the town's gossip mill. Do you think you can handle a simple cut?"

The authority in his voice whipped Nat's head back as though he'd struck her.

"Whoa. Sure thing, Nash. Sorry if I trod on your toes. I like to get to know my customers."

Nash remained silent. Even Beryl, whose eyes had gone wide, didn't say a word. Nash's heart plummeted. In trying to avoid adding to the gossip about Danielle, he'd given them a whole new angle because of the way he had spoken to the hairdresser.

He sat rigidly. It seemed the hairdresser got the message because she started prattling inanely about her own story.

"Hamlet Brae is a great little town, isn't it? I came here about three years ago when Donna decided it was time to hang up her clippers. Isn't that right, Donna?"

A grunt of what could have been assent came from the direction of the washbasins.

"My apprenticeship in Ballarat finished and I wanted my own place. Ballarat already has a gazillion salons so when I saw the Quiff and Curl for sale in the trade magazine, I jumped at the chance. My biggest challenge was convincing the community bank I was worth the investment." Her hands didn't pause as she continued dealing with Nash's hair.

"It's been a great change for me. Most," she emphasized, "most of the people here have been absolutely wonderful."

Nash gained the impression her patter would have said, 'all the people' until he arrived in the salon this morning.

"Located where we are, it's less than an hour down to Geelong for the footy and the beach and less than an hour to Ballarat for the art galleries or the nightlife. It's only an hour and a half to Melbourne too, if you're driving."

Did this fire hydrant have no stop button? He knew all this stuff. He'd lived in this town for eighteen years.

"I bought a Miner's Right a couple of years ago. I go gold prospecting on my days off if I want to. There's still plenty of gold to find along the creeks if you know where to look.

"There now. What do you think?"

Nash looked up at the sudden change in the rhythm of the chatter. Natalie was framing each side of his head with her hands. "You can leave the top messy and natural, so you have the crop look." She fluffed the hair with her fingers. "Or you can quiff it with a bit of product to hold it in place." She combed it back on a diagonal as if to demonstrate her meaning.

"If you go back to the crop style, you can tug a few strands onto your forehead for the bad boy look."

Nash intercepted her pleased look with a feeling of irritation bordering on contempt.

"It's fine. Comb it back but no goo." He'd never aspired to being a James Dean. He wanted his flamin' hair cut in an ordinary style so he could wash it and let it dry and it would be fine.

Natalie humphed. "Well, it won't hold like that. It will bounce back into the crop as soon as you walk out the door."

"I'll live with it." *Until I get back to somewhere I can find a barber.*

"Then we're done!" Natalie flung off the protective cape with a flourish and a big smile.

Nash stood and looked down at her. "Thank you for the cut." The least he could do was to mend some of the damage he knew his testiness over the mention of Danielle and her baby had caused.

He reached into his back pocket for his wallet as he strode over to the counter and handed Natalie a credit card.

"It's good to see you back, Nash," Donna called to him. "Give my regards to your grandmother."

Nash turned towards the older woman and gave her a wave with the hand holding the credit card. "I will, Donna."

He opened the door. The bell tinkled as if it was pleased to see the back of him and his bad temper.

Chapter Seventeen

Nash exited the salon with a will to shake off the cloying sense too many gossipy women gave him.

He needed male company. The town boasted two pubs, "The Golden Nugget" and "The Rising Sun". Both had been built during the period of the gold rushes in the area. He'd had his first legal drink in the Nugget. His grandfather had taken him on his eighteenth birthday.

Grandpa reminded him it was something Nash's dad had been looking forward to almost from the day his son was born. Gordon had done it for Adam, and Adam wanted to do it for Nash. But Nash's parents, Adam and Frances were dead, so Gordon took it on himself to introduce Nash to the mores of men in pubs.

Nash headed to the Nugget. Faces angle toward him as he strolled to the bar. Ted Wilkins had been the proprietor of this establishment for nearly forty years and swiped a cloth across the bar in front of where Nash took a seat.

"Hey Ted."

"Nash. Heard you were home." There was no welcoming smile.

Another man walked to the bar and stood beside Nash. "So, the prodigal war hero returns, eh? You here to do the right thing, finally?"

"What do you mean, Phil?"

"Well, I don't reckon there're many folks around this town who are too impressed with the man you've grown into."

"Yeah? And why's that?" He was serving his country, wasn't that enough for his hometown?

"Maybe, just maybe it's because of the way you left our Dee high and dry. Or maybe because it seemed like you couldn't give a flying fig when they took your Grandma to hospital."

"I see." Nash's hackles rose.

"Hey Brodo!" His football nickname had Nash swinging around to the source of the call. "Come and have a drink with me. Your shout."

"A red or a beer, Tom?"

"Oh, a good red always."

"I'll have a schooner of the local and a glass of Tom's preferred, thanks Ted."

"So, you gunna marry the girl, Broderick?"

"That's between me and the girl, Phil. I'll bet you'll be amongst the first to know." He flattened a twenty dollar note on the bar, collected the drinks from Ted and headed over to Tom Nicholls, ignoring the irritation wrought by the self-styled local enforcer.

"Thanks lad. How's it going?" Tom was in his mid to late thirties but appeared far older.

"It was fine till I walked in here."

"Don't you mind Phil Thomshon. He's always gots to have his shay." Ted's speech was more than a little slurred. "I hear you're some kind of war hero these days."

"Not really. I didn't have much to live for, I reckoned, but the other guys did. I just tried to keep them out of harm's way."

Tom squinted at him. "I reckon it'd be more than that. They don't give out those bravery medals for sittin' on your bum."

"What do you do with yourself these days, Tom?"

"Me? I keep the wheels turning, my boy."

"Still writing?"

"Nah. No scope for an old hack like me in a town like thish. Nah, I'm general factotum. I mend the roads. I dig the gravesh. Occasionally I'll do the obits for a client's preferred newspaper. Keeps me alive and thankfully, it doesn't keep me sober."

He closed one eye and looked at Nash. "If I was sober, I'd have to evaluate my life—not good for my morale. Say, I got an invit... invitashun to this Naming Day out at your place. That was nice of your Grandma."

"You've been special to Grandma for a long time."

"Yeah, well... Is Siobhan coming?"

"I'm not sure, Tom. I'm not part of the organizing committee."

Tom's chin touched his chest.

"Would that affect your decision to come?"

"Might."

"You still got a thing for Aunty Shiv, Tom?"

"Might." The chin bobbed on Tom's chest a couple of times.

"You want me to let you know if I find out anything?"

"Nah!" A great sigh rumbled from Tom's chest before he raised his head.

"What's the bee in Phil Thomson's bonnet?"

"You don't know?" Tom blinked as if trying to focus on an idea just out of reach.

Nash shook his head.

"Well," Tom leaned forward to grasp the stem of his wine glass, "the way the town views it is that you got one of our young girls preggers and high-tailed it outta here to avoid the consequences. The consequences maybe including being on the wrong end of your own Granddad's shotgun."

"I went into the army, Tom. We'd planned it before my parents were killed."

"Mebbe, but the timing was sure suspicious."

"The baby wasn't mine anyhow."

"How do you figure? You're the only guy around here the girl ever spent any time with. Didn't they let you know she was knocked up? Was that the problem?"

"Don't talk about Danielle that way."

Tom closed one eye. "Like that, is it?"

"It's like nothing. Yes, I got word Danielle was pregnant. I also got the message someone else was the father and she wanted nothing more to do with her teenage crush."

Tom's eyes went round. "She told you so, did she?"

"It's the message she sent me."

Tom's face collapsed into a frown as he lifted his chin. "Doesn't make sense. If my investigative skills were still working, I could sift through this information. Let me think. We had the going away party for you and the two of you were tight as a knot. Then you went away, and she did lots of crying and stuff." Tom rolled his hand on his wrist. He sat back and blew a fetid breath between nearly closed lips.

"Then she was waitressing out at the truck stop."

"I knew about her working there."

"Then she started increasing, as they say."

"There you have it," frowned Nash. "She met a truckie at the servo like her mother did."

"Nah. Doesn't wash. The one thing she didn't want to be was her mother. She was contemptuous of truckies. Still is, I reckon. Do you think she mighta been raped? She's a lovely girl and an almighty temptation to those randy bastards."

Nash felt the blood drain from his face and the room spun around him. The beer roiled in his stomach. He swallowed, determined to stave off the embarrassment of losing not only the beer but this morning's breakfast over the floor of the pub.

She would have told him, surely? No. Not if it was going to distract him from his studies and the foundation he was building for them.

"If she was, she would have reported it, wouldn't she?"

"Nah. The young things I used to interview said following through with a complaint was worse than the assault itself. Then everyone knows really personal stuff about you. How would it have played out for Dee, do you think? Mother ran off with a truckie when she was a kid. Father hightailed it leaving her high and dry not much later. Then she was fostered unofficially and therefore illegally by your grandparents. Everyone knew you two were in a relationship without marriage. You've seen the short skirts Emma puts the girls in. Askin' for it. Loose morals."

Oh my God, wasn't it what Nash himself had said to her. He clutched his gut.

He looked up as Ted dropped the change for the drinks on the table. "You don't look too good, Broderick. Beer not to your liking?"

"It's fine." He stood. "I'll be seeing you, Tom."

"Sure Nash."

Nash walked away. "What about your change?" Ted demanded.

"Tom will look after it." He didn't stop until he was out in the brilliant sunshine of the late spring day.

"Shit!" he muttered. "Shit! Shit! Shit!"

Chapter Eighteen

Nash nursed his first beer of the night sitting on a plastic chair near the pool in his sister's back yard on Saturday evening, mulling over what he had done and learned in the time he'd been back, including Tom's inference about Danielle's pregnancy. He threw it into the mix of things to ponder.

The day working on the sheds last Saturday and helping Frank during the week reminded him of the good stuff about country life. It also reminded him, lately, he wasn't used to so much physical activity. He kept fit. He had to. It was part of his job description. This was different labor. Maybe he was getting soft.

Even as his muscles ached, he felt the deep satisfaction of a day's work well done. Frank accepted him as the same guy who left nearly seven years ago.

He couldn't say the same for his brother-in-law. Even this evening, Robbie had taken his hand in greeting, but it was the greeting you'd give to someone you met at a social gathering whom you didn't really know or trust.

Robbie's reaction was as if Nash disappointed him. He knew he hadn't been back, but surely Robbie realized Danielle having someone else's baby was enough to keep Nash away.

He could have been a better correspondent. Hell, he could have written a lot more than he had, but it never felt quite right. Every time he started a letter to send home, thoughts of Danielle intruded. She was the one he should have been writing to, as he'd promised during those afternoons down by the creek.

Cassie was wary around him. like Robbie, but underneath, she was still his little sister and her hug registered the fact, even as the look in her eyes told a different story.

They'd all been close as kids. They'd done everything together. Danielle squared off the foursome.

He and Robbie even talked about going into the army together, but then Robbie hadn't wanted to leave Cassie for however long it would be. Instead, he'd stayed behind and gone to university in Ballarat to do information technology, married Cassie while Nash was in Afghanistan and now, they had a son.

A clutch of envy wrapped around Nash's gut.

The day remained warm and Robbie was in the pool keeping an unobtrusive eye on the two young boys.

Danielle's boy was alternately challenging and protecting his younger playmate. "Try this, Jacob! Oh no. Are you okay? It's all right, I've got you." He was a caring kid, Nash would give him that much, no matter who his father was. The boys could almost be brothers. The similarity was striking.

He was missing something here.

The kid didn't seem to like him much. The feeling was mutual. Too much attitude for a six-year-old.

The appearance of Danielle with exhaustion evident through her dropping shoulders pulled from his musings. She carried a bowl of salad and stuttered to a halt when she saw him.

With her light brown hair hanging loose around her shoulders, she was so much like the girl he'd left behind. He swallowed hard, thinking about whether some bastard had abused her in the most fundamental and intimate way.

"Need a hand?" he offered.

"It's cool, thanks."

"You put a lot of effort into getting the quarters cleaned and stocked." He aimed for neutral.

"Mmm. If push comes to shove, and I run out of time, I can leave the quarters as they are after what I got done last Saturday. It's a point of pride though, to offer the shearers the best we can. Plus, it lifts the load for later in the week when the family starts arriving for the Naming. I'll get back to it tomorrow."

"How many are you expecting?"

"We're not sure yet. Your Uncle Sean and Jenn, your cousins Michael and Connor, Connor's wife Caroline and their two little ones. Aibreann is coming too, but I'm not sure whether she's bringing a partner. Your Aunty Siobhan is flying into Avalon on Thursday so one of us will go down to collect her. There's Caroline's family, her parents, and some aunts, uncles, cousins, friends."

"Why Calypso? Why not Uncle Sean's place?"

"We have better facilities here than on the Mount Mercer place."

She might not have rolled her eyes, but he could hear it implied in her voice.

"Will you fit them all in?" he asked.

"We can house forty in beds in the quarters, thanks to your parents' improvements. Then I have space, as do Anna and Cassie. After that, those who bring swags can bunk in the shed or in the living area of the quarters. It'll work out."

She glanced over her shoulder as Cassie stepped out of the house and Dee hurried over to take a large bowl from her.

"Is that where you got to, Nash? You can give Robbie a hand with the meat. Rob? You want to get the boys in, now? I'll give them a warm shower."

Rob responded with a wave and herded the boys to the shallow end of the pool. Danielle's kid stood behind Jacob and helped push the little guy up the ladder before climbing out himself.

"They look alike," Nash offered.

"Yeah. Funny, that." Sarcasm dripped from the words as Danielle moved away to help Anna to a seat at the outdoor table on the patio.

What the hell did that mean?

He stood and moved to where a towel-dried Robbie was donning a polo shirt over his damp swimming trunks.

"What can I do, mate?" The hard, sideways look that Rob sent him startled him. "Look, what is it? I feel that there's a conversation going on all around me and I'm the only one left out of the loop."

"Mate, we've known each other a hell of a long time. You're a different man than I thought you'd be, but that's none of my business. It's between you and Dee. Talk to her about it. Let's have a pleasant family dinner. Right? Here, put the sausages on for the kids and I'll fetch the onion. Can I get you another beer?"

"I'm right for now."

Nash was more puzzled now than he had been earlier. What could he possibly have to talk with Danielle about?

He arranged the sausages in regimented formation on the barbecue grill.

"Jacob! Stop!" the young voice came from nearby. "The barbie's on. It's dangerous!"

Nash looked up in time to swing out an arm and scoop up the smaller of the boys before he followed a ball into the legs of the barbecue.

Danielle's kid was standing looking up at him with a worried-relieved frown while the child in his arms was laughing hysterically and squirming wildly. "Thanks Mister. I tried to stop him."

"What's up?" Cassie asked as she approached the group.

"Nothing much, Aunty Cassie, but Jacob is a little bit starving to death."

"A little bit, huh?"

Danielle's kid nodded. He wasn't a dobber. Nash could respect that in a fellow male.

"The sausages have just gone on, mate," he said to the kid. "Do you think you can keep him occupied for another five minutes."

"It'll be a struggle, I reckon, but I'll try."

"Good man! Do you think it's safe for me to let him down?"

The kid shook his head. "Give him to Aunty Cassie and she can take him back to the house. I'll take over from there."

The seriousness of the child's face and the thoughtfulness of his strategy impressed Nash. Maybe he could get to like this kid after all.

"Here you go, Cass. All yours." Nash handed Jacob across to his sister and watched the kid follow along. What was his name? Brodie? Was that a diminutive or the whole name? Nash turned each sausage a quarter rotation, working from left to right.

Robbie returned with the onions and steak. Nash put out a hand to protect the sausages from invasion. "Can I do that for you?" He took the onions from Robbie before he responded and layered them carefully on the central solid grill plate and then took the steaks and spread them evenly across the grate.

"You do know it's not polite to completely take over another man's barbecue, don't you mate?" Robbie queried.

Nash punched his shoulder with a wry smile. "You're not a man, though. You're my kid brother."

Robbie snorted. "In law," he corrected.

"Does Danielle still eat her steak cooked till it's leather?"

"Pretty much."

"Should have put in on first, eh?"

"Turn down the heat on these and put hers over the hot spot. She'll be jake."

The meal passed quietly except for a spirited discussion of the upcoming trade picks for the Australian Rules football league. A local lad was in the mix for his shot at the big time and each of the adults around the table had their own views on which team should choose him.

The children finished their meal and wandered back into the house.

The adults sat over their coffee until they heard the bark of a dog and Brodie call out, "Jacob! Stop!" There was a screech of tires and a thump. All the adults except Anna sprang to their feet and hurried through the house and out the front door.

A young driver was getting out of a small hatchback. Brodie was standing, shaking, on the footpath with his arms tightly wrapped around the smaller figure of Jacob.

He let out a panicked yell, "Mum!"

"I'm here, Little Bit. What's happened?"

"Meggs. She stopped Jacob from running onto the street, but then the car hit her." He began to cry.

Nash stepped forward to confront the driver.

"I'm sorry mate, I didn't even see what I hit. I wasn't going fast."

"Back the car up and put your lights on low beam so they shine down on the road."

The youth scampered to follow the orders barked at him. "Robbie, have you got a hard board we can lift the dog onto?"

"Um.. I can't think. Is Jacob hurt?"

"No. Focus, man! A board?"

Cassie stepped forward, tugging her son from the arms of the terrified Brodie. Calmly, she directed her husband to go and fetch the door to the new playhouse he was building.

"The door?"

"The door … you haven't put it in yet, have you? So, go."

Robbie focused on her face for a moment and then sprinted around the back of the house.

Danielle came over to squat next to her prone dog. Meggs whimpered and Danielle went to pat her. The dog snarled. Nash heaved Danielle to her feet. "Don't you know better than to touch an injured animal? I'll deal with this. Robbie put the door here. Now, from the back so she's got less chance to take a bite out of us. Ready? One, two, three."

Together they eased the dog onto the door.

"Undo the tray of your ute, Danielle. Robbie, lift. One, two, three."
They slid the door into the vehicle. "I'll take her to the vet. Is McPherson still in Smith Street?"

"Ah, no. The surgery is still there, but it's a new guy. Um.."

Brodie spoke up. "Malcolm James. I'll come with you." The fierceness of the boy's tone communicated a strong attitude of 'don't mess with me'. Nash glanced at Danielle. She was focused on her son.

"I'm going, Mum!"

Danielle nodded. "I'll handle things here and follow in Anna's car and I'll phone ahead to let Mal know you're coming." She withdrew her car keys from her jeans pocket and handed them to Nash.

Nash wasn't sure it was a good idea for the six-year-old to be part of the visit to the veterinary surgeon, but he wasn't the parent here.

"Right, kid, in you get." Nash rounded the vehicle and climbed in. "Put your seat belt on."

"I know the rules, Mister."

"And don't call me Mister. Grandma told you to call me Uncle Nash. If that doesn't work for you, kid, call me Nash or Captain." He looked in the rear-view mirror and saw Danielle approach the young driver and draw him into her arms. Nash's gut tightened as it always did when he thought of any man other than himself touching Danielle.

"Why did you want to come? This might not have a happy ending, you know?" His harsh tone didn't seem to faze the boy.

"She's my dog. If Mal has to put her down, do you think it should happen without anyone there who loves her? It would be like it nearly was for Anna Nana, if we hadn't arrived in time for mum to blow into her mouth."

"Your mother resuscitated my grandmother?"

Brodie nodded furiously. "And I rang triple zero."

Nash's emotions were in a whirl. Was this when Grandma had the heart attack or something else? Why the hell didn't anyone let him know what was going on? He wasn't totally incommunicado, surely. The kid wouldn't be able to give him answers. It would have to wait.

"What happened back there at the house?"

"Jacob chased a ball and nearly ran onto the road. Meggs herded him like he was a sheep, but then the car came around the corner and hit her."

Nash registered the quaver in the boy's voice. He might be full of front, this kid, but he was still a child.

The vet was dressed in jeans and polo shirt and exited the residence attached to the surgery as they arrived.

"Hey Brodie."

"Hey Mal. Captain Nash is Aunty Cassie's brother."

A smile broke out on the man's face. He was about ten years older than Nash. He held out his hand. "Hello, Captain Nash, I'm Malcolm James. Let's take a look."

They lowered the gate on the ute and between them, Nash and Mal carried the dog towards the surgery. "Open the door will you Brodie, mate?"

The men carried the door and the dog through to the stainless-steel bench in the surgery.

Meggs lifted her head to scent the air and whimpered. "It's okay, Meggsy girl. We're just going to look. Brodie, you come up here, not too close, so Meggs can see you. Nash, you gently place your hands there so she's less likely to jump up."

The vet took his time examining the underlip of the dog. "I'm checking for shock here, Brodie. Do you see how it's taking a little while for the blood to come back in? That can mean she's suffering from shock. I'll check her lungs, then we'll get a drip set up quickly before we do anything else." He dropped his stethoscope onto the bench.

"Lungs sound fine. We call this needle thing a catheter. I'll stick it into her leg and use a drip to get fluids into her."

"Won't it hurt?"

"It might, but she's in shock so she's less likely to feel anything. The biggie we must worry about is the fluid running out of her blood vessels. When that happens, she won't have enough oxygen moving to her brain or her vital organs. Do you know what happens if there's not enough oxygen going to her brain?"

"She dies?"

"Probably. So, we work on that first to keep her alive, then we'll look for broken bones and stuff like that."

"Okay, Mal." The little boy's stoicism touched a barren space around Nash's heart. He was a good kid.

The vet moved efficiently around the space. When the fluid was pumping into the animal, he methodically assessed the dog's injuries.

"I can't feel any breaks and there's no puckering of her abdomen, so we might be lucky here. She'll be bruised in a few places, but if we can keep the shock under control, I think she'll be okay."

"Really?"

"Now, don't get your hopes too high. We won't know anything much for a few hours. I'll put her on a hot pad in a cage and keep the fluids going so I can check her urine overnight. We'll know by morning. But," the vet swung his head on his shoulders from right to left and back again, "I think she'll be fine."

Brodie swung his eyes from one adult male to the other as if searching for something. In the end, he threw himself against Nash's legs and burst into tears. Nash hauled him up. The child clung to him like a limpet and Nash carried him to the waiting room.

Just like his mother, Nash thought. Toughs it out until the danger's past, then falls into a heap. It felt so right having this child in his arms. Danielle's son should have been his.

The physical embodiment of his thoughts skidded to a halt inside the surgery door. Her questioning eyes were panicked.

"Go through. I'll keep Brodie out here for a while."

Nash heard low murmurs coming from the examination area. He sat on a couch in the waiting area with the boy on his lap. The child didn't let go even when the wracking sobs abated.

Danielle returned with Mal on her heels. A cautious smile played on her face.

"Call me in the morning, Dee." Mal patted Brodie's back. "You're one strong soldier, Brodie Tillson. I can see your dad's proud of you too."

"But..." Nash began.

Danielle cut him off. "Thanks Mal. We'll talk tomorrow. I'll get this one home. Brodie, are you going back to Cassie's with me or Nash?"

"Nash," he muttered.

"Right. I'll see you there."

"Thanks again, Malcolm," Nash shook the vet's hand while still balancing the clinging child.

Back at the ute, he leaned down and prized the child's arms from around his neck and put his seat belt on. "Hey Brodie. Do I need to take you back to Mal to put you on a drip? You're not going into shock on me, are you?"

The child whispered, "I don't think so, but it was really scary."

"And you handled it well—the same way I would have done."

"Yeah?" Brodie looked up at him.

"Yeah. You're one tough cookie. Proud of you." Nash ruffled the child's hair, swung around the vehicle and into the cab.

He wasn't sure what had happened tonight, but this child had opened a chasm in his chest he hadn't known was there. He couldn't remember the last time someone had placed so much trust in him.

Chapter Nineteen

Dee called Malcolm first thing on Sunday morning.

"She's doing okay, Dee. No obvious blood in her urine. Still a bit dopey, could be the drugs I fed into her system to keep her calm overnight. I'd say leave her be for another day or so. She'll recover better lying on the hot pack and not moving around."

"Right, Mal. If you think it's for the best... Would it be okay to bring Brodie by later in the day to reassure him?"

"That'd be good for both of them. Meggs might be a little less confused if she sees some familiar faces."

"Thanks. We'll see you before lunch."

With Meggs sorted, Danielle turned her attention to other matters at hand. The shearers were coming, not on Monday as she'd requested but on Tuesday, which would make things tight to have everything shipshape before Sunday's event. Still, she'd make it work.

Shearers, sheep, no sheep dog!

Perhaps Sean had a dog she could borrow at short notice.

An hour later, her head was spinning. Nash's Uncle Sean didn't have a dog available, but his son, Connor would bring his two and work them himself.

The phone rang in her hand.

"Dee! It's Caroline. Connor and I had a chat and, if it's okay with you, we'll bring the family over today. That way, I can help Grandma organize the party stuff while you're dealing with the shearers."

"We'd love to have you, but don't you have work to do on your own place?"

"Not yet. While we're only an hour from you, our ripening season is late. Our harvest won't kick off for another month so we're all sitting around twiddling our thumbs, waiting for some action." Her laugh tinkled through the phone.

"Then come and stay here, not in the quarters."

"Oh no, we don't want to be a bother."

"No bother at all. You'll be more comfortable than sharing with the shearers. Think of the little ones."

"I guess you're right about the kids. They'd be confused with a horde of men tromping through their space."

"Great. You'll be here in time for dinner?"

"We should be. I'll call if we're delayed. Shall I bring a cot for Catherine?"

"Don't bother. I've still got Brodie's. I'll get it out to make sure it's clean. See you soon!"

Okay Dee. Think! Connor and Caroline are arriving today. They take priority. Then there's Meggs. You have tomorrow to do a final check on the quarters for the shearers and get the food organized. Connor is bringing the dogs, so that's settled. There's the plan!

"Mum?" Brodie's frightened voice cut into her thoughts. "You look upset. Was that about Meggs?"

"Sorry, Little Bit. Did I look worried? I'm planning. Meggs will be fine. We'll see her in a couple of hours. Aunty Caroline and Uncle Connor will arrive later today so their dogs can take Meggs' place to bring in the sheep for the shearers."

"Are they bringing Ciaran?" Brodie's face lit up.

"Yes, and Catherine. I've invited them to stay here in the house."

"Cool! Can Ciaran sleep in my room? I'll move to the top bunk and he can have the bottom one."

"If that's okay with Aunty Caroline, then it's okay with me."

"Yay! Meggs will really be all right?"

"Let's not be definite until we see her. Mal thinks she should be fine."

"Yippee!"

"Would you like some breakfast?"

"Yes, please. A big one, like Aunty Cassie's. I think so much worry has chewed up all my energy."

Dee's heart swelled with love for this caring, wonderful child. "Come, show me what you want."

After breakfast, Brodie directed himself to check his room was tidy and to pull the sheets from his bed, while Dee checked the readiness of the guest room with the queen-sized bed and the adjacent smaller one she used as a study. She retrieved the cot from where she stored it in the wardrobe and wiped it over with disinfectant.

Dee's ingrained need for neatness was born out of the times she lived alone while her father was away, and she had to maintain the facade of adult supervision. It served her well now. There was little to do to prepare for her guests except to ensure there were fresh linens on the beds, clean towels on the towel rails and sufficient bathroom condiments.

"Well done, Brodie. Your room looks lovely. Let's go visit Meggs."

It gave Dee the feeling that she was missing something, getting into the ute without calling for the ginger dog. She turned the ute into Anna's driveway.

Brodie bounded out of the car and into Anna's house. Dee followed more slowly.

"Anna Nana, Ciaran's coming!"

"Brodie, darlin'. Slow down. What's this about Ciaran?"

"I rang Sean to borrow a dog. Instead, Connor and Caroline are bringing down two dogs and the children this afternoon," Dee said as she took a couple of steps into the house. "They'll be here about dinner time if you'd like to come over."

"They're staying in the quarters?" Anna frowned.

"No. they'll stay with me. They might want to move down to the quarters when the rest of the family comes, otherwise they're welcome to stay put. We're on our way into town to check on Meggs and to pick up some extra supplies. Is there anything you need?"

"Not that I can think of. Will you do another barbecue?"

"I was thinking of doing a big pot of beef burgundy and another of pineapple chicken with vegetables. And," she smiled down at Brodie, "a casserole dish of macaroni cheese."

"Yay! Ciaran and I both love mac 'n' cheese."

"Okay honey, I'll bring some apple pies then. You'll pick up ice cream and cream?"

Dee sensed Nash walk in the door behind her.

"Captain! Meggs will be all right. Mum and I are going to see her now." Brodie glowed up at the tall man.

To Dee's surprise, Nash came down to Brodie's level. "That's great news, Brodie. I'm sure she'll be pleased to see you."

"And Ciaran's coming this afternoon. Isn't this the best day, ever?"

Nash swiveled to face Dee.

"Your cousins will be here before dinner. I'm sure they'd love to see you."

Nash held her gaze. She had no idea what he was thinking.

"Right. I'll be there. Say hello to Meggs for me, Brodie."

"Sure thing, Captain. Let's go Mum. Bye, Anna Nana. Mwah!"

The ride into town was accomplished with a child bouncing excitedly all the way. Dee couldn't help but grin at his antics. When they pulled into the carpark at the veterinary surgery, it amazed Dee how quickly her son could flip open his seat belt, then the car door and be out and heading to the building before she could move. Thank goodness there were no other cars in the vicinity on this quiet Sunday morning.

"Hey Mal," Dee greeted the vet when she caught up with the pair.

"Hi Dee. Right this way."

Meggs was waiting at the front of her cage and wagging her tail as they came through the dormitory doorway. Her yip of pleasure was loud and sharp in the small space.

"Hey Meggs. How are you doing, girl?" Brodie's sing-song excitement matched the dog's frantic body movements.

"I won't open the cage today, Brodie. I don't want Meggs thinking she's well enough to jump down."

"She'll be okay?"

"By the look of this, we have nothing to worry about. She's got quite a few bruises but no breaks or internal injuries I can find. You can usually tell when there are undiagnosed injuries. The animal isn't herself. Our Meggs here is a box of beans."

"We'll leave her with you overnight, Mal. I've got two replacement dogs coming in this afternoon. They were all part of the same litter, so I'm thinking there'd be far too much excitement for her. If you think she's okay tomorrow, I'll take her back to Anna's, so she's away from the other two for a few days."

"Sounds like a perfect plan."

From the vet's, Dee drove to the small independent supermarket to pick up some extra supplies for her guests along with the cream and ice-cream that Anna had requested. She called in to Cassie's on the way back out of town.

"Hey Cassie, we won't stop," she began as Brodie ducked past her and into the house. "I wanted to let you know Connor's family is arriving this afternoon. If you're up to it, you guys are welcome to join us for a casual dinner. Nash will bring Anna."

"Sounds great. Shall I bring some of my usual pre-dinner dips and crudités?"

"Gosh, I hadn't thought of anything to have with drinks. That'd be excellent. I can take Jacob with me now if you like."

"Bliss! I'll have a nap. How's Meggs?"

Dee laughed. "You can't keep a good dog down! Mal says she has some bruising. If the car had been going any faster, she would have been in trouble."

"It impressed me the way you handled young Simon last night. Someone else would have been screaming at him when they hit your dog. You gave him a hug!"

"It wasn't really his fault. The way you kept everyone calm was amazing."

"Second nature to a teacher, Dee. You did it too. Grandma had a cup of tea waiting for all of us when we went back inside. We women rock!"

"Something happened between Nash and Brodie last night too. I'm not sure what. Brodie was clinging to him for dear life by the time I got to Malcolm's. There was a strong dose of hero worship for him when we called into Anna's on the way into town."

"It'll all work out in the end, Dee. Don't put up barriers, don't push either. Let it evolve."

"I can't help thinking of the 'if onlys'."

"Waste of time. Go with the flow."

Dee nodded. "I'll get the boys. I want to go down to the quarters and make up the beds and get everything squared away so I'm free to bring up the sheep tomorrow."

Back at the house, Dee prepared the main course dishes and put them in the oven to cook on low heat. The beauty of slow cooking was the flavors were great. Better than that, by the time she sat down to eat, it felt like someone else prepared the meal.

Dee set the boys to re-dusting the areas she'd already done in the shearers' quarters while she began making the beds. She'd completed two of the two-bed rooms when she registered a quad bike pulling up outside.

Nash knocked dust from his boots before he walked in. "I'll give you a hand." His voice was neutral and his face impassive.

"Thanks. I could use the help."

"I called into your house on the way down. Something smells good."

Dee smiled. "Just making sure I don't have to panic about dinner after I've finished here."

The boys came barreling through the door from the bedrooms.

"We've finished dusting, Mum. What's next? Hello Captain. Are you helping too?"

"Yep. Teamwork."

"Cool." Brodie looked to his mother.

"Towels. If you go to the linen cupboard, you can put a towel on each bed as I finish making it. Jacob, if you put a bar of soap with the towel Brodie puts down, we'll be finished in no time. Thank you, guys."

With Nash's brooding, though all but silent, assistance the beds were completed. Dee's fingers fumbled with nerves a few times in the confined space of each of the bedrooms. She doubted that Nash would have noticed. She checked the boys presented the towels and soaps neatly, and the job was done.

"What have you got on tomorrow?" Nash's voice rumbled. His beautiful eyes were free of the accusatory glint she'd come to expect. Instead, there was a softness there enough to melt her heart.

"Bringing the sheep to the big paddock, so they're ready for drafting into the holding pens on Tuesday morning when Jim's team arrives."

"Right. I'll go clean up then. I'll bring Grandma over shortly." His departure left Dee wondering what prompted his appearance in the first place. It had been an eerie, intimate sort of thing making the beds with him. Something like a long-married couple might do together. No point wishing for the moon, she chastised herself.

She gathered the boys and drove to the house as a large SUV came through the gate from the road.

Dee swung the ute around to park alongside it. The boys from each car barreled out.

The child emerging from the other vehicle was almost identical to Brodie and Jacob and fitted neatly in the middle in terms of age and height. Ciaran was five years old and looked as pleased to see Brodie and Jacob as they were to see him.

Caroline climbed from the car looking pristine. "I envy you so much," Danielle hugged her friend. "You always look gorgeous and elegant, no matter what. I'm a scruff. We've been finishing the quarters for the shearers."

"You're naturally beautiful, Dee. You don't have to be anything else," Caroline said.

Connor rounded the vehicle and caught Dee in a quick embrace before leaning into the vehicle to unstrap the baby seat carrying six-month-old Catherine.

"Come on in. The rest of the family is coming over tonight, but it won't be a late one. There's work and school tomorrow."

Connor handed the baby seat to Dee and retreated to the rear of the vehicle to open the travelling cages for the two red kelpies waiting there. Mitzy and Beau sprang out of the boxes like horses from a racing gate. They circumnavigated the house at breakneck speed before taking a more leisurely approach to sniffing around the place.

With the dogs out of the way, Connor picked up two medium-sized suitcases and turned to follow Dee into the house.

"Thanks for coming, Connor. I would have been up the creek without a paddle if I had no dog when the shearers get here on Tuesday."

"My dogs need the practice," Connor laughed. "They've been lazy lately. I'm still trying to get Mitzy to do as she's told. This should be a good workout for her. It works for me, Dee. Besides, that's what family is for."

Another car jounced over the cattle grid from the main road into Dee's yard.

"Gosh, I'm not even in yet. I'd better check on dinner." She hefted the baby carrier a little higher to check on the precious cargo nestled there and strode inside.

With the baby deposited in the guest bedroom where Caroline had gone to leave her bag of baby paraphernalia, Dee dashed to the kitchen to check on the meal, then hurried to her en suite bathroom for a quick shower to remove the grime of the day.

Caroline took over getting Brodie and Jacob washed and dressed. Dee returned to the kitchen as Connor's brother, Michael, walked through the back door.

"Michael." Dee squealed. "It's so good to see you. How come you're here too?"

"When my brother said he was coming over here ahead of time, I thought why should he have all the fun? Spending time with my best girl is never a drag, even if it involves mustering and shearing." He wrapped his arms around her and smiled into her face.

"I'm glad you're here," she said sliding out of his embrace. "Where would you like to sleep? I can move Brodie in with me and you can have his bed, a swag on the lounge room floor or the shearers' quarters. We finished those, so they're ready to go."

"The quarters will be fine."

"Okay, but there's no food down there yet. I'll give you a carton of basics for the night. You can come here for breakfast."

"Sweet. Hey, here's Cassie." He wandered over to greet the newcomers. Dee waved a hello to her friend before turning to prepare vegetables to accompany the casseroles.

It felt good to have so many of the family around—even if it meant Nash was here too and catching sight of him made her skin tighten in the instinctive way it did when danger was near, like when she handled Billy.

The evening passed in a blur for Dee. The family was fed, dessert and coffee served, children put to bed and the second lot of dishes piled into the dishwasher. By the time Dee crawled under her lightweight summer bed-covers, she was exhausted. Sleep came quickly.

Chapter Twenty

Nash climbed out of bed on Monday morning, rubbing sleep from his eyes. It hadn't been a restful night.

Images of Danielle swirled through his dreams. Danielle with Michael. Danielle with Connor. Bloody hell, even Danielle with his Uncle Sean. What explanation could there be for the boys being so similar. He could see why Ciaran and Jacob were alike, they shared the Broderick blood line. For Brodie to fit so neatly, he was a Broderick too.

After seeing Danielle and Robbie in the shop, he'd thought it might have been Robbie who had fathered Danielle's child. There was a closeness way beyond platonic friendship.

He sat on the side of the bed. Tom's theory that Danielle had been raped was seeming less likely. His limited knowledge of people who had been assaulted was they shied away from physical contact. Both Michael and Connor were free with their hugs with Danielle during the evening, with Michael keeping his arm around her shoulders while coffee was being drunk. Danielle didn't seem to mind one bit.

Danielle was accepted as a part of his family. Connor made it clear. Even his grandmother said things like, "Blood will out." If she knew who the father was, why didn't she say something? Why didn't she flat out tell him who the arsehole was so he could knock his block off? Then he could go back to Canberra with his own sense of honor restored. He'd get some satisfaction, at least.

It wouldn't change his anger towards Danielle. The fact she chose someone who looked like him might be some consolation, if you looked at it that way. She didn't pick up any dick that walked through the door. She wanted someone like him.

Watching her sitting there with the baby in her arms... he wanted that. He wanted their dreams back. He wanted to see her with their baby. He wanted the whole box and dice.

Could he make a go of it with Danielle again? He could raise her child if he was related to him. He was getting to like the kid. He was stoic and caring. He disarmed disputes between the younger boys. He adored baby Catherine. If nothing else, Danielle had done a great job of raising her son.

It didn't alter the fact she'd tried to claim the baby was his after she'd told Gillian, a fellow cadet, about the other man.

He pulled himself into an upright position as the encrypted phone in his bedside drawer began to chirrup. The ring tone was the one reserved for work colleagues. He snatched it up and found Mitchell's avatar grinning at him.

"Morning, bro. You up and running? My guess is you've already done ten k around the Broderick hectares," Mitch said.

"Hey Mitch. Good to hear from you, buddy. How's things?"

"Good. Good. How's your Grandma?"

"She's doing well. Better than I expected, given the reports I got. I'm worried about her though. Shearing's coming up and then harvest. She pushes herself way beyond the limits even for a fully healthy person half her age."

"Right. Right. Listen, mate, we need you back here. There's shit happening and you're the one with the strategic brain."

"No can do, buddy. I've got three months up my sleeve and I haven't started sorting the stuff with Danielle," Nash said.

"Forget that bitch, Nash. Remember the shit you went through all those years ago? If you don't, I can remind you. You were a basket case, mate. You'd put yourself through that again? It's not happening! If I need to come down there myself and knock some sense into you personally, I will."

"The kid looks like me. That is, he looks like my sister's kid and my cousin's son. He's related. Gotta be."

"Don't do it, Nash. *Do not* go thinking you have any responsibility here. You need Gill to give you the message that bitch left for you? She can tell you verbatim. She can! The bitch down there couldn't even tell you direct. She left a friggin' message. What sort of low life sends a Dear John through a third party she's never met?

"For fuck's sake, Nash. Think, man. Keep your dick in your pants and use your brain to work it through. There's gotta be a simple explanation. She was probably fucking your whole fucking family. Isn't that what they do in them thar hills?"

"Watch it, mate. You're not just heaping shit on Danielle. Watch your mouth."

"Right. Right. I get a bit riled up when I can't be there to have your back. A man with your intelligence should use it for God and country, bro. It's why I rang. You got us out of serious shit with the Cambodian situation and now the Chinese are trying something in Indonesia. We have to get it sorted soon otherwise we're in for another major military and diplomatic SNAFU."

"Look mate, Danielle aside, I can't be anywhere but here for at least another month. You'll have to work around it."

Nash heard Mitchell moving things around on his desk, a swallow, and the thump of a coffee mug on the desktop. The scene was familiar to him. Mitch would then swipe his mouth with the back of his hand and stare down whatever hapless soul was within range. He did not like not getting his own way.

"Is video chat secure? Could we use video to show you what we've got?" Mitch asked.

"It'd work fine if you wanted every other intelligence agency knowing what we're looking at," Nash warned.

"They'd have to get lucky though, wouldn't they?"

"In the normal scheme of things, but mate, our Division is under constant surveillance. There'd be no luck involved unless their guy needed to take a piss at the same time we were online. If you need to get classified stuff to me, it must be by secure courier."

"Right. Right. I'll think of something. You sure you can't get back? I might only need you for a couple of days."

There was no way Nash would fall into the trap. There was no such thing in their business as 'a couple of days'.

"I'm positive. Send me what you've got, and I'll take a look. Make sure the courier is someone I know and trust."

"Right. Right. I'll pull your grandma's address from your file. I'd better go and deal with this shit. You look after yourself, bro. Don't think with your dick and remember what I said. I don't want to be dragging you out of the depths of despair by your fucking fingernails ever again. Come back, mate. Your country needs you."

The phone went dead in Nash's hand. Despite Mitchell's protestations, Nash knew there were other strategic analysts with great minds in the Division. He'd trained them himself.

He tapped, "Aviator, Byron, Princess" into a message on the phone. Mitchell would recognize the code names and know what he was getting at. Any of these could discern what political agenda was at play. Nash's input would be redundant if Mitchell had the sense to use the others.

It wouldn't be the last he'd hear from Mitch. The guy wouldn't trust one of Nash's 'students' to fly solo on a crisis as serious as the one Mitch had intimated.

Mitch might not have had any success as a work colleague in convincing Nash to return to Canberra, but he had succeeded as a mate. Getting back together with Danielle would not work. Mitch was right. He couldn't go through that hell again.

Chapter Twenty-one

Dee was wrapping Brodie's school lunch in plastic film when her son stumbled into the kitchen.

"Hey, Little Bit. How did you sleep?"

"Mph phuoc bleah."

"Are you able to give me a translation, please? Is it Vietnamese we're speaking today?"

Brodie climbed onto a chair and stretched his arms across the kitchen table. His head dropped to the table with a thump. "Too tired!"

"Whining about it won't make it better. Do you recall I gave you fair warning last night?"

"Yeah, but..."

"No buts. I told you Ciaran would still be here today. You didn't have to fit a week of fun into a few hours. Come on. Have a shower. It'll help you wake up."

"Mu-u-u-um..."

"I'm doing a full breakfast today because Uncle Connor and Uncle Michael and I have to spend a long day rounding up sheep for the shearers. Would you like me to cook extra for you or do you want your muesli?"

Brodie cracked one eye open in her direction.

"I think I'll need a big breakfast too. I need the energy."

"You're right, you will. It's a tough gig being a big cousin to two boys instead of one, isn't it?"

"It's nice though." His smile peeked out as he pulled himself off the table and leaned back in the chair. "We're a cool team. I reckon the three of us together could be awesome."

"You're already awesome. When you get older, you'll be unstoppable. Into the shower with you."

"Okay..." He dragged himself off the chair and wrapped his arms around his mother before wandering back down the hall to the bathroom.

Michael stepped through the kitchen door as Brodie left. "Good morning, Sunshine!"

"Hey Michael. How did you sleep?"

"Like a log. Might not be the same tomorrow night when I have company down there, but last night was good."

"You might have company tonight. Sometimes Jim's team like to finish one job and arrive at the next place ready for the new day. They could be at the quarters any time. Was there anything missing down there? Anything I should have organized? I've been distracted by finishing at school for the last few weeks."

"Nothing I saw."

"Well, let me know if you notice anything. Three eggs or four?"

"Two, if you're doing those sausages and bacon too. How are you getting on with Nash?"

"Warily. One moment he's my knight in shining armor, like he used to be. Next, we're at daggers drawn. Did I tell you he used a stocking to jury-rig a fan belt for me to get home from Ballarat? When he does things like that, he's like the old Nash. I dunno. I just have to see it through till he goes back to Canberra, I guess."

Brodie came back into the kitchen dressed for school. "Good morning, Uncle Michael!" he beamed.

"G'day kiddo. You ready for another day of studying hard."

Brodie screwed up his nose. "If it's interesting."

"Make it interesting. You've got another eleven years of it, at least."

Brodie's eyes went wide. "I'm not even six yet."

"See what I mean. You've got to make it interesting, so you can get through it. You wanna be bored for the next eleven years of your life?" Michael asked.

"Uncle Connor, how do you make school interesting?"

"Good morning to you, too, Brodie."

"Sorry. Good morning. But how?"

"Well," Connor looked to Dee for help. She raised her brows at him. "Your teacher will make it interesting. I'll bet your mum's classes are the best."

"Miss Brown's classes are okay, but sometimes I get bored."

"Then look at things from a different angle. If the teacher says, plant a seed and it will grow, think, 'Why? What makes it grow?' If that doesn't work, you could think about how you would explain something to Ciaran or Jacob, so they understand it as well as you do," Connor said.

"Does that work for spelling? I hate spelling. I always get stuff wrong."

Connor heaved a breath, bit the inside of his bottom lip, before venturing forth. "It's not wrong, exactly. It's how you see it now. It might be different from the way everyone else spells a word. You work out how yours is different and make it better. Always look at how things can be better, and you'll never be bored again."

Brodie frowned and nodded. "Okay, I'll try."

Dee placed a plate in front of Brodie with an egg, a sausage, and some bacon. She handed the men a plate each with two eggs and invited them to help themselves to everything else. She turned to greet a sleepy Ciaran, who walked over and slumped against his father's side.

"What would you like for brekky, Ciaran?"

He mumbled into his father's arm, "Toast and vegemite."

"Please," his father tacked on.

"Please," the boy echoed.

"Coming right up. Brodie, I'll be way out with the sheep today. If there's an emergency, Aunty Cassie should be your first point of contact. Aunty Caroline will take you to the school bus this morning, but you'll need to get the bus back to Anna Nana's on your own this afternoon. You cool?"

"Yes, mum," he replied with a world-weary drawl.

"If I have enough phone signal during the day, I'll find out how Meggs is going. Oh, and talk to Aunty Caroline about some ideas for your birthday cake. You know she's excellent with those sorts of things."

His eyes brightened. "Yeah. Is that Catherine making a noise? Can I say good morning?"

"Check with Uncle Connor." The boy's pleading gaze swung to the man.

"Sure, but wait for Aunty Caroline or me. Don't pick her up even if she insists," Connor said.

"Coming, Ciaran?"

The younger boy shook his head. Dee smiled to herself. Greeting his baby sister was routine for Ciaran, not so Brodie. Everything about his visitors was exciting for him. Brodie sped down the hall to Dee's study.

"Good morning, Catherine." The singsong greeting wafted back to those in the kitchen and raised a smile on each of the faces of the adults.

Dee handed Connor a plate of toast spread with vegemite and he maneuvered Ciaran away from his side and up onto the chair next to him.

Dee finally served herself a hearty meal, popped some extra bread into the toaster and sat down.

"A thousand and fifty sheep all up, Dee?" Michael asked.

"Mmm. We need to keep the coloreds separate from the Saxons. I can't decide whether it would be better to do them first or last." She glanced at Connor.

"Last. Leave them where they are until the Saxons are back in the lower paddock. It won't matter if you get bits of white fleece amongst the colored wool, but your Saxon clients will be unimpressed if there are fragments of black wool mixed with the ultra-fine," Connor said.

"Makes sense, thanks. We need them to do the alpacas too, but they'll only slow them down for an hour, I should think. Since you'll be working the dogs, are you okay to run the show out there today? There can't be two bosses." Connor nodded. Dee stopped speaking as booted feet tramped up the back steps. Nash swung through the door.

His cousins greeted him. Dee stood to clear away the breakfast things. "Have you eaten?" she asked.

He aimed a narrow-eyed nod at her and went on speaking to Michael. Connor dropped his plate on the sink beside her before going to check on his daughter.

Dee cleaned the kitchen, loaded the dishwasher and placed Brodie's school lunch in his backpack before she walked outside to load the quad into the back of the ute. The loading ramps were in place and she was retrieving the quad bike from the shed when Nash joined her.

"Are you taking the ute? You can't muster sheep with a car."

Dee rolled her eyes and held her temper. "Wow. Really? I might fancy a spot of paddock-bashing. You're in my way, Nash."

She backed the quad out of the shed, aimed for the ramps and drove straight onto the bed of the ute. She'd done this before.

Nash was the one clenching his teeth now.

"Where does the second quad go, then?"

"If you're asking to have your bike loaded and to ride with me, then you can pull the flat-bed out of the shed and hook it up to the ute when I get back. I'm going over to Anna's to get the food for smoko."

She left him standing as she drove off.

Anna had the eskies, the large cold-water jugs and the vacuum flasks waiting. "I couldn't give them to Nash, dear. He wouldn't be able to carry them on the bike."

"That's okay, Anna. I needed a break from all the testosterone at my place. What's between Nash and Michael? They seem friendly enough on the surface, but there's an edge there. A bit of tension?"

"Mmm. I noticed that Nash seemed none too pleased Michael had his arm around your shoulders last night."

"There's nothing in it. We're mates. What's it to Nash, anyway?" She paused. "Ohhh. He's worried I'll contaminate his cousin. Phoo. Whatever! Thanks for the food, Anna. We should be back in range for lunch. I'll call you to let you know. Um. Do you think you could ring the vet to check on Meggs? If you send me a text message, it'll come through as soon as there's a tiny bit of signal."

"Sure thing, honey. If she's right to come home, I'll bring her here so she's away from the active dogs. She'll have Old Nell for company."

"Thanks Anna. I'll see you later." Dee gave Anna a quick hug and drove back the way she'd come.

The men were standing in the yard as she approached. The flat bed was out, and the quad loaded onto it.

"You can hitch it while I say good-bye to Brodie, then we'll go."

Minutes later, the two cars and trailers cavalcade moved off. Connor and Caroline's vehicle stayed behind for Caroline to use and Michael's truck was hitched with a quad-laden trailer in a similar fashion to Dee's. Frank was waiting down by the sheds and pulled in behind the others.

Silent tension reigned in Dee's vehicle for the entire time they took to get to the flock. Nash's proximity had her hormones doing acrobatics. She was glad to leave the cab as soon as the car stopped.

"What's the spread, Dee?" Connor asked.

"They'd be out of bounds to the east. They should all be in this arc." She moved her arm like a sundial from the north, through west and to the south.

"Right. Mick and Dee, you go to the far south and start bringing them up. Take Mitzy with you. The rest of us will get this lot into the holding yard and move from north to west."

"I'd be better with Michael," Nash interrupted, "instead of Danielle."

"We worked well together last year, and the year before," Michael contradicted. "You're a bit out of touch, mate."

Connor ignored the by-play. "Let's get started."

Dee glared at Nash and went to retrieve her quad. She backed Nash's bike off so she could unhitch the trailer then moved the ute forward to access her own all-terrain vehicle.

Nash was still in conversation with Connor when she looked to where she'd left them. Nash's body was tense while Connor's wide leg stance was relaxed.

Michael gave a sharp 'whee-whee-wheet' whistle to bring Mitzy to him. She sprang into the storage bay. Together Dee and Michael drove past the other three men and headed in the direction Connor had directed.

"If looks could kill, I'd be six foot under," Dee muttered to herself when she caught the look on Nash's face. His problem.

Several minutes of riding brought them to the first sub-flock of more than four hundred sheep. They gave the group a wide berth to check there were no stragglers further out and then began working them back. Dee took the left flank while Michael drove right and Mitzy ran back and forth at the direction of Michael's shrill instructions, preventing attempts by some sheep to break away and relentlessly guiding the flock forward.

More than two hours passed before Michael and Dee moved to within sight of the temporary holding yards. Frank was waiting to open the gates and make a rough count of the sheep going as they passed.

"Thanks Frank. We'll break for smoko and if Connor isn't back by then, we'll do a run in the eastern quadrant to check for runaways."

She unstrapped her helmet, left it sitting on the quad and wandered to her ute. She twitched her panama from the front seat and onto her head before pulling some folding chairs from the dog pen. She dragged one of the eskies to the edge of the tail gate and started dragging the water jug. Twenty liters of water resisted her efforts until Michael put a hand on her shoulder to steer her to one side so he could heave it out.

"Thanks Michael." They both looked toward a shrill 'wheet-wheeeo' as Beau worked a flock of about the same number that Michael and

Dee had brought in. Beau followed Connor's whistled commands and moved the sheep toward the yard in a clockwise direction.

With the mob contained, the three men strolled across to Dee and Michael. Each of them used some cold water to wash their hands. Nash lifted the thermos flask down and poured a mug of tea. The others followed suit and helped themselves to wrapped sandwiches. They sat in companionable silence until Frank ruminated, "I figure we've got the bulk of them, Dee. Do you still want to skirt around to the east?"

"Yes. I'd like to do a run to be sure. They're too valuable to ignore. What do you think, Connor?"

"Why don't you do the run with Nash after smoko? We'll count these through and start driving them home. You can join us with whatever you get. Take Beau."

Dee's heart thudded. *Working with Nash. This should be interesting.*

Chapter Twenty-two

Dee sat a while longer finishing her coffee, musing how they still referred to the break as 'smoko' but none of them smoked. She shook her head and stood, tossing the dregs from her cup onto the hard earth. Grabbing an empty water bottle from the door of the ute, she filled it from the large water carrier. She'd forgotten to take it with her this morning and castigated herself for her stupidity. Distracted by Nash's presence once more? She wouldn't make the mistake again. She flipped her panama into the cab, took a moment to check her phone messages, learning Meggs was now home with Anna, and strolled over to her quad.

She called, "Beau. Whee wheet." The kelpie's ears pricked. He stood to attention looking at her and glanced to Connor. Connor drew his arm around in an arc and pointed to Dee. The dog bounded to her and jumped into the storage bay of the quad.

Dee saw Nash was ready and surprised a questioning look on his face. She raised one eyebrow at him and pivoted to don her helmet. The motor of his quad roared to life as she moved off.

After fifteen minutes of seeing no sheep, Dee pulled up. She thought she heard bleating. Cutting her motor, she swiped her hand across her throat to tell Nash to do the same. Then she listened. She heard what sounded like several sheep nearby, but she couldn't see them. She started the bike again and edged forward. This was a part of the property she rarely visited, so she was unsure of what lay ahead.

She came to a small but deep gully. Two dozen of the expensive Saxon sheep were huddled in a vertical cave formed when the creek folded back on itself over many floods. The natural silo had one entry point. One sheep had probably wandered into it and the others followed the leader till the last one in wouldn't fit but blocked the only opening allowing them to escape.

"Dammit," Dee muttered.

Nash came and stood beside her surveying the problem.

"Let's think this through." Nash advised.

"We don't have time to write a proposal on this, Nash," she snapped. "Pushed up against each other in the confined space could cause a trampling or suffocation issue. They won't get out without intervention. They're becoming more distressed by the moment. We need to move fast to manually pull the first couple free."

"Don't get on your high horse, Danielle. If we don't plan carefully, we'll have a mini-stampede because of panicked animals as soon as they've got some space. We have to pull the first one free without startling the others any more than they are."

Nash walked further along the creek bank.

"It's not so steep here and we can get down fairly close. I'll go first," Nash said.

Dee opened her mouth to disagree, Nash forestalled her. "Don't waste more time arguing."

Dee grimaced and demonstrated a be-my-guest gesture. Nash sat on the edge of the bank and dug in his heels and let his weight fall. He slid in a straight line to the bottom and landed on his feet. He turned and signaled for her to join him. "Unless you want me to handle it?"

Dee rolled her eyes for his benefit, then followed his lead to slide down the embankment. Her descent didn't feel as gracious as his appeared as her backside hit rocks. She jounced around the place, but she got there, stumbling into his arms.

He caught her and held her close while she regained her balance. Instant need shot through her. It was a panicked feeling. As if she'd found something that she'd long lost and couldn't lose again. Why was it that only this man had ever been the one who could make her feel this way?

She glanced up at him. Her eyes snagged on his mouth. Forcing her gaze to his eyes, she watched them darken. The world stopped turning, advancing one frame at a time, as Nash dropped his mouth to hers.

She had time to turn away. Of course, she had. But she didn't. She couldn't. Lord help her, she wanted this. She'd wanted it the night in Ballarat and every day since. She leaned into him.

The kiss exploded a tsunami of memories—of days of laughing as they learned about loving, of Nash teaching her not to be scared. How he'd held her, kissed her, loved her, and made promises to her.

Dee's whole body pressed against his. Her arms clenched around him as she felt his encompass her. She didn't want to let go, ever.

The kiss went deeper, his arms wound tighter and his mouth forced her neck to stretch backwards. She was in another world until the frantic bleating of the sheep intruded.

The kiss might have lasted mere moments, but it left her spinning.

She dragged herself out of his arms. He seemed as reluctant as she to break the contact.

The silence between them stretched.

"Um..." she gulped. "Um, thanks for catching me." She strove for some level of normal behavior. She tried tamping her body's reaction, but her hand shook when she lifted it to smooth back her hair.

She cleared her throat. "Let's get this done," she said. She focused on a button of his shirt before risking a glance at his face.

Nash's face was full of confusion, as his arms relaxed to let her go. "And that's it?"

She straightened her spine, willing the tension back into it and grit into her voice. "I don't know what your agenda is Nash, but you walked away from Brodie and me seven years ago and I'm not opening myself up to hurt like that again. We have work to do here. There're sheep in trouble, remember?"

She needed to focus on what she was doing, otherwise there could be serious consequences for any or all the living creatures in the gully.

He spun away and stomped around the bend in the creek with Dee on his tail. There wasn't space for both of them, so she stood back and watched as he gripped the fleece on the protruding rump of a sheep and hauled it backwards as though ready to throw it for shearing.

When it was clear of the opening, the sheep stumbled, regained its footing and shot into the gully.

Nash grinned. "One down," he said delving into the silo for another.

Danielle felt her body relax a little in response to his conciliatory tone.

He repeated the process three more times and called Dee in to help turn the sheep from the far wall so they could see their escape route.

When the last one moved out, Nash and Dee followed. The sheep were still restless, but the noise had died down. The small flock turned as one to stare down the humans. Dee moved further along the higher side of the gully to whistle for Beau. The dog responded with a short bark as if to say, "Where are you?" Dee waved a hand above her head and the dog peered over the edge. He sped down to the far end of the gully, and down to where she waited.

She signaled wheet wheeeo for the dog to move in and circle around the sheep. Immediately Dee followed up with pee-pee to slow the dog down. The sheep were still distraught.

Dee and Nash scooted back up the gully to get up top ahead of the sheep. Nash put a hand on her arm. She tensed. "This, you and me, it isn't over."

Dee gave herself a mental shake against the warning.

He strode on to his quad, while she returned to the top of the escarpment to direct Beau.

The dog got most of the sheep moving as he tracked behind them, but there were still three huddled close together out of the main pack.

Dee whistled, who-hee-who. Beau spun, at her command, to look for those left behind. His sharp bark turned the sheep to look at him and he was able to work behind them to herd them to join the rest.

Nash was waiting as they emerged to head them home while Dee jogged back to get her bike. By the time they returned to the smoko site, the others had moved on. It wasn't much later their small band of Saxons sighted the larger flock and took off towards them.

Dee pulled up away from the moving flock to take out her phone. She made a brief call to Anna giving her a rough rendezvous point for lunch and then aimed for Connor.

"I'll double back and ferry up the cars." He gave her a quick salute and Dee peeled off. Three cars meant three trips. It would give her some time alone to sort out what happened in the damned gully.

She hadn't gone far when Michael zipped alongside her with a cheeky grin on his face. When Dee pulled up next to the trio of vehicles at the smoko site, Michael rode up and cut the engine. The grin was still in place.

Dee returned the expression, wondering why she couldn't fall for someone like Michael. He was her age, easy to get along with, as drop dead gorgeous as all the other Brodericks and he got on well with Brodie. But her heart didn't sing, even when he grinned at her as he was doing now. Electrical currents didn't zap her into senselessness. She could hug him all day and still not feel the need, the demand, to take it further.

It was so different from being with Nash. Even a gully full of panicked sheep had done nothing to stop her reaction to him, dammit.

She heaved out the loading ramps so she could drive her quad onto the ute.

"What's it to be, Dee Dee?" Dee couldn't help but laugh at the expression Michael had used for years.

"Why are you here?'

"Gotta have two people together at all times–basic occupational health and safety and I know how serious you are about the good old

O.H. and S. Besides, I like spending time with you and annoying the crap out of Nash while I'm doing it." He grinned again.

"Right. Okay. Hitch the flat bed and load your bike onto it. You can drive Frank's car, I'll drive mine. We'll leave the second flat-bed here for when we come back to get your car."

"You're the boss."

Michael moved off and Dee drove in a wide arc to turn her ute and trailer around to follow him. They caught up with and skirted the moving flock of sheep, driving a further few kilometers to the spot Dee had set for Anna to meet them.

They went through the process of off-loading the bikes again and drove back towards the flock. Michael gave Nash a wave as they swept past him. Nash's face was thunderous.

Within half an hour, Michael and Dee collected Michael's truck and ranged it as part of a barrier to hold the sheep together while the team ate their lunch.

With the sheep patrolled by the dogs, the musterers sluiced their faces and hands with cold water, unloaded chairs and prepared to relax for half an hour as Anna and Caroline arrived with lunch.

Chapter Twenty-three

Nash carried his chair and followed the others to where Caroline had set up a shade gazebo for Catherine and Ciaran. The baby was bouncing happily in her spring-loaded seat while her big brother slept soundly on a sheepskin rug spread on top of the tarp that separated the children from the dusty earth.

Connor walked to Caroline and kissed her with his arms out at his sides. She ignored Connor's attempts to keep her free of his work-soiled self. She stepped in and wrapped her arms around him anyway. The look of love and acceptance that passed between his cousin and his wife left a strange yearning in Nash's soul.

The entire morning had been like that. He felt part of, but separate from, the activity. His heart said he belonged here. His head warned him he had to earn his place again.

He wanted to be closer to the action here, integral. The team had worked together previously, it seemed, and he'd tagged on today. If he were honest with himself, he was out of touch with sheep handling. It had been seven years since he had done it and even then, he'd never taken the lead role.

He'd worked with his parents when they were alive and, in the three years after their deaths, it had been Frank who'd kept things moving under his grandfather's direction. His grandfather insisted that there'd be plenty of time for Nash to take responsibility when he came home from his stint in the army, so Nash had fitted in where he was told, while storing up his grandfather's wisdom.

Perhaps it was this that drove him today. He needed to be part of this place again. He couldn't let it pass out of his hands. The early morning phone call from Mitch and the work he had wanted Nash to do seemed important then, but it was another routine assignment that Mitch could delegate to others.

This place was his heritage. He wanted to be the one to make the decisions. Danielle was the manager, according to his grandmother, but she'd ceded leadership to Connor this morning. Was it because of the dogs or because it always happened that way?

Danielle Dawn.

Watching her work had sparked the sense that she truly was part of this place. She didn't look for kudos or special consideration. She got the job done. She handled the quad like a pro, bumping over hillocks and potholes as if she were born to it. And the way she handled the dog—that took a truckload of commitment and hours of practice.

Holding her again had rocked him to his foundations. He'd wanted to keep her in his arms forever. She was the piece missing from the puzzle of his heart. The hole in his soul. Mitch's warnings should have doused the re-emergence of his feelings for her, but the kiss had rekindled everything hotter, harder, higher. She'd been the one to pull back.

He glanced over to where she sat next to Michael—again. There was a closeness there that irritated the bejesus out of him. Minutes after she had shared a heart stopping kiss with him, she was off mucking around with Michael. Bringing up the cars, indeed. Sounded like an excuse to him. Was she playing him?

Mitch's words came back to haunt him. He was right. He couldn't let Danielle get under his skin again. He flung the dregs of his mug of tea to the ground beside him.

Danielle's head snapped up. She stared at him, stood, and approached.

"If this is all too much for you, Nash, you can head on back to the house with Anna and Caroline."

Nash bristled. "What do you mean?"

"Now don't you go rousing on the boy, Dee!" Frank's voice came from left field. "A man needs a bit of time to himself. There's no need to get cranky about it."

Nash cast a half smile in his defender's direction before narrowing his gaze on Danielle. "What do you mean?" he demanded again.

"You've been sitting there on your own for the last twenty minutes, scowling so everyone knows you would rather be anywhere else than here, and ignoring Connor and Anna when they've spoken to you. So, I'll say it again. If you can't handle it, go. Don't hang around making others feel uncomfortable. It's not the way we work here."

Nash pulled himself up to his full height. Danielle didn't step back, so there was less than twenty centimeters between their bodies. He gazed into her stubborn, set face, and on to that demanding kissable mouth.

Words rattled around his head. Experience warned him to keep his mouth shut until he thought through the consequences. His body was reacting to her nearness even as he wanted to shout at her, *"Of course, I can bloody well handle it. It's you, I can't deal with!"*

He put his hands on her upper arms, big mistake as he felt her jolt of reaction as if it were his own, and physically set her to one side. He stretched his mouth into a facsimile of a smile as he looked down into her angry face. From the corner of his eye, he saw Michael, too, come to his feet. What? He thought Danielle needed protection? From him?

Nash held Danielle's eyes for a moment more and then he brushed past her to speak to his grandmother.

"Sorry, Grandma." This time, a real smile formed. "Danielle tells me you said something to me. I've been off in a world of my own."

"Oh, it wasn't important, dear, just including you in our discussion."

"What were you discussing?"

"Whether it's worthwhile keeping the alpacas we have with the black sheep or if we should sell them off."

"Are they any bother?"

"Only when we have to pay the shearers extra because they're more difficult to handle than sheep."

Nash frowned. "Go back to why you and Grandad got them in the first place. What made you buy them?"

"To guard the smaller flock. A small flock is less able to look after its own than a larger one, and the alpacas are effective guardians. They protect the chooks too."

"If that's still important and you have evidence they're doing what you expect of them, then keep them. If you've lost sheep anyway, get rid of them. Do you have an emotional attachment to them?"

"No, well... only that they were Gordon's way of helping to lighten the load for us."

"Grandad usually had things the right way around, Grandma. If it's time to let them go, then that's business. Stick to the facts and the decision will be easy." He ticked off on his fingers, "Do they do the job you need them to do? Do they pay their own way in other ways, like the value of their fleece? Would the shearing costs be less per beast if you had more of them? You know how this works, Grandma. You've been farming your whole life."

He tilted his head to one side. "On the other hand, not business-wise, do you like them? I mean, does it give you extra satisfaction to have them here when other people don't. Are they a fashion statement?" He chuckled.

"All right, all right, young man. I know where you're heading. You think women make decisions with their hearts. Sometimes we do, but when we're building for our families, we can be pretty darn hard-headed." The grin didn't leave his face. "Go on with you." Anna flicked her hand in dismissal.

Nash held the grin as he strolled across to where his cousin sat with Caroline. "Caro," he acknowledged before turning to Connor. "The schoolmarm," he tossed his head in Danielle's direction, "tells me I haven't been paying attention in class. What did I miss?"

"Mate, don't worry about it. You looked like you were trying to solve all the problems of the world at once, or you had a woman on your mind, or you were working out what you would do with your life or all three. Nothing there I wanted to interfere with. You okay?"

"Yeah. You got it in one—or should I say three."

Nash squatted on his haunches next to where Connor and Caroline were resting on a piece of tarpaulin. "You guys, Michael, Danielle, work well as a team."

"And you fitted in again like you'd never been away. You used some quad maneuvers I haven't seen since your dad used to do them. You were great, man. Time yet for you to be thinking about coming home and living the life you were meant for?"

Nash's grin was lop-sided. "One of the things I was thinking about. I still have responsibilities in Canberra, too."

Caroline flipped herself into a standing position and drifted off toward the children.

"Nash, seriously, this place needs you. I won't take anything away from Dee. She's been doing a mighty job, but she's finished her studies now. The Department could send her anywhere from Bordertown to Mallacoota," he named the west to the eastern-most points of the state. "Just quietly, I wonder how Grandma will cope without her. Dee makes her do things to keep her involved and active and part of the place at the same time as she keeps a check on her to make sure she's okay."

"But Danielle is still an outsider," Nash put in.

"Might have been once, but that has well and truly changed over the years and came to an abrupt full stop the afternoon she saved Grandma's life. If she'd been even five minutes later, Grandma would have been with your parents and Grandad that day. Dee runs around after her, getting her to appointments, pushing her into seeing people who can help keep her healthy. She doesn't quit." Connor shook his head. "That's not what an outsider does, mate."

"What's with her and Michael?"

"Not as much as my kid brother would like, but that's for them to work out. Ready for the afternoon? You take the lead. I'll work the dogs, but you take us home."

"Will the manager allow that?"

"I think she'll give you a go to see if you fall flat on your face."

Nash had received plenty of military accolades during his time as an army officer, but they always felt a bit... he couldn't find the words.... like being rewarded for doing his job. Connor's words and confidence put a warm glow in his heart. It felt like a welcome home and a statement of belief in him as a person and it cleared any suspicions he might have harbored that his cousin coveted Calypso for himself. It was a big step towards belonging again. "Right," he grinned again. "Let's do it."

Chapter Twenty-four

Caroline drove to meet the droving team for afternoon smoko. She brought with her a batch of Anna's freshly made scones and lamb sandwiches.

"The shearers are arriving right now," she announced happily. "Jim wants to know if you have anything ready for him to do this afternoon."

Dee frowned. She needed to get the main flock of sheep home, but she couldn't leave the shearers hanging either. Nash had taken over from Connor after lunch. Maybe that was the solution. She could let them finish here.

She turned to Caroline, "You up for a bit of mustering with me? We could bring in the alpacas and get them through this afternoon. The team wouldn't be able to finish the coloreds today and Connor pointed out that there'd be too much cleaning to do to make sure it didn't contaminate the superfine. If we get the alpacas done, we'll have made progress."

"Yes!" Caroline's eyes gleamed with pleasure. Dee watched Connor's eyes narrow in their direction.

"Caro, are you sure?" Connor queried.

"Yes," she repeated. "Anna has the kids and I ne-e-ed to get back in the saddle—even if it's a quad bike. I'm not pregnant anymore and this will soften me up for our own muster. It's only an hour or so. I won't even have the chance to overdo things."

"Nash, are you okay to bring in the main flock? You've got Connor and Michael for back-up so you should be okay."

Nash nodded in response to Dee's initial question but scowled as she added the rider to imply he might be out of his depth. Dee didn't give him a chance to say anything before she turned back to Connor. "May I take one of the dogs?"

"Better be Beau, I reckon. Mitzy is still a bit scatterbrained. You can bring him back when you've finished, if we're not home by then."

"Thanks. I'll hitch the flatbed to your car, Caro, so the guys have all the vehicles they need to get home. Let's go."

"What about your afternoon tea?" Caro asked.

"It can wait. I'll make do with some water."

With Caroline riding the quad and Dee on foot giving the dog directions, Beau cut the alpacas from the flock and herded them into the pens within the hour.

Dee rode to the shearers' quarters to meet Jim. The shearing boss held out his massive, heavy-knuckled hand.

"Jim! It's good to see you again."

"You too, Dee. You got some work for us to start today?"

"I've brought up the alpacas."

"Mongrel things."

"I knew you'd say that. I figured if you got through them today, you wouldn't have to look forward to doing them at the end of the week."

"Yeah. There is that, I guess. They ready to go?"

"Ready and waiting. They've been in the pens for ten minutes now. By the time you get down there, they should be cleaned out. I know how fond you are of not being peed on." Dee chuckled. "Have you eaten?"

"Yep. You know Anna. She had food here before we'd unpacked the truck."

"Good. I'll leave you to get organized. I'll take Connor's dog back to the main flock. I'll see you down at the sheds." She gave a half salute and whistled for the dog.

Her body was aching all over, but the day wasn't done yet. She pointed the bike toward where she'd left the main flock and let her mind go as blank as she could while negotiating the terrain on her quad bike.

Nash had moved the flock quickly, so her ride only took twenty minutes although it would take much longer than that for the flock to cover the same distance. She whistled to the dog and pointed to Connor. Beau bounded off the quad and over to his master. Connor looked up and gave her a wave as she spun the machine and headed to the sheds.

Dee arrived to find Jim scowling at the small group of alpacas. Like the other members of his team, he stood with one booted foot on the lower rung of the fence, and his arms spread on the upper railing.

"The bloody things look so gentle, don't they? Gentle, my Aunt Nellie! They kick and spit worse than bloody camels. Who's your catcher, Dee?"

"That would be me. I'll bring them in one at a time. You have a thrower?"

"Young Blake is learning to do that. He's getting pretty good considering he has only got yours and a larger group up near Buninyong to practice on. Jess will secure the front legs. Dave's on the hinds. I'll do the bloody shearing myself. Okay, let's get this over with. Give me sheep any day of the week."

Despite Jim's misgivings, they sheared the alpacas without incident and the beasts were back with the colored merinos before they heard Connor's whistles to the dogs.

Dee did a final check to make sure the boards and tables were clear of alpaca fleece so there could be a clean start in the morning. She was tired but there were another two and a half days of frantic activity with the shearing before they turned around and drove the Saxons back to where they'd come from.

Nash walked into the shed. Dee felt his eyes following her as she moved around. "How did you go?" Dee asked to break the tense silence. "Did you lose any along the way?"

"Don't trust me, Dee?" Dee's heart skipped a beat.

"Are we talking sheep here?"

"That's what you asked about."

Dee's fists landed on her hips as she met his narrowed regard.

"There's always the possibility for stragglers to go off on their own or for there to be a major breakaway. With Connor's dogs there, it would have been less likely."

"Well, we didn't lose any today. They're in the close paddock ready for drafting into the holding pens in the morning."

"Are you planning to be here or was today too much for you?" Until this minute, Dee hadn't recognized for herself how much Nash taking over this afternoon had irked her. She was tired, yes, but she wasn't usually argumentative. Maybe the kiss had something to do with it too. Did she want to feel like that teenager in love again? Hell yeah! Did she want it to be with Nash? That thought had her feeling like she was standing on the edge of a very high precipice, and he was the only one she trusted to catch her. Dangerous.

Right now, danger was all he was offering. The scowl on his face would have a lesser person quivering in her shoes. Dee didn't flinch. He turned and left without a word. Dee let loose with a long, long sigh.

She headed towards home to have a shower and hug her son.

"Mum! Mum. Anna Nana says they're having dinner in the quarters tonight to welcome the shearers. Can we go too?" Brodie asked.

"That's the plan. Have you been good for Aunty Caroline?"

"Yes, and I've been teaching Ciaran how to play my new computer game so when he goes home, we can play together online. He's good for a little kid."

Dee smiled at this wonderful child, thinking, not for the first time of how much Nash had missed by choosing not to be a part of his life.

"I desperately need one of your delicious hugs, Little Bit, but I'll have a shower first."

Brodie screwed up his nose. "I think that would be a good idea, Mum."

Dee laughed out loud, ruffled his hair, and strode down the hall to the master bedroom.

The first night of the shearers being on site was a big deal. Anna had taught Dee it was important for everyone to eat together so the shearers, too, felt like they were part of the place even for a short while. Like so many other life and social occasions, Dee depended entirely on Anna's guidance. Even when they'd been around, Dee's parents had not been people who entertained or welcomed others to their home. She had not learned how to entertain or what protocols to follow if she was a guest.

Dee followed Anna's instructions as a hostess and closely watched her hosts when she was invited to anyone else's home. She'd probably go into a panic if she were required to entertain totally on her own, but she would manage it.

Tonight, tired as she was, she wore a soft, knee-length dress with sandals. She tied half of her freshly washed and dried hair in a ponytail with the rest flowing loosely around her shoulders. A touch of lipstick and mascara and she was ready.

Brodie appeared in a collared shirt and jeans with his dark wavy hair brushed as flat as he could make it. Dee didn't have the heart to tell him that the hair on his crown was standing to attention. It was the same for all the Broderick men, his father included.

"I'll have that hug now, Little Bit." The smile he bestowed on her could have melted ice as he stepped into her arms.

"Love you, Mum."

"Love you too, Brodie."

Caroline came down the hall carrying Catherine. "I took three of your cheesecakes out of the freezer as per your instructions. I haven't topped them. I whipped cream and prepared fruit, so people can add what they like. Is that okay?"

"Perfect, thanks. I know Anna will have everything under control, but I like to contribute too. I make a big batch of things like cheesecakes, sticky date puddings and so on so they're ready and waiting in the freezer."

"Good thinking. They're delicious."

"There are still a few left for the naming party?"

"There are another four there. That'll be plenty along with all the other food Grandma and I have been working on."

"You must fill me in on that when we get a minute. Have you changed the latest version of the ceremony?"

"No, but I have been wondering whether we should make Nash one of Catherine's Life Guardians. What do you think? He's missed out on so many other family things and he's here for this one."

"Hmm, tough call. I'd say he could take a running jump off the nearest cliff, but that's me."

"Mum! The Captain's great. I don't want him to get hurt."

"Just joking, Little Bit. Sorry if didn't respect your hero." *If Nash only knew how much his son cared about him.* To Caroline, she said, "Will you still include Cassie and Michael or replace one of them?"

"Is three too many? I wanted to keep the others and add Nash."

"Why don't you ask him. If he's not comfortable with it, he'll tell you. He can't have changed that much."

"Are you okay with it, Dee?"

"As the celebrant, I'm fine. As Dee... it's not for me to say. Ask him, Caro. He should feel he still belongs here."

"I will then. Is there anything else we have to take to the quarters apart from dessert?"

"There's a carton of beer in the cool room. I'll give Anna a call to remind Nash to bring it from the homestead."

With the call completed, Dee saw Caroline and Connor's family off for them to drive to the quarters before she and Brodie piled into the ute to follow.

Brodie's conversation during the short drive worked its magic. Fatigue forgotten, Dee walked into the quarters carrying two of the plastic boxes of cheesecake with laughter playing on her face and in her eyes.

The room was abuzz with carefree voices and she felt great!

Chapter Twenty-five

Another sleepless night. That woman would do him in. It was just on five and daylight was peeking through the curtains. He had to get moving if he was going to be first down to the sheds as he wanted.

Anna was at the stove boiling water as Nash walked into the kitchen.

"Good morning, dear." How could his aging grandmother sound so cheery at this hour of the morning?

"Did you sleep well?"

"Yes, thanks," he lied. Like the night before, visions of Danielle had haunted his dreams, this time colored by the memory of the kiss in the gully. His tired brain had taken the body and the kiss and morphed it into a re-enactment of their teenaged love making. He'd woken with a rock-hard member and no way of relieving his discomfort.

Being awake gave him no respite either. Instead, he had the very real memory of her face as she'd walked into the building last night. His heart had screamed, "Mine!" but then he'd had to sit back and watch as all the males from Jim to Michael felt they had the right to flirt with her. The only one who didn't join in, but stayed chuckling on the sidelines, was Connor.

Nash ground his teeth.

"It was a lovely evening, wasn't it and didn't Dee look lovely?"

"It was good to catch up with Jim's team again. It's changed a lot. I never thought I'd see the time when Jim would have a female on his squad."

Anna followed the redirection. "Mmm. I'm not sure, but I think Jess might be some sort of family member. She seems very definite about learning the shearing trade. Mind you, I don't think Jim would stand for it, family member or not, if she weren't able to do the job. Jim sent her out to do the crutching with Frank, so he's making sure she learns every step of the job. How many poached eggs would you like this morning? It will be a long day."

"Two as usual, please Grandma. You'll be out for smoko?"

"Uh huh. I'll have a carrot cake, a fruitcake and the regular scones and sandwiches. The crew can't get enough of those."

"You can't blame them. Everything you produce is magic, Grandma."

"Go on with you, boy. Enough of that nonsense. Here's your breakfast. I'll give you the big water container to take with you. Is Dee collecting you? That sounds like her ute now."

He heard Danielle tromping up the back steps and talking to Meggs. Dee hadn't allowed the kelpie back to her own home yet in case she got too excited by the other working dogs. Here with Anna's aged canine companion, she had company but a calm life.

"Hey Anna! Nash." Nash felt the whip of her glance. She'd destroyed his sleep and now here she was putting him off his breakfast. She looked fully rested and glowing with good health. "Are you travelling down with me?"

"Will we need the quad?"

"I've got mine on board. It's all we'll need in a pinch if the dogs can't handle the sheep. Is there anything we can take with us, Anna? Is Caroline helping today?"

"We didn't have time to discuss it last night. If I need a hand, I'll call you."

"Don't you go lifting anything you shouldn't," Dee warned.

"And don't you fret so much, child. I know my limits these days. I've already asked Nash to take the water. I think I can manage a few cakes for smoko. I'll need some help with lunch though, okay?"

"All right. We can sort it then. You right to go?" Nash nodded and stood.

"Thanks Grandma. I'll see you later." He bent and kissed her soft weathered cheek. He picked up two insulated water buckets into which Anna had loaded ice. He filled them, made sure the taps on the containers were closed firmly and carted them around to the ute.

He and Danielle were at the sheds well ahead of anyone else and set up hoists, shearing harnesses, hessian bags that would become wool bales once filled, and other necessary paraphernalia ahead of the shearers. Nash tracked Danielle's efficiency as she moved around the building.

When they were kids, she'd promised to learn whatever she needed to so that could work together to rebuild Calypso Station into the prosperity it had been when his parents were alive. They had such plans.

It looked like she'd made good on her side of the promise, but to what end? When he came back, he'd make sure she was nowhere near the place ever again.

The kiss yesterday had nearly sent him over the edge and back into her clutches. He'd wanted it so much. He had to keep his wits about him. She was likely still on the lookout for someone to play happy families. It wouldn't be him!

He'd be happy enough to fuck her again, but he would not be caught in her daddy-snare.

Connor and Michael pulled in beside Danielle's ute. They'd brought James, the wool classer, with them. James went to inspect the sheep and Nash tagged along. He told himself it was because he wanted to reacquaint himself with what everyone did. It had nothing to do with getting out of Danielle's magnetic orbit.

With the sheep passed for shearing by the wool classer, Nash worked with Connor to cut out a group of thirty and bring them into the holding pens for half an hour before the shearers began work at seven thirty.

Once the shearers appeared, the day became hectic. Nash had forgotten how frantic shearing days were. It was exhilarating. He moved from loading animals from the holding pens into the races to the catching pens and around to clearing the shorn sheep back out into the side paddock.

Anna and Caroline arrived with morning tea and one by one the shears fell silent. The half hour smoko gave the shearers a chance to compare tallies, tease the rouseabouts and quiz the wool classer. It was a familiar routine, but one time had assigned to the recesses of Nash's memory.

"How's it going, Jim?" Nash asked as he sat next to the man he'd known for most of his childhood.

"Good. It's good. Blake, here, is in training for the Ballarat Show next week. He's made it to 'gun shearer' category now and wants to try out against the interstate talent. I think he's got the State Champs in his sights for next year."

"He shears more than two hundred head in one day?"

"That's it. With Mack, the other gun, he'll help to clear half this lot, I reckon. He's focusing on clean sheep, no cuts, and plenty of speed. In this trade, a man's got to set his own goals, or the work gets on top of him."

"How long can a person maintain that workload?" Nash asked.

Jim shrugged. "It'll be okay so long as he looks after himself in between, eats the right food and gets plenty of rest."

"You're using Jess as a rouseabout?"

"Yeah. She's a good rousie. Strong. Gathers up a fleece and gives it a great throw onto the tables. I'll give her another couple of months till the boys forget she's female, then I'll let her go with shears on the board. Not a bad little shearer, but too much of a distraction just yet. Your Danielle ain't no slug, neither."

Nash's body jolted at the mention of Danielle. She was so not 'his' Danielle anymore, but it wasn't worth commenting on that to Jim.

"To answer your original question, we could be through the Saxons and onto the coloreds by lunch time tomorrow, if Blake keeps up his pace. You thinking of coming back to build up the flock again?"

"Maybe. I haven't looked that far ahead yet. But it's a distinct possibility," Nash said.

"Stick with the Saxons. They pay off better than the rest in terms of the fleece. And there's a small meat market in some high-end Melbourne restaurants. I can put you in touch with an agent if you're thinking of developing that side of the business into something bigger."

"Thanks, Jim. I'll let you know."

Nash sensed Jim sizing him up. "Your dad and your grandfather were good men, Nash. I think they'd be pleased to see you back where you belong." His words hit Nash with a thump in the solar plexus as whorls of emotion roiled in his gut. Jim stood. "Right. I'll get these guys moving again. All aboard!"

Jim's shout galvanized his troop into action. Coffee mugs were replaced onto the table, a last slice of cake was snatched and stuffed into a mouth, and moccasins shuffled as the shearers made their way back up onto the shearing board.

By the end of the day, the gun shearers showed they were definitely in form. They'd cleared more than their target of four hundred and the rest of the team had combined to equal them.

Nash approached Danielle. He'd stayed clear of her all day. It wasn't hard. She'd worked diligently as one of the rousies, gathering fleeces, cleaning skirtings away from the tables and maintaining the workspaces around the shearers. He'd been outside working the sheep.

"Looks like Jim will have this lot done early tomorrow. How do you want to handle the movement of the flocks?" he asked. Her eyes spoke of a bone deep weariness and he wanted to gather her up and hold her safe. He couldn't work out the pendulum of his emotions where this woman was concerned.

"Umm. The priority is to get the Saxons off and away before we bring the colored merinos around. If you guys can get them moving as soon as they're finished, I'll ask Caro to help me bring the colored into the holding pens. The extra day to clean the shed and quarters will be a bonus so we can get organized for the weekend. That sound okay to you?"

"Sure thing, boss." He gave her a lop-sided grin and her eyes seemed drawn to it. His body tightened in response. He sensed rather than saw her sway towards him before she snapped her spine erect and took a step back, leaving him bereft again.

"Can you finish here? I'll lay out some hay for the shorn sheep, then I'll go clean up and help Anna with the meal for Jim and co," Dee said.

"Sure, but..."

"What? You need me?"

Yes!

"No. I can handle it. You need a bit of a break."

Her eyes turned stormy. "I'll know when I need a break, Nash, and the middle of shearing is not the time. I'll see you later."

Nash shook his head as he watched her walk away, whether at her or at himself, he couldn't be sure.

Chapter Twenty-six

What was Nash playing at? He called her boss but seemed to resent it when she gave him instructions.

He threw out contradictory signals. One minute he was all care and concern, and in another moment, scowling at her like she was a rabid dog he had no clue about handling. Then to say she looked like she needed a break—in the middle of shearing—hah! The man was so out of touch.

Shearing might finish earlier than she expected, but there was the Naming Day to get through and then harvest should start next week so long as the rain held off. Plus, she still needed to submit the last two written assignments for her university course.

She pulled her phone from her pocket. That was something else she still had to check—whether Robbie had replaced her phone. She was about to put a call through to Caro and stopped. She'd see her in fifteen minutes. She replaced the phone, climbed into the ute, leaving the quad for Nash to ride home.

She'd loaded two of the ten hay bales required into the back of the ute when Nash rode up.

"Don't you ever ask for help?" he barked at her.

"Do you ask someone else to do your job for you?" she countered, grasping the next bale.

"I have a team. We all work together." He hefted a bale as he spoke. It landed neatly on top of the first bale she'd loaded. "You take on too much, Danielle."

"This is my job, Nash. It comes with a home for my son and food on the table." She kept moving.

"Why doesn't the kid's father help?"

"You'd have to ask him that, I guess. I didn't get to speak to him directly at the time, but he sent me a message to say that he wasn't interested, or words to that effect. Remember?"

"Why would I? Who was he?"

"Don't give me that bullshit, Nash...." She stopped as Michael rode up.

"Need a hand?"

Nash spoke for her. "Yeah. If you help me feed out the bales, Danielle can go up and help Grandma."

Michael tossed his glance between them as if sensing the tension there. "That what you want, Dee?"

"It would be an enormous help. Thanks, Michael." She turned to Nash. "I'll take the quad then." She strode over, adjusted the internal straps on the helmet and rode to the homestead.

Now what was he playing at, pretending that he didn't know that he was Brodie's father? The man made her so angry. The nights and days she'd spent crying over him, their lost love, the child that he wouldn't acknowledge and now... what? What the hell was going on?

She pulled into the turnout in front of Anna's place and went around to the back door.

"Hey Anna. I'm heading home to clean up. Is there something you need me to do now?"

"Hello, Dee." Anna's worried frown was a clear indication all was not as it should be. "My oven and stove top died half an hour ago full of half-cooked roasts. I called Josh, but he reckons I'll need an expert for this, not an auto electrician-come-motor mechanic. The Geelong crowd can't get anyone out here till Friday and the Ballarat crew charge an arm, a leg and an extra pound of flesh."

"Anna, stop. We've got this. We'll bundle up the roasts and everything else and carry it down to the shearers' quarters. It'll be on site then. We'll tell the family we're eating down there again. It'll be fine. If dinner is a little later than usual tonight, we'll offer some chippies and dips and bowls of nuts to start with. We'll call it a celebration for the excellent progress the shearers have made and to congratulate Blake on his new-found status. Did you know he's officially a gun shearer now?"

Anna burst into tears.

"Hey. Blake being a gun shearer upsets you?"

Anna shook her head. A wan smile peeked through the tears.

"Hey, darlin'. Don't cry. I'd give you a hug, but I'm all stinky and dusty. Is it the dinner or is there something else bothering you?" Dee rubbed a hand up Anna's arm.

Anna dragged her hands over her face. "To be honest, I've been in a panic since that call from the hospital last week, or maybe it was when Nash walked through the door. I don't know. I feel as though I've been on tenterhooks for a lifetime and the stress is getting to me."

"You put the kettle on, and I'll wash my hands."

Dee walked back into the kitchen from the bathroom and took down two cups and saucers and pulled the carton of milk from the fridge. Anna made the tea and brought it to the table.

"Let's clear some things off your list. Your heart is fine, so there'll be no more trips to the hospital for a while if you look after yourself. It might mean saying no sometimes—even to me or the family, but you can do it. Nash is home. We don't know for how long, but he's well, grouchy and hard to live with, but he's alive and safe."

Anna nodded and wrapped her hands around her teacup. "But he should do something about getting to know Brodie. He was a young man when Brodie was born, like you were, but he's old enough to know better now."

"About that... This afternoon, he asked me why Brodie's father didn't help. Do you think he didn't understand that Brodie is his son? Could the messages have gotten twisted or mixed up?"

"I have wondered too. But his message back to you about not being a convenient father had to show he understood. Surely?"

"I'll have a talk with him to be certain. I told him he was talking rubbish this afternoon, but Michael arrived, and I didn't take it any further. What else is bothering you?"

"You and Nash. You were always meant to be together. There was that soul connection long before you got to boyfriend and girlfriend stage. You trusted each other. You talked to each other about a lot of things neither of you would talk to me or anyone else about.

"Nash knows more about you than anyone and you were the only one he would talk to after his parents were killed that terrible night. I have a hunch it's probably still the same if either of you could see it.

"You have protected him all these years when others would condemn him. You'd tell anyone his career in the army was something Adam panned with him and Nash wanted to honor his father's wishes. Then you'd come home and cry yourself to sleep again."

"Well, it's all in the past now, Anna. Nobody cares any more that Nash wasn't around when Brodie was born. The world has moved on. Being a single parent in a small town doesn't have the stigma it did, even five years ago. That has a lot to do with the way you stared people down back in the day." Dee grinned.

"Brodie is loved and happy. He's a positive leader for his cousins and he's such a wonderfully caring kid. Again, a lot of that is down to your influence. If I'd ever thought I could have dreamed up a great-grandmother for any child I had, she would have been you. You are the miracle in my life. Because of you, everything else has time to work itself out."

"And you'll talk to Nash?"

"I will, as soon as there's space when we won't be interrupted. It will happen at its own pace, Anna. Isn't that what you taught me? Now what else has you all hot and bothered?"

"This blasted oven. I had all the cooking planned for once the shearers left and now, I have no oven."

"Well, the good news is that the shearers will finish tomorrow, thanks to Blake's exceptional skill, so we have an extra day. We can do the baking at my place or down in the quarters. My place would be better. I could work on my assignments for uni and aim to get them away by the end of the week at the same time as I'm keeping an eye on anything you have cooking."

"They'll finish tomorrow? Are they leaving then?" Anna asked.

"I'll invite them to stay but Jim likes to be back on the road as soon as one job is done so he can get on to the next place. It's how they managed to be here early."

"You're right. We should invite them to stay because it might be their accommodation plan for this week, but if they go, it'll will ease the pressure a bit until harvest."

"We might have to start the harvest next week, too. Will you be okay for that? The canola is ready to go and the chickpeas likewise. I haven't been over to check on the wheat. I'll go tomorrow if I get a chance. I must organize a crew. If Nash is staying on, he can help. It would be one less pay packet we need to fill this year."

"Things are getting better, though?"

"Much better, thankfully. With a good return this year, we can pay off the remaining debt and start to expand again," Dee said.

"What about your teaching?"

"There are no guarantees there either, Anna. I'll get what teaching work I can within an eighty-kilometer radius. Any further, it would make life difficult for all of us—you, me and Brodie. Travelling time, meeting time, preparation and making sure things were okay here. It wouldn't work. It's not something we need to worry about at this moment. Let's focus on the here and now. Are you feeling any better?"

Anna nodded, but still with a frown.

"Don't fret, Anna. We're big kids now. Everything will work out as it should—with or without Nash and with or without me. Let's feed these shearers. I'll drop you down to the quarters with the food and then head to the house." Dee stood. "Sounds like my ute arriving," she said.

A car door slammed, and boots tromped up the steps.

Dee saw Nash toeing off his dusty work boots outside the kitchen door. He walked in and stopped when he noticed her.

"I thought you were going to clean up." His eyes narrowed.

Dee lifted her chin. "We have a small crisis here so you would better serve the situation if you gave us a hand to load this food into the cars and save your interrogation for later. Put your boots back on and carry these heavy trays of meat out to Anna's car. I'll bring the vegies. We have to get it down to the quarters right away or we won't eat tonight."

She picked up a tray of prepared vegetables and set it down again. "Is Michael down there?"

She could sense Nash bristle at the mention of his cousin's name. "He said he was going back there."

"Good." She pulled out her old phone and pressed one of the speed-dial buttons. "Hey Mick. Could get you get the ovens turned on down there, please? Yeah, about two hundred Celsius on each one. No. No dramas—merely an inconvenience. I'll tell you later. Thanks."

With the ovens organized, she turned back to Anna and grabbed the tray of vegetables once more.

"Anna, if you head down with Nash, I'll follow right behind. Do you want me to bring desserts now or can I come back for those later?"

"Well, since you both need to clean yourselves up before dinner, you could bring them down as you come then. There are trifles, custard, and cans of tinned peaches. Oh, and that big extra bowl of whipped cream. If Michael is already down there, I don't need either of you once you stow everything in my car. Michael and Jim's lads can help me carry it in. You bring Nash when you're both ready."

"Okay," Dee agreed narrowing her eyes at Anna's innocent expression. "Brodie and I will pick you up in fifteen minutes, Nash." Dee smiled to herself as she watched Anna's smile slip. Yes, Anna was trying to set up that talking time. Well, it couldn't happen with Brodie in the car.

Besides, Dee was way too tired to contemplate an emotionally draining conversation with the father of her child. She wouldn't be able to think straight. Not tonight.

Chapter Twenty-seven

Nash was ready when Danielle's ute bounced off the road and into the yard. She jumped out and pulled a large Styrofoam box off the tray of the ute and headed into the house.

Brodie emerged from the passenger side door and arrived at the door of the house before Danielle. "Hey Captain. Do you think next year I can help with the sheep at shearing time? I'll be nearly seven and Aunty Cassie said you used to help when you were seven. Did you ride the quad bikes then?"

"Hello, Brodie. We didn't use quads until I was about twelve or so. We used to have horses."

The kid's eyes grew round. "You can ride a horse? I'd love to ride a horse. Mum says it's too dangerous."

"Sometimes, if you're not careful. Horses are big animals. If you don't respect them, you can find yourself in the wrong place at the wrong time and get a kick to knock you flying, or worse."

"You could teach me, couldn't you? Please, Captain?"

Nash liked this kid. He knew what he wanted and was prepared to use all available resources to achieve his ends. Even a relative stranger.

"We don't have horses on 'Calypso' anymore."

"Not right now. But Anna Nana says horses are good for mustering because they can go where quad bikes can't, like in the scrub. So, we should have one or two, don't you think? P'raps you could explain to my mum?"

Nash smiled at the boy's doggedness. He glanced to where Dee stood holding the box, waiting to go into the house. There was an expression of wistfulness on her face as she looked between Nash and her son.

She cleared her throat and looked to Nash.

"I brought this for the trifles. If you get the large esky from the top shelf in the pantry, we'll use it for the extras. The cans will go in a shopping bag."

Organized. Danielle was always organized. She thought things through. Except for falling pregnant.

The idea caught Nash's imagination. They hadn't thought things through when they were teenagers in love. Consequences were the last things on their minds when their hearts and bodies craved each other. That she could have found that level of mindlessness with someone else so soon after he had left shattered his peace.

He pivoted to find the goddamned cool box she wanted, pulled it down and set it on the kitchen table while she pulled dishes from the refrigerator. The two largest bowls fitted neatly in the Styrofoam box. A third dish of trifle and the whipped cream went into the esky. She directed Brodie to stash two large cans of peaches into one calico shopping bag and another two into a separate bag.

Nash picked up the Styrofoam box and headed out, but paused as she spoke.

"When you put that one in, could you get another carton of beer from the cool room please? If dinner is still a while off, we'll need extra supplies."

He didn't answer but kept walking, deposited the box on the tray of the ute and headed to the cool room. When he returned with the carton of beer, she was carrying one of the calico bags hitched over one arm with the grip of the esky in the other. Brodie was determinedly struggling with the other bag of tinned peaches.

Nash slid the beer carton onto the ute tray, took the bag from Brodie and the esky from Danielle. "Gee, thanks, Captain, they're heavy," Brodie said.

Danielle hefted her remaining load into the back and walked to the driver's seat, as though her mind was elsewhere.

There were times, Nash thought, he couldn't get a handle on the woman Danielle had become. He directed Brodie into the cab to sit next to his mother, while he took the edge of the seat next to the door.

"Captain, my birthday party is on the weekend after the Naming. Jacob and I are sharing. Can you come? Will you still be here? Jacob will be four and I will be six years old. It will be fancy dress. Anna Nana is making a pirate costume for me. She always makes great costumes. Did she make costumes for you, too? We're having the party at the community hall so the kids from town can come."

Nash realized the boy didn't require a response, but kept up an endless stream of chatter until they arrived at the quarters. He bounded from the vehicle as soon as Nash cleared the way, and dashed inside.

"Sorry," Danielle muttered. "He gets excited when the family is here."

Unsure how to respond, Nash nodded and dragged the carton of beer towards himself as Michael joined them.

Nash tensed as Michael threw a casual arm around Danielle's shoulders. "Need a hand?"

"You can take this box. I'll bring the esky," Danielle said as she looped both calico bags onto one arm and picked up the esky with the other and led the way inside.

One of Jim's team came and relieved Nash of his load. "Just in time, mate. We ran out before I nabbed a can. Thanks." He wandered back to where the rest of the team sat.

Nash was going through that feeling again—part of the scene but not really belonging. Young Ciaran brushed past him as he entered the building, and Nash turned to greet Connor and Caroline. Danielle moved to join them.

"Dee," Connor greeted her. "What's the plan for tomorrow?"

"Jim reckons they'll finish the Saxons early, probably soon after smoko. So, if you guys took them back to where they came from, Caro and I can handle the blacks. They'll be done after lunch. Jim tells me they want to pack up and leave straight away. They're going ten k's up the road to Jamieson's."

"You need Beau?"

"What do you think, Caroline? Can we do it with or without Beau?"

"With is safer, I think. The coloreds can be difficult, and Beau keeps them in line. I can take him down to Connor with afternoon smoko," Caroline said.

"Good plan,'" Dee said. "Thanks Connor. Meggs is probably not too far off from being better, but I can't risk her yet."

"I've got another proposition for you, Dee."

"Oooh, sounds exciting." Danielle batted her eyelashes at Connor.

Connor laughed. Caroline said, "I think I'll walk away now..."

"Bye." Danielle twiddled her fingers at the other woman.

Caroline chuckled. "Just remember, he comes home with me."

Danielle grinned.

"So, Connor. What did you have in mind?"

"Harvest."

Danielle cracked out a laugh. "Darn it, just when I thought I was going to get lucky."

Nash's gut twisted as Danielle flirted with his cousin. He ignored the evidence of the innocence of it given Caro had wandered off unconcerned.

"Your canola is ready, and you haven't done any windrowing," Connor frowned.

"That's right. The research I've been reading indicates windrowing is counterproductive on low yield paddocks. You lose seed through windrowing attrition and you lose fuel having to go over the same paddock twice. This year, I will direct head to see how it goes. I have an anticipated yield in mind. If it isn't as high as I expect, I might go back to windrowing next year. If it's close, then I've saved a small fortune in fuel and equipment."

"Research, eh?" Connor smiled.

"Yep. This isn't something I was born to, Connor, so I learn as I go and reading research helps me. It also means I can be flexible with my ideas and not fixed on something because of the way it's always been done.

"I plan to make a start on Monday with the canola, then the chick-peas. I haven't checked the wheat, but it can't be far off."

"The wheat will be ready within the week," Nash interposed. "I had a look at it the other afternoon."

"You still know how to assess ripeness, do you mate?" Connor asked with a grin.

Nash scratched the side of his neck with the edge of his index finger and looked at his cousin from under his brows. "Well, I *was* born to it. I was assessing wheat readiness when I was Brodie's age and I don't reckon research will have changed that measure."

"So, Dee, this is what I propose," his cousin turned back to his initial conversation piece. "My crops won't be ready for at least another couple of weeks. We can stay on here and give you a hand if you and Frank could do the same for us later. I can get my blokes to bring over some more equipment and we would halve the time."

"Connor, that would be amazing. If Nash is right, we could get onto the wheat by Wednesday and finish in time for Brodie's party next Saturday. It'd be wonderful to have you here then. Your place will take a lot longer to harvest, but we'd still be done ahead of Christmas so long as the rain stays away."

"We've got six weeks before Christmas so, yes, we could finish by then if the weather holds. What about you, mate?" Connor turned to Nash. "You up for the harvest or do you need to get back to serve the nation?"

"The nation is in good hands."

"You know how to drive a harvester?"

Nash scratched the side of his neck again and smiled. "I reckon so."

Caroline arrived and linked her arm through her husband's. "Time to break up this little ménage," she chuckled. "Dinner's ready."

There were only two seats left at the table by the time Nash had brought in the last dessert box. Danielle walked through with a bowl of roast potatoes and took one seat, leaving him with the seat next to hers. Twenty people was a bit of a crush around the table, but it saved setting up a trestle for the overflow.

The trouble was his body in constant contact with Danielle's. Her essence surrounded him, and he was reminded of the night in Ballarat. It had been the best night's sleep he'd had in years. It was if all the pieces of his world were aligned where they should be, and he could rest. Danielle had relaxed into him and slept soundly.

She wasn't relaxed now. She had a fixed smile on her face, and her left hand was clenched so tightly around her fork, he thought she would bend it. Anna was on her other side and he didn't think her closeness would be what was putting Danielle on edge.

He might be strung as tight as a bow string, but it was a little satisfying to know she was equally affected. Even better, Michael's eyes were flinging daggers from across the table.

As dessert was served, Nash stood, in the way he remembered his father doing on similar occasions. He thanked the shearers for their work, congratulated Blake on his success and wished the team safe travels until they visited Calypso again. He'd thank his family members privately.

When he sat down, Danielle's hand brushed his thigh. "Well said," she whispered. Her hand might have easily reached in and squeezed his heart, such was the impact of that one little bit of praise.

Chapter Twenty-eight

Anna and Nash arrived at Dee's place early on Wednesday morning. Dee finished wrapping Brodie's lunch sandwiches and set them aside as Nash placed one of Anna's baskets on the table.

Anna bustled around lighting the stovetop and warming the oven.

Having Nash in such proximity when she hadn't the chance to set up her defenses for the day was unsettling for Dee. Nevertheless, she pulled out the words to thank him for the speech he'd made the night before.

"I know the manager is meant to do stuff like speeches, but I never know what to say. Your words were perfect."

"I've had the advantage of watching my father do it over the years. It's no big deal, but it needs to be done so the shearers know we appreciate and respect their work."

A sleepy Brodie wandered up the hall in his pajamas. He brightened a little when he saw Nash. He stumbled to where Nash sat and slumped against his side. "Good morning, Captain." Dee's heart clenched as Nash dropped an arm on Brodie's shoulders and smiled down at him.

"Good morning to you, too."

"Since you're up so early, do you want breakfast with the workers today, Little Bit?" Dee struggled to keep her voice steady.

"You mean eggs and sausage and bacon and tomato and stuff?"

"If it's what you think you need. You can check with Anna Nana to see if she has enough for you," Dee said.

"Do you, Anna Nana? I'm really hungry this morning."

"Sure thing, Brodie," Anna said. "You sit up there. We'll have breakfast ready for you in no time."

The child climbed onto the chair next to his hero and beamed a smile. "Mum never has time to cook a proper breakfast when we're on our own. What are you doing today, Captain?"

"We'll be finishing the shearing and droving the shorn sheep back to the far paddocks. We can bring them back onto the canola stubble as soon as we've harvested."

"Yeah, about the harvest," Connor said as he walked into the kitchen dressed for the day ahead. "With the shearing done, there's nothing to stop us getting straight onto the canola tomorrow. What do you think, Dee?"

"It's not an option for me. I have the next couple of days fully committed."

"Hmm. But you agree the canola's ready?" Connor asked.

Dee nodded.

"And you don't mind if we get started?"

Dee was torn. The harvest did need to get underway. It was her job to oversee it, but she had too much to do on Thursday and Friday finishing her university work and preparing for the naming day.

"If you start, you'll have to quit again on Saturday afternoon, and usually you like to work through," Dee said.

Nash's deep voice joined the discussion. "We don't have to focus on getting the entire job done, just the canola or the chickpeas. I agree, Connor. Instead of sitting twiddling our thumbs, we could get some done before the end of the week. If Michael's not doing anything else, we can clear one or the other, maybe both. I've seen chickpeas on the Nicholson Road paddocks. Are they the only ones?"

"Yes." Dee was cautious.

"The harvesters have been checked because I helped Frank with that last week. Is the storage ready?" Nash asked.

"Frank checked that last week, too."

"Do you have Frank doing anything else this week?" Nash asked.

"Helping with cleaning and set up for the naming day."

Nash drew his jaw up to compress his top lip and puckered his chin. Dee's stomach dropped. He was the image of the young man she'd fallen so deeply in love with.

"Teamwork. What Frank would have achieved over two days, the four of us can achieve on Sunday morning, if it's still needed, well ahead of when you want things organized for the afternoon," Nash said.

"Good plan, Nash. And it gets us from under the feet of the women for the next few days." Connor looked pleased.

Anna set plates of food in front of Nash and Brodie. "Same for you, Connor?"

"Nash size, please Grandma," Connor grinned.

Dee felt fingers of fear tingle over her spine. It seemed that a manager wasn't required if these guys were going to swan in and take over. She held her tongue though, because the property needed these things to be done and she couldn't do it on her own or even with Frank. Casual labor had been hard to come by since the drought.

She focused on her son sitting between the men, looking so much a part of their lives. "Brodie, I'm going down to the shed. You'll be okay with Aunty Caroline again?"

"Of course, Mum. I'll be six next week. You don't need to worry about me."

"Okay, Little Bit. Give me a hug then and I'll be off," Dee said.

"Aw Mum, you didn't ask the Captain or Uncle Connor to give you a hug. Why me?"

"Brodie Tillson," Anna chipped in. "You will give your mother a hug so she can get on with her day's work. If she chooses to hug anyone else, it will be up to her."

Dee hid a smile as her son climbed down from the chair and sauntered over. "Love you, Little Bit. Have a good day at school. Mwah."

"Love you too, Mum." His hug was comfortingly firm.

Dee gave Anna a quick hug and headed for the door.

"What about me?" Connor whined.

"Rain check." Dee grinned.

Nash's face was tight. Dee had no idea what was going through his head and she wasn't going to hang around and find out.

"I'll come with you," Nash's voice rumbled.

"Finish your breakfast and bring down the ute. I'll take the quad," Dee said.

She tweaked her panama from its peg, grabbed her helmet and scampered.

Even a few minutes totally on her own in the sheds sounded like a piece of heaven. It wasn't to be.

Michael's track from the shearers' quarters converged with hers and they rode together for the rest of the way.

Michael's face was strained. "Something wrong?" Dee asked as she dismounted from the quad.

"I don't like Nash hanging around you so much."

"It's not for you to say, Mick. This place belongs to him mostly, so technically, I'm his employee. He has every right to keep an eye on things."

"I don't know how you can be like that, Dee. He led you up the garden path and left you standing before you got anywhere near the church door. Up the duff, broke and not long out of high school. Has he ever asked if you needed support for Brodie?"

His words were like a punch in the gut for Dee. The memory of those early days of dread and panic were enough to undermine everything she had built. The days after she learned she was pregnant and then realized Nash wanted nothing to do with her or their child were some of the darkest in her life.

She must have paled because Michael reached out and grabbed her by the arm as her ute rumbled over the ground towards them with Nash at the wheel.

Dee pulled her arm away and straightened her spine. "Brodie and I don't need his support or any man's."

She spun on her heel to walk away. Michael called after her. "He'll have to come home for good soon if he wants to hold onto Calypso. What happens then?"

She turned and faced him as Nash climbed from the car. "There's never any point in buying trouble ahead of time, Mick. I'll see you later." She risked a glance in Nash's direction and encountered an assessing stare. She cast a fleeting look at Michael and back to Nash. "Nash, if you have time during the day, we need to talk."

This time she managed to escape and headed up onto the board to check on readiness for the work to begin.

Blake kept up his punishing pace and cleared fifty-two sheep before morning smoko. His achievement seemed to lift the rest of the team and Jim approached Dee to delay the morning break for an extra fifteen minutes so they could finish the Saxons.

Things were going well, and the wool classer was pleased with the grade of fleeces coming through. There would be a good return for the property. Dee was quietly satisfied the gamble she'd taken on behalf of the business was paying off so well.

The Broderick men and Frank took their smoko as soon as the last sheep were on their way to the shearers. They were ready to move the shorn flock when the shearing finished.

While Jim's team took their break, Dee went to Jim. "The boys are heading out with the Saxons. Caroline and I will go and bring over the colored sheep. Will your rousies be able to finish the clean through while we're busy?"

"Sure can, Dee."

"Thanks Jim. Your team is remarkable."

The man narrowed his gaze on her. "You know," he drawled. "I kinda reckon you're the remarkable one. You could have walked away from this place and left Anna in a hell of a pickle after Gordon passed, but you stayed, and you've built a good business here. I hope the Brodericks realize what you've done for them, Dee."

"Anna took a heck of a risk giving me a go to test my untried ideas. And she gave me a home for Brodie while I did it."

"Anna's nobody's fool, Dee. Remember that. If she'd had any doubts, she would have stepped in. It was her confidence in you that persuaded me to take on your flock the first time. We have more work than we can handle so we don't waste time on poorly husbanded sheep." He scratched the stubble on his chin.

"You checked me out?" Dee's eyes widened.

"Had to. Your business is my business. If I waste time on crap animals, I lose money and I end up with a cranky team. Not worth it from my end. As you can see, you've kept us coming back." He grinned.

"Thanks Jim. That means more to me than I can say."

"You're good people, Dee Tillson. And if a certain hard-headed Broderick doesn't realize it, it's his loss. Big time."

Dee laughed. "I don't want you giving me any more of a big head, Jim, so I'll go and round up a few sheep for you."

Jim grinned again. "You do that. And in case you missed it, you're a damn good rousie too."

Dee couldn't help the smile blooming on her face as she walked away.

Caro was packing away smoko with Mitzy lying close by in the shade.

"Hey Dee. Connor reckoned we would only need Mitzy for fifty."

"Sorry I missed the boys. I was setting things up with Jim. Did they say how they were going to handle the pick-up."

"Michael has taken his truck and trailer and Nash said you could bring yours when we've finished here. He said they might not take the flock all the way back since you want them on the stubble after harvest."

"It was Nash's idea, and it's a good one."

"Connor rang his dad and instead of driving over on Saturday morning, Sean will come over with the combine and Bruce and Ryan will bring the catchers this afternoon."

"What about road permits?" Dee asked.

"The new regs are a lot easier to handle lately. He's got annual permits on all the heavy vehicles."

"Will Sean be okay in the quarters? I can't really fit him in with me."

"Do you think Anna would let her precious son sleep anywhere other than in her home?" Caroline chuckled. "I'd like to see it. Bruce and Ryan will be fine down there. They might need a lift back to the Mount on Friday arvo if they don't want to stay for the weekend."

"We'll sort something out. Are you right to leave this and help me with the next lot of sheep?"

"I'll let Grandma know."

Dee called Mitzy, picked up her helmet and climbed aboard the bike. The main flock was already moving into the distance as she swung right toward the home paddocks.

She decided not to waste time cutting out the alpacas. If they came too, it wouldn't be a major issue, she'd keep them from going up to the board again. She smiled to herself. Jim would probably freak if he saw one of the beasts up there again so soon.

Caro rode around to join her taking the left flank. Dee positioned herself on the right and used Mitzy to keep the small flock moving into the holding pens. The exercise was much smoother than she'd feared. Caro waved as she left to go back to the house to relieve Anna of child-minding duties. Dee went in search of Jim to let him know the sheep were in and should be clean and ready to go in fifteen minutes.

The colored sheep didn't have the wrinkle free hides of the Saxons, so the pace of shearing slowed. Nevertheless, fifteen had been shorn by the time the shearers broke for lunch and the rest were done not much later.

"The Saxon bales are on their way to the wool store in Geelong. What do you want done with the rest?"

"Anna has a market for the colored wool amongst the local artisans. She handles the coloreds and the alpaca. There's not a lot there."

"Nah, don't know why you bother."

"Could be just to annoy you, Jim?" Dee smiled.

"Yeah. Could be." He chuckled. "Lucky I like you then, hey?"

Dee laughed. "Mutual."

Jim declined Dee's offer to return to the quarters for smoko and to shower when the shearing was done.

"A bit of dust and good, honest sweat never hurt anyone, Dee," he chortled. "We'll have a cuppa and get on the road."

It seemed only minutes later the shearing team was gone.

Dee called Mitzy to round up the newly shorn sheep. They were keen to return to the greenery of the home paddock and took off at trot. There was little for Dee to do except to follow and close the gate behind them.

She called Mitzy into the storage unit of the quad and spun the bike to drive to where the men were travelling with the main flock. At the end of the day, she'd bring Nash home. The thought of it brought on a fizz of sensation in her lower belly and a feathery feeling in her upper chest. It must nearly be time for him to return to Canberra and leave her in peace.

Chapter Twenty-nine

Nash was conscious of every jostle of Danielle's body as she steered the ute and quad-laden trailer towards Anna's place. He had been trying to puzzle through the little information that Mitch had given him to offer some long-distance advice on the situation back in Canberra. Thinking about anything but Danielle while she was this close, even when she wasn't nearby for that matter, was impossible.

Coming home, he hadn't bargained on her being the manager of the property or seeing her and the boy on a daily basis.

"Earlier, you said you wanted to talk," he prompted. "What about?"

"I thought it was time to clear the air about Brodie."

"Anything in particular?"

"I figured you might want me to spell out the role I thought his father should be playing in his life. Just so you know you're not standing on anyone's toes."

"Not interested."

"Well, that's what you said seven years ago but I thought you might have had time to reflect on that decision now that you've met him."

"Nope. Don't get me wrong, Danielle. He's a great kid. You've done wonders with him on your own but I'm not the one who's going to be playing daddy."

"You are his daddy..."

"You've tried that line before and it didn't work then, either. What crops did you want the harvest to start with tomorrow?"

Nash knew that the decision had already been made to start with the canola, but he needed to change the subject away from the boy. As he'd told Danielle, Brodie was a great kid, but he was also a constant reminder of how little Nash had meant to Danielle once he was out of sight. Even as a grown man, the hurt still rankled. For her to suggest he was Brodie's father? It rubbed salt in the still raw wound.

"You're not even going to address this?"

Nash moved his head from staring out the passenger side window, slowly rotating it until he faced Danielle's profile. He caught her glance.

"Since I'm staying on for the harvest, I'm going to need some night-time work gear. Do you know what happened to Dad's pullovers?" He kept his voice emotionless.

"You are kidding me!" Danielle's voice lashed across him. He could almost taste her anger in the fragrance she exuded.

"I'm not kidding. I do want to know if there are any of my Dad's work clothes still about. I wouldn't fit into any of Grandpa's. Since you're living in Mum and Dad's house, I thought you might know what happened to them."

Danielle thumped the wheel. Nash might have heard an expletive or two muttered beneath her breath. He ignored them as he noticed her face tighten further.

"They're still where they were."

"What do you mean?"

"Exactly what I said. Disposing of them is a family responsibility and Cassie and Anna didn't want to do that without you having a say, so there they've remained."

"You packed them up though, right?"

"Nope. No need. It's a huge room. I bought a small wardrobe and tall-boy for myself."

"Then you'd better take me there now instead of straight back to Grandma's."

"You want to go through them now, this afternoon, right now?"

"Is it a problem?" His ploy to divert the conversation from the kid seemed to be working so far so he ploughed straight on. "If there's nothing there I can use, I'll have to ask Connor for something. It gets cold during harvest nights."

"No problem, but there had better not be any sarcastic comments about my housekeeping. I have a full house of guests."

"I wouldn't dream of commenting on anything so personal." She shot him another of those lacerating looks. If he hadn't already faced wartime conditions, this woman could scare him to hell and back.

He let his head sway back towards the view beyond the vehicle and tried to keep his mind anywhere but on the jouncing of Danielle's breasts as the ute lurched over the uneven track.

He felt rather than saw her intermittent glances in his direction and the occasional shake of her head. Whether it was disgust or lack of understanding, he couldn't be sure, but it did signal she wasn't happy with him.

There were no other vehicles in sight as they pulled into the space in front of the Dee's house.

Danielle pulled the keys from the ignition and sifted through them before latching onto one and headed to the door.

"You lock the house? We never had to do that."

"Those were the days before methamphetamine users scoured rural properties for anything, preferably firearms, they could sell on the black market for a quick buck and an even quicker hit."

"You have a drugs problem out here? In Hamlet Brae?"

"Ballarat, Geelong. Ironically, addicts will travel long distances to get what they can. Even the dogs aren't always a deterrent. Come in."

Nash followed her into the house through the back door, scuffed off his shoes, following her example, and walked in his socks into the kitchen.

Now that the place was empty apart from the two of them, memories of his own family around the table rushed to meet him. It probably wasn't true that his mother was always smiling. Who does that? But it felt like she did. He and Cassie weren't perfect. There was always trouble to be had, but his memories of his mother always had her smiling, her blue-green eyes sparkling from something inside.

He walked behind Danielle as she moved down the hallway. He couldn't see any reason for her to comment on her housekeeping. The house was pristine. They progressed past what used to be the guest bedroom, his own bedroom, Cassie's. He tuned into her commentary. "Connor and Caro are in the guest room, the boys are in your room, Catherine is in Cassie's. Here's where I sleep," she said stepping into what had been his parents' bedroom.

If Danielle thought this room was huge, she hadn't been inside any decent sized homes. The room was modest in its proportions. Sure, there was room to move about, but he'd been in homes where the master bedroom was the size of a small apartment. Tucked over in one corner was a white cupboard of the style that came as flat-packs from a dollar shop. It could be used it as a broom cupboard or as Danielle had done here, a miniscule wardrobe. Next to it was a similarly utilitarian set of drawers, the tall-boy she mentioned.

In the other corner sat the dressing table his mother used. His mother's brushes and jewelry boxes were no longer there, replaced by a small white pot holding a snake plant and a single black hairbrush.

The bed looked the same, but the doona cover was newish.

"You'll find your parents' things in here." Danielle led him to the walk-in robe next to the en-suite bathroom and stepped back to let him by as she flicked on the light switch.

Nash could feel his heart pounding. It started speeding up as he walked down the hall. Now it was thundering.

He stood at the door, his hands clenched at his sides. His teeth were clamped so tightly a macadamia shell would have stood no chance against them.

His mother's dresses, blouses, trousers, and jackets all hung where they had been left nine years ago. Facing them were his father's shirts and dress pants, and a couple of suits. The dresser drawers were closed but he knew what he would find there. On the right-hand side would be his mother's intimate wear, socks and then in the lower drawers would be her warmer clothes.

On the left-hand side top drawer would be his father's reading glasses, a few pairs of cufflinks, an old compass in a leather case, an ancient snake bite kit in a tiny pouch no use for anything except as an historical peculiarity. The descending drawers would hold his underwear and socks, pajamas, jeans and finally the bottom two drawers would hold hand-knitted pullovers in various states of degradation with the very oldest in the bottom.

These were what he had come to find, but he couldn't move.

His parents' scents still seemed to hang about the clothes. He could reach out and touch them as if the clothes still held them. He could rant at his father and say that at sixteen years of age, of course he was old enough to make his own decisions about his life. He could absorb the understanding in his mother's eyes.

His eyes welled and he bit his tongue to stem the flow. It didn't work.

Stumbling out of the closet, he sat heavily on the side of the bed, his head in his hands and his right knee mechanically jumping up and down, a response he believed his army training had abolished.

Moments, minutes later the mattress depressed as Danielle sat beside him and placed her hand on the hammering limb, as she'd done when they were younger and he was upset.

"Nash?"

He lifted his face to her concerned eyes and the years melted away. He threw himself into her arms with an anguished groan.

Her hug was a vice, squeezing the anxiety out of him. He held on for dear life in the same way he had when they'd been awoken at his grandmother's house, on a freezing winter's night, to be told his parents were dead.

The memories assailed him. The fear, the denial, the guilt, the absolute certainty it was all some sort of weird joke. He remembered hugging his mother and saying, "I love you," before she got into the car that afternoon but, even now, he couldn't remember doing the same for his father. They'd had some petty disagreement and Nash couldn't recall whether he had continued to sulk at his father's intransigence or whether he'd been son enough to set it aside and wish his father well on the journey.

It should have been a routine trip to the farmers' meeting in Warrnambool. It was one his parents had undertaken on many occasions. The children would stay at Grandma's and Mum and Dad would pick them up the next morning.

"I didn't say goodbye." His voice was muffled against her neck.

"You couldn't have known they would die. That some truck would break down on the highway in the fog, waiting for them to drive into it."

"I didn't tell him I loved him."

"Yes, you did!"

Nash lifted his head as Danielle's arms loosened.

"I told Mum I loved her when I said goodbye, but I don't remember doing it for Dad."

"Well, you did. I was there, remember. You were grumpy with your Dad, but that wasn't unusual. Your Dad gave you the tolerant half-smile thing he used a lot with you. You remember the one, don't you? He pulled you into a hug. He said, 'Love you, son!' and you mumbled, 'Love you, Dad.' It wasn't too enthusiastic, but you said it. Your dad knew you loved him, anyhow."

Nash grasped Danielle's upper arms. "Are you sure?"

"Nash, what is this? Of course, I'm sure. Because then your Dad gave me a hug and rolled his eyes in your direction as if to say, 'keep an eye or him,' or 'apologies for the brat' or something. It was a special moment for me because your Dad made me feel it was okay for me to be part of the family."

Nash scoured her face looking for clues of a deception and found none, just a lot of concern and a bit of the love that used to shine from her eyes for him. He jerked back.

There was the deception. She never had really loved him otherwise she wouldn't have gone behind his back so easily with another man. The alluring scent of her even after a day's work, the kindness and caring in her eyes, enough so he wanted to lay her down on that bed and revisit her body in the way they used to do. It was all deception.

He pulled himself upright off the bed and dragged his hands down his face. He steeled his spine and strode towards the dresser. He pulled out the bottom drawer dragging out a pullover at random. It was from his grandmother's colored fleeces she had spun and knitted. It was redolent of lanolin and his Dad. His knees buckled again, and a wracking sob burst from his throat as he lifted the pullover to gauge its size. This time sadness and grief rumbled from rather than the guilt he experienced earlier. He wanted to bury his face in the fabric and be with his father one more time.

Danielle's arms came around him again and he shrugged her off. "I'm fine. I don't need you or your sympathy. This one will do." He barreled from the room ignoring the look of shock and concern on Danielle's face.

"Nash!" Danielle called from behind him.

"I'll take the quad off the trailer and take it back to Grandma's."

He stuffed his feet back into his boots and almost ran back to the ute, followed the procedures he'd learned from watching Danielle, threw the pullover into the storage well, mounted the quad and rode off.

There were demons here to unman even a war-hardened soldier—the memories of his parents, the concern in Danielle's face, his own lust. He had to leave.

Chapter Thirty

Dee was up early the next morning to make breakfast for Connor before he went to start the harvest. She'd declined joining the family get-together the night before when Michael and Connor's parents, Sean and Jennifer, arrived.

The oven repair people from Geelong had called Anna early in the afternoon to say one of their technicians was going to Ballarat to pick up some spare parts. He could stop and check on her appliance on the way if it was convenient. With the efficiency of experience, the technician had the oven and stove top repaired in no time and Anna was back cooking for the family in her own kitchen, relieving Dee of the responsibility to play host. A night alone with Brodie was what she needed after the emotional scene with Nash.

She'd gone through the rest of the day on autopilot, checking on the shearers' quarters and making sure supper and breakfast essentials were available for those who were staying there. Michael wasn't around, which was a blessed relief. She didn't want to answer his questions about how things had gone with Nash.

She reloaded toilet rolls, gathered used towels, replacing them with fresh ones before collecting the laundry to take back home. She cleaned the bathrooms and the kitchen and barely registered what she had done.

Caro and Connor and their children were leaving to go to Anna's as Dee arrived at the manager's house. She waved them off and, after checking on Brodie, she went into the kitchen to make hamburgers for Brodie and herself. The quiet routine soothed her soul as she sat with her son to eat the meal. Brodie wandered off to find something to watch on television and Dee went to her study to organize the material she would need to complete her university work before the end of the week.

She skirted the cot Catherine was using, pulled out her laptop and some reference books and left them on the sideboard in the lounge room, ready for the next day. With her organization in place, there was nothing left to do. An early night was in order.

She and Brodie were in bed long before Caro's family returned.

The general hubbub of the morning kept her mind off the discussion with Nash, but not for long. She kept returning to it, trying to figure out what she had done to create such a level of bitter disinterest from Nash for his son. Why did he think she deceived him? She simply could not understand it.

Once Brodie was on his way to school, she drove with Anna and Caroline and the babies down to the shearing shed to start the preparations for Sunday's naming day. The last few days had shown the work was better done in the morning before the temperatures rose.

The numbers of guests had firmed to be sixty coming for the celebration. Not quite as many as for a wedding or a funeral, but a naming day was as good an excuse as most to get together with family and friends, especially when those family and friends were geographically remote for most of the year.

The team left the sheds in good condition after the shearing, but the cleaners still had to dust and sweep them. Then they'd put a wet mop over the floor. A hosing down would be less back-breaking, but with memories of the prolonged drought still in their minds, the women weren't prepared to sacrifice precious water when a bit of elbow-grease would achieve a similar result.

When they stopped for morning tea, Caroline outlined her vision for the decorations and set-up for the barbecue dinner on Saturday night and then the afternoon tea and supper on Sunday. A bush band from Mount Mercer would provide the entertainment. Like the rest of the overflow guests, the musicians would either bunk inside the shed or in their swags or utes nearby. The women agreed it would be best to have all the interior organization done the next day before guests began arriving on Saturday.

They worked on until lunchtime when the children got crotchety and the interior temperature of the shed rose to uncomfortable levels. They headed back to the house and had a simple lunch around Anna's table.

Dee desperately wanted to talk to Anna about the non-discussion with Nash, but not with Caro present. Caro, she feared, would tell Connor and then Connor would feel obliged to confront Nash. It was like acid eating at her gut, but it could wait. She'd been through worse.

Caro and Anna were preparing food for the weekend. Dee had her university work to complete. She offered to take the children back to her place so they could nap in the cool and be out from under the feet of the others.

Caro threw her arms in the air crying, "Thank you! Thank you!" She quickly bundled up the children's gear for Dee to take with her.

Once she was home, Dee settled Catherine in the cot in her study before checking Ciaran had enough to eat and was ready to nap too. She followed him into Brodie's room and helped him take off his shoes. He wrapped his arms around her neck for a hug and a kiss and flopped back onto his bed. He dozed off without another word.

With the children asleep, Dee had three clear hours to do her university assignments. She seated herself at the kitchen table and got to work. She finished one and had made a good start on the final submission as Brodie came through the door, leaving it to bang behind him.

"Sshh!" Dee pleaded. "The babies are asleep."

"Oh! My bad! Sorry mum," Brodie whispered as he ran to give her a hug.

A cry came from Dee's study. Brodie gave her a wry look. "Catherine is awake now." The tromp of Ciaran's feet sounded like they were heading from Brodie's room into his sister. His soothing voice confirmed it.

"You check on your cousins while I put my stuff away, okay? Then I'll make some afternoon tea."

"Okay, Mum. You've got it."

'You've got it?' 'My bad?' Where had they come from?

She stacked her materials out of the way and followed the path Brodie had taken down the hall. She could hear Catherine's giggles before she got to the door. Both boys were playing at hiding out of the baby's sight before popping back up to reveal their positions.

"What wonderful baby-sitters you boys are! Thank you for looking after Catherine so well. Go and wash up and we'll have something to eat in a minute after I get this one changed."

The boys scampered off as Dee lowered the side of the cot to change the baby's disposable. Catherine was still giggling and chattering away as if telling Dee all about what the boys had been doing. Dee felt the love for this child wrap around her and, not for the first time, she wished for another child, perhaps a daughter like this one.

She gathered up the little bundle and carried her to the kitchen and lowered her into her bouncinette where Catherine kicked her legs and jiggled her weight until the support chair bounced up and down.

The boys had a quick afternoon tea of sultana cake with a glass of milk before dashing back to their shared room to play on Brodie's laptop.

Dee on the other hand, reveled in the time to play with Catherine on her own. She counted fingers and clapped hands and then sat and read her one of Brodie's favourite picture books, 'The Very Hungry Caterpillar'. Her university studies taught her it was important for their development to read to very young children, especially because of language, cadence and word recognition.

When Catherine tired again, Dee positioned the bouncinette out of danger in the lounge room but where Catherine could watch Dee in the kitchen. Dee gathered ingredients for a meal but was interrupted when Anna and Caro came through the back door each carrying a pot.

Caro looked excited. "We wanted you to try some of the stuff we've prepared for Sunday. We took a load out to the men and they seemed okay with it. Now it's down to you. In this pot we've got spring rolls, samosas, Chinese dumplings, and Thai fish cakes. Grandma's got a fish curry. We figured we could cook some rice when we got here."

"Sounds great," Dee said. "The boys will be over the moon." She moved to take a heavy pot from Anna.

"Did you get your work done, dear?" Anna asked as she bustled into the kitchen to prepare a pot of rice.

"I emailed in one assignment and the last one is well under way. I'll finish it in the morning when Brodie goes to school. Then I'm finished—if the submissions are satisfactory."

"They will be, dear. Everything you've done in the course has been excellent. These will be no different. I'm so proud of you."

"We're all proud of you, Dee," Caro said. "I've never once seen you curl up in a ball in the corner and say, 'Poor Me!'" Caro laughed as she leaned down to pick up her daughter. "You're amazing!"

"Not really. Anna and Cassie kept me on task, and what else do you do when you're responsible for a little one? The whole family has been wonderful and supportive. Look at your men out there doing the harvest for us!"

Caro laughed again. "They love harvest, though. It gives them a sense of pride, all this male-bonding, competing with each other, and working through the night to get the job done. Then they come home exhausted, expecting loads of tender loving care, and waiting for the laurels of appreciation to be heaped on them. They're such boys, aren't they?"

"They come through when needed. I hope Brodie grows up with those values," Dee said.

Anna nodded, "It's in the genes, dear."

"I know, that's why… no, don't worry about that. Boys, could you wash your hands and come to the table, please? Anna Nana and Aunty Caro have some wonderful surprises for you."

"If you mean Nash. We don't get it either." Caro intuited what Dee had been about to say.

"There's a missing piece there somewhere," Anna mused. "It will all come out one day."

As the boys came to the table, Caro turned the conversation. "I've got all these name cards for Sunday printed. I need some helpers to put them into their card holders for people to wear. Do you boys think you'd be able to do that? I'm sure Catherine would help if she could, but she's still a bit little…"

Ciaran looked at Brodie. When Brodie agreed they would help, Ciaran nodded enthusiastically.

"Great. We'll have it done in no time. What do you think of the food, boys? Will our guests enjoy it?"

"Oh yeah. I looove the spring rolls. What do you think, Ciaran?" Brodie said.

Ciaran repeated Brodie's verdict word for word, inflection for inflection.

"Good," said Caro. "And what does Dee think?"

"Dee thinks she could live on this and never get bored," Dee said. "What else is on the list?"

"We have some more curries, casseroles, salads, etc., and then we've made tiramisu and trifles," Caro said. "Tomorrow we'll work on pavlovas. For the barbecue, it'll be mostly salads and meat with the first round of desserts. At afternoon tea, we'll serve sandwiches and some of the finger food we've had here and finish with the Naming Cake. All the other hot foods and desserts will be for Sunday night's supper when we'll need your cheesecakes. What do you think?"

"I think it's as well you ordered the extra cool room to store all this stuff, Anna," Dee said.

"Yes dear. It arrived this afternoon and is working like a dream. I've got Ted coming out in the morning. He'll bring one of his boys to unload the beer and wine straight into it."

"It sounds like you're organized. My guess is Ted's crew will need to be back at the pub by ten for opening, and I should finish my last assignment by then. Shall we plan on putting up the decorations after that? Caro, could you do one more review of the ceremony now I've added in Nash as a Life Guardian? I'll print it and the certificates tomorrow too."

"Okay. For now, I'll get these boys organized with the name tags."

Anna and Dee cleared away the meal and Dee listened as Brodie tried reading the names from the list. "There are a lot of Brodericks, Aunty Caroline. Who is this one? Ay .. Ab...?"

"Aibreann?"

"It doesn't look like Ab-rawn."

"It's tricky, Brodie," Anna explained from the kitchen. "That's why we call her Aunty Abby."

"Oh, I know Aunty Abby!" Brodie confirmed. "I didn't know she had a weird name."

"It's not so weird," Anna explained. "All the Brodericks have a little bit of Irish in them so we use quite a few Irish names. Even Aunty Cassie's dad was really Abban but everyone called him Adam. Have you come across Aunty Siobhan yet?"

"No, but I found Sergeant Hamilton. Why is he coming? Are we expecting trouble?"

Anna laughed. "Don Hamilton is a really good family friend. He rescued your mum when she was little and made sure she could stay here with me. He's special to us."

"Okaaay."

"Is there a name card for me, Aunty Caro? What name did you put on it? Brodie or Broderick?"

"I used Brodie because it's how people know you. It would be confusing with all these other Brodericks."

"Ah huh." The boy's eyes widened as though in alarm. "Really confusing."

Anna smiled at the boy. "It can be sometimes, Little Bit. Dee, if you have time, could you drop me home? I want to clean the kitchen and get an early night. It'll be another big day tomorrow, I'm thinking. Good night everyone."

The boys rushed to hug her and kiss her goodnight. "Love you, Anna Nana." "Love you, Grandma!"

As Anna's great-grandsons hugged either side of her body and brought such a smile to the older woman's face, Dee wished in that moment she had a camera in her hands to capture, for eternity, the picture of unconditional love.

Chapter Thirty-one

The harvest left Nash elated but absolutely exhausted. Since Thursday morning, the team had taken off the canola and prepared for the chickpeas at the start of the week. They'd stopped only to eat the food that Anna or Danielle had ferried down to them or to catch an hour's sleep here and there.

He felt great. This was the work he loved, part of who he was. The past few days decided his future for him. He was coming home—for good. It wasn't just the threat of losing his birthright forever that decided him but the inner belief that this was his destiny—a belief he'd been able to hide in his subconscious while he was away but refused to be denied once he was home.

He stepped into the shower for the first time in three days. As he lifted his arm to adjust the shower head, the gritty, pungent odor from his body filled the shower cubicle. He hadn't smelled as bad since he'd spent weeks on patrol in Afghanistan. He lathered his body, washed his hair, rinsed off and repeated the process. The stream of hot water helped to ease the kinks from his muscles.

He slapped the towel against his back as he dried off, but stilled as he heard a car pulling into the gravel driveway. So far as he was aware, everyone was down at the shearing shed preparing for this evening's barbecue.

Dressing hurriedly, he arrived at the door as a familiar figure emerged from a vehicle with defense force plates.

Lieutenant Gillian Wallis of the Royal Australian Navy had been with him during Officer Training and it was she who had broken the news to him of Danielle's treachery.

"Gill! What brings you here?" He wrapped the woman in a bear hug.

"Hey to you, too. When you still weren't back in Canberra yesterday afternoon, Mitch figured I should come and try to drag you back. I got as far as Albury last evening before I pulled in for the night."

"Come in. Can I get you a drink? The family is down at the shearing shed about to have a barbecue. My niece's naming day is tomorrow, so family and friends have come from everywhere."

"Is a naming such a big deal in these parts?" Her puzzled look verged on a sneer.

"Any valid excuse for a get-together is a big deal," Nash grinned as he poured two glasses of scotch, handing one to his guest. "Plus, I'm one of the baby's life guardians. I'm glad I'm here. Take a seat. How long are you here? Do you have somewhere to lay your head?"

"My plan was to swoop in, drag you out to the car and be on my way. I hadn't figured on your entire family being around. Do you have space for me?"

"I can put you up in the shearers' quarters with about thirty other family members. Would you be okay with that? I'd invite you to stay in the house, but Grandma already has Uncle Sean and his wife plus Aunty Siobhan and Aunty Abby. If you drive me to the quarters now, I'll take you across to the barbecue."

Nash sensed Gillian's hesitation. "Isn't that an imposition?"

"No more than any of the other guests."

"I've got Mitch's paperwork here. When can we go over it?"

Nash frowned. It was his turn to hesitate. He really didn't want to be drawn back into the intelligence world when he'd decided to leave it all behind.

"Come on, Nash. I've made a two-day trip to get here to consult you."

"It'll have to wait till tomorrow morning. I'm expected down at the sheds."

Gillian nodded. "Okay. Lead on. There'd better be hot water."

At the quarters, Nash levered himself from the sedan and went around to help Gillian retrieve her overnight bag and briefcase. As he stepped into the common area of the quarters, he found Danielle tidying the space.

The shock of seeing her unexpectedly made him miss a step and Gillian glanced at him.

"Danielle, where is everyone?" Nash asked. "All the cars are here. I thought everyone would be at the sheds by now."

"They are. Frank turned the transport into a hayride and took them all at once. Hello, I'm Danielle, the manager here," Dee addressed herself to Gillian. "Everyone, except Nash, calls me Dee."

"I'm sorry," Nash said. "This is Lieutenant Gillian Wallis. She's brought some work from Canberra. I've asked her to stay for the party."

Danielle's smile lit up her face. "Cool. Welcome! Nash, your Aunt Siobhan was looking for you earlier. I can look after your guest if you want to go on over to the sheds?"

"You okay if I take off, Gill?"

"Certainly."

"I'll see you later then."

~ * ~

Dee turned to the visitor. "Come, I'll find you a room."

"I don't want to be a bother." As Gillian spoke, Dee stopped dead.

"Wait, you're that Gillian? The Gillian, from-seven-years-ago-Gillian? Wow! I didn't think I'd ever get the chance to meet you and thank you for your help back then."

"What gave me away?" Gillian raised her brows.

"Your accent. You're Canadian?"

"I'm an Aussie." She pronounced it with the sibilant 's' of someone from North America rather than the harder 'Ozzie' version of a local. "I spent a lot of time in Canada when my dad was serving there."

"That explains it. Double welcome. Nash has probably told you we have everyone here for Catherine's naming day tomorrow. We have the welcome bash tonight. The naming is set for two-thirty with afternoon tea to follow and supper tomorrow night before everyone travels home on Monday. Catherine's mum wanted the naming to be in cocktail dress, but Nash's Grandma won't be wearing a frock, so anything you have with you will be fine."

"I'm not sure I'll be staying. I have some things to discuss with Nash in the morning. Then I'll probably jump in the car and get on my way, and stop in Albury or Gundagai tomorrow night if need be."

"If you change your mind, you're more than welcome to stay. It's not all family here. There are lots of friends too."

"Where do you fit?"

"I'm a bit of both, I guess, as you would realize. Mainly, I'm the property manager."

"Well, I'm a bit of both too, then, since Nash and I are going to be married."

"What?" Dee prayed her face didn't register her shock. "You're engaged? Nash hasn't mentioned anything, but then he's been out working on the property for most of the time he's been home."

"Well, please don't say a word. He'll want to tell people in his own time. You know what men are like."

"No, no. Of course not. Um, congratulations. Here's your room. Look, I'll wait out in the common area and when you're ready, I'll take you across to the party. Shared facilities are further down on your left."

Dee scurried back to the common area and out into the night, heaving lungsful of healing air.

Nash was engaged. No wonder he wanted nothing to do with his son. He was setting out to start a whole new family with someone who was not Dee.

Sensations swirled through Dee's heart and mind. She didn't know what to feel. Should she be angry? She was too heart-sore. Should she be shattered? Naïve. Nash let her know seven years ago they were over. Should she be grateful the door marked 'Nash' was now firmly closed? Her head said yes, but her heart cracked wide at the thought.

She swallowed hard and willed herself into hostess mode as she Gillian's door closed and footsteps sounded in the hall. Taking a deep breath, she unwrapped the arms she'd clamped around her middle and walked inside.

Chapter Thirty-two

Nash stood with a beer in one hand, speaking with his father's sister, Siobhan, more relaxed than he had in a long time. Siobhan and Aibreann were his grandparents' unexpected twin bonus babies, born when Nash's father was fifteen or sixteen.

"What are your plans now, Nash?" his aunt asked.

"These last couple of weeks I've been back on Calypso have been great."

"Back to your roots, eh?"

"Yeah. It feels right being home. I know someone else has done all the work leading up to it, but the shearing and then the harvest... it's me, it's my work."

"Your dad would be pleased."

"Would you be okay with me coming back, Aunty Shiv?"

"Nash, for fuck's sake, there's less than eight years between us, so skip the 'Aunty' crap, would you? It makes me feel old and I'm not ready yet."

Nash laughed. "Whoa! Sorry!"

"To answer your question, my responsibilities, obligations and rights in relation to Calypso Station ceased when I accepted the family exit package at age twenty-one. I thought I would be married, remember? When that didn't happen, I took the money and went to Sydney. I have no say at all. Neither has Abby. On a personal level, though, it would be wonderful for you to be here and continue the legacy. For your own sanity, you should remember it's still a parcel of dirt, Nash, so if you have other goals in life, go for them. You can take the package the rest of us did and live a good life. Calypso will survive. Remember, you own the land, not the other way around. Don't be swayed by people who want to dump a shit load of emotional guilt on you. You'd never be happy. Do what's right for you."

"You always tell it like it is, Aun... er Shiv. I reckon I've about decided to resign from the Army and come home."

"Would you live with Mum?"

"I reckon I should move into my parents' place. I could still keep an eye on Grandma."

Nash sensed Danielle behind him. He turned to find both Gill and Danielle staring at him with set faces. There was tension here. Was it between them or had they overheard him?

Danielle stepped forward. "Siobhan Broderick, I'd like to introduce Gillian Wallis. Gillian is a friend of Nash's from Canberra."

"Jillian, is it?"

"No, ma'am. It's a hard 'g' like golly gosh Gillian, not jim jam Jillian. It's nice to meet you ma'am." Gillian extended her hand for Siobhan to take.

"What brings you all the way from Canberra, Golly Gosh?"

Gillian's smile was tight.

"I had to speak to Captain Broderick on some work matters, ma'am."

"Canadian?"

"No, ma'am. I'm Australian, though I spent a lot of time in that part of the world. What gave it away? Most people assume my accent is American. Both you and Dee picked me as Canadian."

"It's the way you said, 'about'. Canadians say it so it sounds like 'a boat'."

Danielle excused herself from the group and moved through the gathering. Nash's gaze tracked her as she stopped first to accept a kiss from his Uncle Sean and then as Michael hugged her close to his side and directed her away from the rest of the guests. Nash felt his body tense.

"Right, Nash?" Gill said.

Nash forced his attention back to the conversation around him. "Pardon?"

"I was explaining to Ms. Broderick you are in line for another promotion when you get back to work."

"Mmm. Maybe or maybe not. Look, excuse me for a moment, will you?"

Nash moved around the outside of the group to come abreast of where Michael and Danielle were standing close together outside the circle of light.

"Come on, Dee," Michael was saying. "We would be good together. You know how to run a farm. We could work together to set up our own place—in the Riverina, maybe?"

"But..."

"I think Brodie is a great kid. I'd raise him as my own."

"Michael, I love you like a brother, not..."

"Don't say it, Dee. Forget Nash. He's more trouble than he's worth as far as you're concerned."

"No, Michael." Danielle stepped back. "You'd be much more suited with someone like Jess. Remember her? You were very pally when she was here with the shearing team."

"Jealous, much?"

Danielle's shoulders slumped. "I'm not jealous, Michael. I'd be happy for you if you and Jess got together. You and I are friends, Mick. I want it to stay that way."

"Think about it, Dee. Nash will come home and boot you out, quick as look at you. Then what?"

Danielle bit her lip. "I've got to organize the food. I'll see you later, Mick."

"Dee..."

"Later, Michael."

It was then that Michael saw Nash standing in the shadows. "You're a bastard, you know that?"

"What makes you say that, Mick?"

"You left her in the lurch when she needed you. You won't acknowledge your own kid. And she still thinks she loves you. That makes you lower than pond scum, in my opinion."

"Brodie is not my kid."

"You keep telling yourself that, man, if it helps you sleep at night. You're the only one who thinks that way. Ah, why bother?" Michael spun away and headed back to the party, leaving Nash to ponder what he'd said.

Brodie was not his son. He couldn't be, could he? Danielle herself told Gill seven years ago the baby's father was a man she'd met after Nash had left. The kid did look like the Brodericks. He shook his head to clear away the insidiousness of creeping doubts.

The sooner he came back, moved into his family home, and moved Danielle and her kid on, the better it would be for all concerned. His body still recognized when she walked into a room, she still haunted his dreams, and he might have wanted to wring his cousin's neck when he realized what Michael was asking of Danielle. He'd get over it. He would put those feelings to rest when he had a wife and family of his own to shut out the memories.

Chapter Thirty-three

Dee struggled to keep her poise and a smile on her face. What a night. It felt like one bombshell after another had rained on her. She'd have to find a moment to speak with Nash to clarify what she'd overheard about him coming home. She couldn't stay if Nash was returning and bringing Gillian as his bride.

If the job at the school came off, she would find a cottage in town for her and Brodie, and still keep watch on Anna. If it didn't...?

She strode into the shearing shed as the evening wound down and moved to the end of one of the long trestle tables. She was clearing away paper plates and cutlery when Siobhan came to stand beside her.

"Nash and his visitor seem very close, don't they?"

"Yep."

"And if his visitor ma'ams me one more time, I'll scream."

"Yep."

"The party went well. There was heaps of food. We can bundle up some of it and send it back to the quarters for anyone who wants a midnight snack." Shiv set actions to her words.

"Yep."

"You're all organized for the ceremony tomorrow afternoon?"

"Yep."

"Good. And you know it's snowing on the south paddock as we speak."

"Yep." Dee's head snapped up from her task. "What?"

"Just checking. Are you okay?"

"Sorry. I was miles away. What did you say about snow?"

"Ignore it. You're exhausted. Come, take a load off for a while. Grab a beer and we'll let the world go by for ten or fifteen minutes. What?"

Dee cracked a small smile. "Well, I could go all pompous, lower my voice for dramatic effect, and say, 'I don't drink when I'm on duty, *Ma'am!*'"

"But...?"

"I really don't drink when I'm on duty!" Dee's laugh escaped full throttle. It felt good.

Siobhan joined in. "For Chrissake, grab a can of soft stuff, then. You need to get off your feet. Come and tell me your life story or something."

"Boring, as my son would say."

"Not to me. We've never had a chance to sit and natter." They both sat on one of the hay bales.

"You're always busy when I'm here," Siobhan continued. "Tell me how you came to be living with my mother and why my idiot nephew hasn't made 'an honest woman' out of you," she said twiddling her fingers in air quotes.

"Hmm, 'honest woman' is somewhat patriarchal coming from an independent person like yourself."

"Yeah, yeah. You know what I mean. So, give! What's your story?"

"My story, huh? Tall order. I wouldn't know where to start," Dee said.

"You could start with when you came to Hamlet Brae, but the beginning would be better."

Dee's mouth twisted to one side.

"I don't visit that part of my life often and I don't think anyone apart from Anna and Nash know the whole." She hesitated and clamped her lips together as though the words themselves didn't want to be released.

"Look, everyone in the family thinks you walk on water, except my idiot nephew," Siobhan said. "You reportedly saved my mother's life. You are the mother of one of my great-nephews. You run the family farm like it's your own. I want to know more."

"Fair enough." Dee flicked one hand into the air. "The story of Danielle Dawn who arrived in the world when her parents were already having problems. Named Danielle for Daniel, the protector of marriages and Dawn for a brand-new start. It didn't go so well. I figure Daniel, the Archangel that is, knew my mother wasn't serious about the whole deal.

"We arrived in Hamlet Brae shortly after my ninth birthday. I think Dad planned this as a clean break, a fresh beginning for them both. He got farm jobs wherever he could, and Mum worked at the truck stop south of town."

Dee stopped and swallowed a mouthful of her drink.

"Anyway, Mum met a truckie almost as soon as she started work there and they developed a closeness. The upshot was one day she left for work and didn't come home. I was eleven."

"Hmm, tough for you..."

Dee grimaced. "Dad was distraught, but what could he do? He had no idea anything untoward had been happening, no idea who the guy was and no idea which way they'd gone. They could have been in Gundagai, Gippsland, or Adelaide by the time we realized she'd left. And he still had me to worry about.

"He grieved from the bottom of a beer bottle when he was home, but still pulled himself together to go to work every morning. Then the drought didn't break. It kept going. Work dried up alongside every living thing around." Dee paused as she felt the skin across her cheeks tightening. She smoothed it out with her fingertips.

"Yes, it was an awful time for everyone. What did he do?"

"He started going farther afield to find work. He'd leave me behind so I could go to school. I was about thirteen by then. 'In days of old, Dee,' he'd say, 'young women were married and running their own homes by the time they were twelve. You're older and much more capable than they were I reckon, plus you've only got yourself to look after.' He'd leave me some money, warn me not to let anyone know I was on my own and told me to go to school every day."

Dee bounded off the bale of hay and started pacing the space with her arms crossed tightly at her midriff.

"The times away got longer and longer. I soon learned to make sure I kept the house clean and the lawns mown on Saturdays even though there was mostly dirt. It made it look like there was a responsible adult there somewhere. After all, what teenaged kid would willingly go out and start the mower when there were more interesting things to do. I kept a low profile, only going to the shops when I really needed to. A loaf of bread, some sausages and some potatoes could keep me going for nearly a week."

"Shit!" Siobhan said, "and no one realized?"

"Nope. Anyway," she stopped and plopped back onto her seat, swallowing convulsively to stop the glistening tears from falling. Her eyes stared at the corner of the paper-covered trestle where the leg of the table met the top.

"Anyway, one day he told me that there was no work left for him here. He would go up to Cobar in New South Wales to see if he could get some work in the mines. He'd only be gone a week or ten days. As soon as he found work, he'd be back." She took a deep breath, letting it out through the O formed by her lips.

"He left me with seventy-six dollars, an absolute fortune, to keep me going. It must have been pretty well all he had left. He was gone the next morning, and it's the last time I saw him."

"And then...?" Siobhan prompted after several seconds of silence.

Dee shrugged. "It was the normal way of life for me. I did my homework, and the laundry, added some baked beans to my diet..." She grimaced. "It could have gone on a lot longer but in the second week, the real estate agent at the time knocked on the door three nights in a row looking for rent. I told him Dad was at the pub and would be home soon. But he went to the pub looking for him and Ted told him he hadn't seen my dad in weeks. You know Ted? He's still the publican." At Siobhan's nod, Dee continued.

"Well, the agent made a complaint to Don Hamilton. I'm still not sure whether it was a complaint about lost rent, or he suspected I'd been abandoned. Within an hour, Don arrived at the house. He was a Senior Constable then, although he's a sergeant now. Legally, he should have held me until the welfare people came from Ballarat. Instead, he rang Anna because he knew I was friends with Cassie. He told Anna he'd seen this before. The parents usually turned up within a day or two. I refused to say how long I'd been on my own. He told Anna he thought, by the look of the place, it could only have been a few days. I sort of won that round." Her face split into a momentary grin.

"Your mum said she'd be happy to have me until my dad got home and there was no need to go bothering the authorities. I don't know if my dad ever did come back and go looking for me in the Dutton Street house, but I used to sneak off over there from school at lunchtime to check. I left a note for him to say where I was, just in case. Then one day I went over there, the note was gone, and a new family was living there. I pretty much gave up hope that day."

"What happened about Children's Services?" Siobhan demanded.

"Every time Don broached the subject with Anna, she'd say, 'A few more weeks, then we'll see.' She kept saying that till I was sixteen. By then, a car accident had killed Mr. and Mrs. Broderick, so she had Cassie and Nash living with her as well. I owe her everything. She got me through school. She supported me through my pregnancy, she's an amazing Nana to Brodie and then she pushed me to achieve my dream of becoming a teacher."

"You were living here in our house with Nash when you got pregnant?"

"Mmm. But it didn't happen under Anna's nose. We were pretty much a foursome with Robbie and Cassie, and we'd all go out together. Robbie and Cassie would go off on their own and Nash and I were the other pair. As these things happen with older teenagers, we experimented with sex and found we liked it, not even considering the consequences. I don't think Anna even suspected we had a relationship until Nash left, and I was pregnant." Dee stopped and cocked her head on one side.

"I feel like I'm telling tales out of school," she said.

"Nah. It's off the record. What happened next?" Siobhan sounded eager.

"Well, you know Nash's dad encouraged him to join the army and get a trade before coming back to the land, so, he joined up."

"Adam and Frances had been gone for three years by then. No one would have criticized him for staying," Siobhan mused.

"He still looked to his dad for guidance if you know what I mean. He said he'd go into the army for a few years and then he'd come back, and we'd build Calypso Station into the best sheep and wheat property around." A sad smile touched her face.

"Did you let him know you were pregnant?" Siobhan asked.

"That's a whole other story, but yes, I did."

"So, the army was more of a pull for him than the girlfriend he'd left behind?"

"One possibility, I guess. Now he's home, I'm sure I'll eventually find out exactly what happened and why. Don't look so outraged, Shiv. We'll work it out or we won't. And that's me. All there is to know. Someone abandoned by her parents without a backward glance and abandoned again when she was pregnant."

She raised the back of her hand to her forehead. "Poor me! Damaged goods! The psychologists would have a field day."

Siobhan humphed, unimpressed by the theatrics. "Have you ever tried to locate your parents?"

"I did an internet search of both their names. I figured if they were dead, then death notices would show up somewhere. And I did a whitepages search, but I doubt either of them would bother to have their phone numbers listed in the directory. I'm no further along. I have no idea what I would say to either of them if they should turn up on my doorstep.

"I'm not the scared little girl I was. I'm not angry at them anymore, either. I'm not even curious, I don't think. I'm just not... anything. Brodie is my life and he will never feel abandoned as long as I can help it."

"Good for you. It's an amazing story. You should know, though, I don't think I can concur with your assessment of yourself as damaged goods. You're a pretty well put together young woman."

"If I am, it's down to your mum."

"And now Nash is thinking of coming home. How do you feel about that, Dee?"

"I can't really say, tonight. First, I must check with him on his plans and his timeline."

"The family is on your side in all of this, you know?"

"Thanks, Siobhan, but blood is thicker than water. It might be easier if I make plans now to move on. I can apply for teaching jobs anywhere in the state. I hear Gippsland is a lovely part of the world."

"You finished your degree?"

The question cracked a smile on Dee's face. "I sent the last assignment in yesterday. So, yes, I've finished. I can soon start applying for work."

Siobhan reached over and took Dee in her arms. "Wonderful! Congratulations! You should have said, and we could have raised a toast to you with all the family here. They'll be so proud of you."

Dee returned the hug and stood to go back to clearing the table.

"I wouldn't want to put the mockers on myself. My lecturers might want me to redo one or other of the assignments, then where would I be?"

Siobhan laughed. "Not much chance."

"How's life for you in Sydney?" Dee was desperate to turn any further conversation away from herself.

"Lonely. If you were to repeat that to anyone, I would deny it." Siobhan snorted. "Print media is not what it used to be. I've been thinking for a while now of moving back to Victoria, maybe Geelong, and writing what I want to write. It might be freelance news, or it could as easily be a Broderick memoir or a romance novel."

"You could afford to give up your day job?"

"When I cashed in my Broderick legacy, I invested well and got out before the crash, so yeah, I live comfortably since there's just me."

"It would be great for Anna to have you closer."

"I thought so, too. Plus, Abby's in Strathbogie these days. On top of all that, it's time for me to confront my past so I don't have a panic attack every time I even consider coming back to this place. Mum's more important anyhow."

"I don't know your story. You'd left before I came to Hamlet Brae."

"It's not very edifying. The usual story of love gone wrong over something that seems petty with hindsight."

"He's still around?"

"So far as I know—but I'm not asking, yet."

"Okay. If you need a listening ear anytime, come on over."

"Thanks. You're a good person, Danielle. Life's a bitch sometimes, ain't it?"

They began working methodically along the trestle tables—clear food, dump plates and cutlery, roll up paper tablecloth, trash it. Move on.

"Well," Caroline broke in as she came to join them. "You guys have been busy!"

"Many hands, as they say," Siobhan responded.

"I'll get Connor to organize the hay-ride back to the quarters. That'll move everyone out in a hurry, and we'll have a clear run. They can party on over there if they want to."

Siobhan nodded, and Caroline went to set her plan in motion.

"Let's finish up here and get to bed," Siobhan suggested.

"Okay. It won't take long. I'll come back in the morning to do any extra decorations and stuff," Dee said.

True to Dee's prediction, it took less than half an hour to clear the area ready for the onslaught the next day.

Siobhan straightened. "With that done, I'm for my bed unless there's anything else I can do for you?"

"I can give you a lift up to the house, if you like, since I have to collect Brodie," Dee offered.

"Thanks. Abby and I came down with Mum, but she went back with all the littlies."

"Let me drop the rest of these bags in the skip bin and we're finished," Dee said.

Dee drove Siobhan from the shearing shed to the main house. They found Anna knitting with the television on low and the children sprawled on makeshift beds of sofa cushions.

Dee noticed Jacob wasn't amongst the group. "Has Cassie gone already? I hardly got to speak to her tonight."

"Yes. They called by forty minutes ago. She has some work she needs to do in the morning. She apologized if she'd left you in the lurch with the cleaning."

"Oh, we managed. I'm sorry I missed her," Dee said.

"Goodnight everyone," Siobhan called quietly as she edged around the carpet of sleeping children.

"Night!" Anna and Dee responded.

"Have the children been okay for you, Anna? Not too much for you to handle?" Dee asked.

"Goodness, no, dear. They were pooped. As soon as we got here, Brodie pulled the sofas apart and organized the boys into their camping beds and they were sound asleep in no time. They haven't stirred since. Nor has Catherine."

They paused as the door swung open again and admitted Abby along with Sean and Jennifer.

"Shall I put the kettle on, Mum?" Sean asked.

"Yes please, dear. I didn't bother earlier. It's been so peaceful here with the kiddos, I didn't want to move."

"I'll grab Brodie and get him home. Thanks again, Anna." Dee stooped and collected her youngster in her arms. She was tired, or he was getting bigger. His weight was almost too much for her tonight.

She stood and mouthed 'Goodnight' and headed to the door as Nash was about to enter. He took the child from her without asking, trod down the steps and over to Dee's car. She opened the passenger door. He deposited Brodie on the seat and strapped his seatbelt over him.

"Thank you." Dee paused. "Nash—you've decided to come home?"

"I think so."

"You'll want your parents' place?"

"We won't need two managers, Danielle Dawn."

"What's your timeline?"

"I'll go back to Canberra the week after harvest to sort it out. I should be home by Christmas. You'll need to be out by then. I'll be sending in some people to do some land surveys, look over the place, see what improvements are needed."

Tiredness weighed heavily on Dee, but his comment stiffened her backbone. Nash's plans affected her son.

"I'm entitled to sixty days' notice on the job and on the house."

"You would be if you had a proper contract, but Grandma hasn't been able to produce one for me, so I don't think I have to worry."

"On the other hand, you're not my employer either. Anna and Cassie are. You ceded your proxy to Anna indefinitely when you went into the Army, so unless you have formally rescinded it, you have no rights over my employment."

She watched as Nash clenched his jaw. "Cassie cashed in her legacy when she married. The property belongs to me and Grandma now."

It was Dee's turn to bite her tongue. That would explain why the property had a sudden shortfall in cash five years ago if it bought out Cassie's stake. Family business, not something that involved the 'manager'.

"Then you'll have to speak to your grandmother, won't you? Good night, Nash."

Dee stomped around to the driver's side of the car.

"There's always Michael's offer, isn't there?" Nash taunted.

Dee dropped her chin to her chest and let out a long sigh. She raised her head and rolled it from side to side.

She whispered, without anger. "Go to hell, Nash Broderick. Just... go to hell."

Dee gunned the engine, enough for the tires to spin on the dry earth. She drove off, leaving him standing in a cloud of dust.

Chapter Thirty-four

Sunday morning dawned clear and bright, which was more than Nash could say for himself. The light coming through the gap in the curtains was too much for his eyes. He grabbed his second pillow and pulled it over his face.

His head was thumping. He should have gone straight to bed after Danielle left last night. Instead, he'd ignored the tea Sean made and sat down with the whisky decanter instead. It wasn't something he did often. The most memorable occasion had been when he'd learned of Danielle's unfaithfulness. His world shattered then, and he'd drunk himself into a stupor.

This morning's headache was nothing compared to then. There was still plenty of liquid in the decanter, so he can't have had that much, but he was out of practice with heavy drinking and there'd been those beers earlier in the night. Ah! Understanding dawned. His grandfather warned him never to mix the hops and the barley unless he wanted the mother of a hangover.

What was it about the woman that still triggered him into being so thoughtless after so many years? His brain said he shouldn't want her, so why was he so upset about Michael's proposal?

He pulled himself upright and drifted to the bathroom in search of medicinal relief. He found some slightly out-of-date painkillers and swallowed two of them with a huge glass of water.

He showered quickly and left the bathroom free.

The house was beginning to stir as he wandered towards the kitchen where his grandmother was organizing breakfast. If it hadn't been impressed upon him how seriously unwell she had been, he would have continued to believe she was totally indomitable.

"Good morning, dear. How are you this morning?"

"Best not go there, Grandma. After one of your breakfasts though, I should be right as rain. Shall I put the kettle on?"

"Yes please. Will your friend be all right getting her own breakfast down in the quarters, or do you want to fetch her?"

"She'll be fine. Besides, she's due up here in a while to go over some work with me. If she's hungry then, we can have some of your scones."

Nash felt healthier with some food in his stomach. After he'd helped to clear away breakfast, he wandered through the house and out the front door to stand in the fresh air. He tilted his head on one side to contemplate the track running between this house and the one where Danielle lived. As soon as he came home permanently, he'd fix the track so it was easier to drive between the houses without going onto the highway.

Danielle! She invaded his mind both day and night.

In the distance, he saw her leave the house with a large box, closely followed by Caroline similarly encumbered. The women dropped their burdens on the tray of the ute and climbed into the cab. Nash tracked the car to the shearing shed.

There seemed to be an awful lot of fuss and bother to name a child who'd been called Catherine since the moment she was born. He wondered briefly if Brodie had a naming day. What sort of name was Brodie, anyway? It was damn close to Broderick. He felt he was missing something here. It wasn't the first time he'd thought about it since he'd come home.

He strolled around inspecting his grandmother's house for potential maintenance issues. There was some cracked paint along the western wall, a common hazard with the blistering summer heat. Some windows weren't closing flush. A water stain ran down one wall which might indicate litter clogged the gutters, so rainwater was overflowing rather than running to the downpipe. He lost track of time as his examination continued until his grandmother hailed him from the back door.

"Gillian's here!"

He dusted off his shoes and re-entered the house. "Good morning. You're early."

"Mmm. There's more to get through than you realize, I think."

"Did you have breakfast? Would you like a cuppa?"

Gillian laughed. "Breakfast was bedlam, but I have eaten, thanks. Coffee would be great."

"I'll make it, Nash. You two get started and I'll bring it through. I'm not sure where you'll find space. The dining table is full of gifts and paraphernalia," Anna said.

"We'll be fine, Grandma. A coffee table in the lounge room is all we'll need."

He directed Gillian to a corner space away from the thoroughfare through the room. "What have we got?"

Gillian withdrew a thick wad of paperwork and dropped it on the table.

Nash scratched his neck with the side of his forefinger. "I see what you mean. These are all stamped 'Top Secret-AUSTEO'—Australian Eyes Only. They shouldn't have left the building. There should be a summary, not the original reports. How did you get them out?"

"Diplomatic pouch. Mitch was moaning he wanted you to see them. I made it work."

Nash felt a tingle of unease. This wasn't the way to do things. Mitch *had* said it was important and Gillian *had* driven eleven or twelve hours to bring the material.

"I'll have them back in the office by tomorrow morning and no one will be any the wiser except we'll have your input to sort through this mess."

These weren't any ordinary office files. They were TOP SECRET containing highly sensitive material about China's plans in the Philippines and Indonesia! Nash quickly thought through the various scenarios and either dismissed them or identified justifications for handling the material in this unorthodox way. He trusted Gillian, and he trusted Mitch. They'd been there when he needed people to rely on.

"Okay, let's get started."

For the next hour, Nash worked through the papers, making annotations and suggestions as he went, until Brodie crashed into the room, shattering his concentration.

"Hi Captain. I'm looking for Jacob's fire engine. Have you seen it? He thinks he left it here last night, but I don't remember."

"Which one is this?" Gillian asked. "I couldn't work out which of the kids was which last night."

"This is Brodie, Danielle's son."

Nash felt Gillian tense beside him. "Oh. He looks just like..."

"Brodie," Danielle said, coming into the room. "Can't you see that Nash and Gillian are trying to work?"

"But Mum..."

"Is this what you're looking for, Brodie?" Nash pulled a toy from under the coffee table.

"Thanks, Captain. Sorry for interrupting."

Nash turned his head towards Gillian, who had placed a hand on his arm and was leaning into him.

She smiled and turned to look at Danielle. Nash was confused.

"Did you find it, Brodie?" Robbie asked as he walked through the door.

"Captain Nash did, Uncle Robbie. Here it is," Brodie said.

"Thank goodness. We've had all sorts of dramas this morning. I had to bring Jacob out here to stop him from driving his mother mad. Before I forget, Dee, your new phone arrived in the shop on Friday. You can get it in the morning. It's time for you to come back into the twenty-first century."

"Thanks Rob. Let's take this to the kitchen. These guys are busy."

"Oops. Okay," Robbie grimaced.

Danielle herded the interlopers out of the lounge room.

"It's like Grand Central Station, isn't it?" said Nash. "We've been lucky until now, but I reckon we should finish this quickly. No one in this house has Top Secret clearance except you and me." Nash took up the next sheet of paper.

Nash worked quickly through what was left of the pile without further family interruptions. "Done!" he declared, shuffling the materials together and binding them with the long piece of pink fabric tape they had travelled with.

"Thanks, Nash. You're a wonder."

"Are you staying for the naming?" he asked.

"No, I have nothing suitable to wear."

"You look all right to me." Nash walked towards the interconnecting door from the lounge room into the kitchen, carrying the empty coffee cups.

"Grandma, Gill reckons she can't stay for the naming because she doesn't have anything to wear," he said.

"Well, nothing that meets the 'cocktail' criterion, anyway," Gillian commented, following behind Nash.

"I think Caro meant that mainly for the official group—the guardians and Dee. Most of the guests will be pretty casual," Anna explained. "I'm wearing a trouser suit. Definitely not cocktail. What about you, Dee?"

Dee turned from stacking plates into the dishwasher.

"Mmm? I've got an above the knee frock Caro has approved," she laughed. "I don't have an extensive wardrobe, Gillian, but you're welcome to find something there if you don't want to wear shorts. We're much the same build."

"I wouldn't want to impose."

"It's no problem," Dee said. "Look, take a key to the house in case no one is there when you decide. My room is the one at the end of the hall. You can return the key to me later or pass it on to Nash. I've got to run."

Gillian accepted the key and slipped it into a pocket of her shorts.

Danielle dashed out of the house, and Gillian frowned.

"Is it normal around here to invite strangers to use your wardrobe?" Gillian asked.

"We help each other out, I guess. You should take her up on the offer. You'd enjoy it, I think," Nash said.

"Hmm. I'll think about it. I'll go and organize my gear. Thanks for your help and thanks for not going ape-shit over the AUSTEO classification. See you in a few."

Chapter Thirty-five

Dee gathered up Brodie as she skirted Anna's house and made her way to the ute. It had been a frantic morning and things would not slow down until they finished the ceremony.

"Hey Brodie, we'll have a quick lunch when we get back to our place, then you can have your shower and get dressed. Do you reckon you can stay clean for the next couple of hours?"

"Sure Mum, if I can take my laptop with me down to the shearing shed?"

"Brodie..." Her tone telegraphed a warning.

"Otherwise, I'll be running around with the other kids and who knows what will happen?"

Dee shook her head, acknowledging she was being conned. "Just this once and only because I'm desperate."

"Yes!" Brodie pumped his arm in the air.

"But you must stay clean!"

After lunch, Dee directed Brodie to her en-suite bathroom so their guests could use the main bathroom without interruption. While he was busy, she did a last-minute check on her briefcase. Today she needed the ceremony, the Naming Certificate and the certificates for the Guardians and the grandparents. As she had done for any of the family ceremonies she had conducted, she had also contrived a special Great-Grandmother memento for Anna.

When Brodie returned to the kitchen, she said, "Gather what you need and put it next to my briefcase. I'll get ready."

She emerged from her bedroom twenty minutes later, dressed in an apricot frock with a fitted bodice and a slightly flared skirt that hung to just above her knees, small pearl earrings and a single pearl pendant on a silver chain. She secured a section of hair from either side of her face with a pearlized hair clip at the back of her head. She made her makeup the best she could. She avoided using liquid foundation because the weather would be quite warm during the ceremony. She wouldn't risk makeup likely to melt, choosing mineral powder instead. It had nothing at all to do with the likelihood of seeing Nash with Gillian and wanting to burst into tears.

Caro was in the kitchen, with her family each at various stages of eating their lunch.

"I'm heading down to make sure everything is working as it should. You guys shouldn't hurry. Arrive about a quarter of an hour before the ceremony so everyone can meet the guest of honor. I'll see you there."

Caro flicked a hand in acknowledgement and kept spooning food into Catherine's mouth.

Dee collected her briefcase and slid Brodie's laptop into it. "Are you sure this is all you need? No other games or anything?"

"Sure."

"Okay. Let's move."

Outside the sheds, Caro and Dee had set up three floral arches to form an open square. One of Anna's floor rugs provided a tidy base. A long, red, carpet runner led into the square. Using the arches as a bit of a disguise, a large, cantilevered umbrella hung over the top, providing shade within the space.

Dee shooed Brodie into the shearing shed out of the sun to play on his own while she set up the music stand she used as a lectern. All the ceremony furniture she needed, she had brought down earlier in the day.

She pulled a white cloth from the box under the little side table and spread it to hang and cover the makeshift storage space underneath.

She set a large candle in a glass jar on top of the table to stabilize the cloth in case of a sudden gust of wind. The certificates went beside it, held down with a holographic angel paper weight. Finally, she scattered white and pink faux rose petals across the cloth. With her headset microphone in place, she was prepared.

As if her readiness was some silent signal, guests began arriving, and she went to greet them. She knew the Broderick family and the friends who had come from Hamlet Brae. The faces she was less familiar with were those from Caroline's family. She moved from group to group, making sure everyone felt comfortable and welcome.

When Caroline and Connor finally arrived to take over hosting duties, Dee retreated to read through the ceremony one more time.

She checked her watch. It was time to begin. She dashed over to the shearing shed and called Brodie to come and went to check that Caroline and Connor were ready.

"Are all the guardians here?" she asked.

"I haven't seen Nash yet, but Cassie and Michael are ready."

"Right. If you'd like to make your way into the ceremonial area, I'll gather the others." She hadn't spoken to Michael since his proposal of the night before, and she hoped it wouldn't be awkward. He was standing with Cassie's family, so she could bring both Cassie and Michael forward together.

"Have you seen Nash?" she asked.

"Um..." Cassie craned her neck to look around the small sea of guests. "Here he comes now."

Dee followed the direction of Cassie's head tilt to find Nash in his brown army dress uniform striding confidently towards them. Dee's knees went to jelly. She swallowed hard to regain her composure. She lifted her chin and drew a hand up to direct him straight to the arches.

Anna was in the front row of seats with Brodie beside her and gave Dee a beaming smile of encouragement.

Dee slid her hand in her pocket to switch on the power pack for her headset and began the ceremony.

"Good afternoon, family and friends. My name is Danielle Tillson, and it is my pleasure to lead you through this afternoon's ceremony to name this child and to welcome her into our community. We'll start by asking her parents to light the candle."

The ceremony proceeded to the point where Cassie and Michael both pledged to provide guidance for the child. Then it was Nash's turn.

"Please read your vow."

"I, Ignatius James Broderick do..."

"Hey!" An indignant Brodie was hushed by Anna.

"...solemnly promise that I will..."

Dee glanced at her son who wore a severe frown. He had questions he wanted answered.

The ceremony progressed through an explanation of the name, 'Catherine' meaning pure and clear, and the name was bestowed. The conclusion to the ceremony came as Catherine's parents extinguished the candle for the wishes and prayers of those present to carry to Heaven on the wisps of smoke as they rose.

Predictably, as soon as he could escape from Anna, Brodie came charging to her.

"The Captain's got my name! How come?"

"Brodie, it's a long story. I'll sit down with you tonight and tell you all about it if you like." Dee tried to infuse her voice with eager anticipation. "Right now, it's Catherine's special day, so we must look after the guests. Okay?"

"I guess."

"Do you know I made sure there was macaroni cheese for you guys?" Dee said.

"Really? That's awesome. Thanks Mum."

"Could you go find Jacob and Ciaran and make sure they're okay? Come and get me if you need help."

"On my way!"

Where were all these sayings coming from?

She unthreaded the headset microphone from her head, retrieved the power pack and stored them in the briefcase. Pulling out her phone, she switched it on and stowed it in her pocket.

Dee headed into the shearing shed to check on what needed to be done. Siobhan was busy laying out the food with Abby, Cassie, Robbie, and Anna. It looked to be a veritable feast, and this was just afternoon tea.

The decorations of white and pink looked stunning and transformed the utilitarian space into a festive fairyland.

Dee moved to the tea and coffee urns and eskies of cold soft drinks and juice. Everything was in order there too, so she came back to touch base with Siobhan.

"A wonderful ceremony, Dee. Your poem about a child living with positive things was inspirational, even for me." She patted Dee's arm.

The pat became a vice-like grip. Dee looked at Nash's aunt to find her staring across at the doorway to where Tom Nicholls had appeared. Tom stood like a deer caught in a pair of headlights for several moments until he seemed to gather himself and walked across to them.

"Shiv. You're looking well."

"Thank you, Thomas. You're still living in Hamlet Brae?"

Tom nodded. "Lovely ceremony, Dee. Good use of words. Well done."

Dee couldn't remember ever seeing such uncertainty, almost embarrassment, in Tom's face. "Well, that's all I wanted to say." He pivoted and walked towards Nash.

The grip on Dee's arm eased.

"Well, now I know," Siobhan muttered inscrutably as she walked off in the opposite direction from the one Tom had taken.

Before Dee had time to consider what happened, Caroline was beside her. "I've left two big bowls of the chicken and macadamia balls in your fridge. I don't feel I can leave right now. Would it be too much of an imposition to ask you to get them?"

"Not at all, ask Cassie to keep an eye on Brodie. I'll only need five or ten minutes. Say, did Gillian turn up?" Dee asked.

"I haven't seen her."

"Me either. Maybe she went straight back to the city. I won't be long."

Dee caught sight of Brodie as she made her way to the car. "Hey Little Bit! I'm going up to the house for some chicken balls Aunty Caro left behind. You can go to Aunty Cassie if you need anything, okay?"

"K."

The phone banged against Dee's thigh as the ute bounced over the track. She went to pull it out, but an unexpected pothole nearly wrenched the steering wheel from her grasp. Moments later she was home.

She strode towards the house, up the few steps onto the porch and stopped. She'd given her key to Gillian and hadn't gotten it back. There was a spare hidden around the back, but she'd have to get down on her hands and knees to retrieve it.

She walked to the door to try the knob. It turned. Her hackles stood on end. She pushed the door open and stood in the space.

Gillian was browsing the photographs on the mantlepiece in the lounge room with candles alight on every conceivable surface.

"Hi Gillian! Didn't you find anything you could wear? We missed you at the ceremony." Dee kept her voice calm and cautious until she could find out what was going on.

Gillian turned slowly to her left, keeping her right hand behind her like some war general in a classic movie.

"Nothing for me in your pathetic little wardrobe." Her tone was cold and flat.

There was danger here. Dee needed backup.

The phone! She bunched her hands in her skirt to disguise her finger pressing against a number on the keypad. She searched for the big enter key and pressed that. She felt the slight vibration as the phone rang at the other end and then stopped.

"Sit down, Danielle Dawn. We need to have a little chat." Gillian withdrew her right hand to display a sinister-looking syringe.

The sight of it had Dee's head spinning. She needed to make a super quick decision. Did she remain calm and rational, or opt for hysterical?

She screamed!

Chapter Thirty-six

Nash glanced down to find Brodie tugging on his sleeve.

"Captain. Is your name really Ignatius Broderick?"

"Uh huh."

"So's mine." He shook his head. "At least it's Broderick Ignatius. It's weird you have the same name."

Nash felt every fiber of his being go taut. The blood drained from his face. Danielle had named her son for him? He felt as though he'd swallowed a rock that lodged itself low in his belly.

"I'm Broderick Ignatius Tillson, so my 'nitials are BIT. That's why Anna Nana and Mum call me Little Bit. I'll be six next week. They shouldn't call me little anymore. What do you think?"

"Where's your mum now, Brodie?" He studied the boy's face. He'd seen the similarities, sure, but pushed them from his mind. Michael said Brodie was his and so did Danielle—more than once. He'd dismissed it, but now the truth hit him like a punishing left hook to his gut.

"She went home for chicken balls or something. She said she'd be back soon. So, what do you think about our names? Only my mum used to say it had something to do with my father, but I don't have a dad. Do you know my father, Captain?"

His brain wouldn't function. From a long way off, he recognized he was probably in shock.

The phone trilled in Nash's pocket. He pulled it out to find Danielle's name displayed on the screen. How did she know he needed to speak to her? Why would she ring him? His brain kicked back into gear.

"Hello?"

He heard shuffling, and someone screamed.

"Gillian! What are you doing with that thing in my house?" It was Danielle's voice.

Was that Danielle screaming? She was always so calm. His senses went on high alert.

"Is that a syringe? Holy fuck, Gillian! Have you been doing drugs in my house?"

"This is for you," Gillian said.

"For me? I don't do drugs. You're standing in my lounge room, threatening me with a syringe. Have you gone mad? Why are my candles all alight?"

"You don't do drugs? Ever? Then this will be a treat for you. Here's what happens. It starts with you dosing up on this little cocktail I've prepared for you. You get high. You'll love it, trust me. You're dancing in the clouds, swinging your arms around." Gillian said.

"The candles are collateral damage. It's a pity you set fire to Nash's childhood home and burned it down. The real tragedy is you were too spaced out to get yourself to safety. Poor Danielle Dawn, poor motherless Brodie."

"You're mad. I'm getting out of here." Danielle said.

There was a rustle of movement through the phone.

"No, you're not. Stop screaming like a banshee and sit down quietly," Gillian instructed in the cold tones of someone in total control. "There's no one here to hear you."

"Let go of me. You want me to sit down so you can stick me with that thing? What the hell? Get it away from my neck."

"STOP screaming. Or I will have to shoot you up to get some peace. That's better. Now take a seat."

"How do you even know that my name is Danielle Dawn?"

"Oh, that's what Nash would moan when he found out that you were an unfaithful slut. 'Danielle Dawn, why?' he would say or 'Danielle Dawn, I loved you.' See what I mean? So pathetic. So sickening. What an awful name. It fits you though."

Nash cringed at the whining imitation of himself. He turned to the boy by his side. "Have you seen Sergeant Hamilton?"

"He's over there talking to Aunty Abby."

"Thanks. And Brodie? I'll talk to your mum. Then I think we all need to have a sit down and work out this name thing. What do you say?"

"'K."

Nash sought the cold calm he carried with him in a war zone, but it deserted him. This was Danielle who was in danger. His pulse was racing, and his nerves were jumping. He strode across to the police sergeant and whispered in his ear. "We have a problem."

Don Hamilton gave a startled nod to Abby and excused himself.

"Don, we need to get over to Danielle's place. Do you have your car handy?"

"What's going on?"

"Danielle's under threat. I have her on an open phone line."

He held the phone for Don to hear.

"Let's go. I've got the unmarked car. It has everything that a marked police vehicle has. I'm not sure you should be along on this. You're not police."

"But I am military, and I outrank the suspect," Nash said as they hurried towards the vehicle.

"Okay. I wouldn't mind having some company. What do you know about the person who's holding Dee?"

They both got into Don's car. "It's Lieutenant Wallis. I don't understand why. I'll put it on speaker." Nash turned his attention to the conversation coming from Danielle's house and ramped up the volume on his phone.

Danielle's voice said. "I'm sitting now, so why don't you tell me what's going on?"

"Let's start by you giving me your phone."

"The only useful phone I have is the landline in the kitchen. You heard Robbie tell me this morning my phone arrived at the shop."

"What do you use when you're out on the property?" Gill asked.

"Satellite phone. It's a brick... in the kitchen." Gillian wouldn't know any better, Nash realized.

There was silence for several seconds until Gillian spoke again.

"You know you're a fool, don't you? You and Nash both. You were so, so easy to manipulate back then."

"What do you mean manipulate?"

Gillian laughed.

"I was with Nash one day you rang, and your name came up with this little heart next to it. It nearly made me puke. He got this dreamy smile on his face, but he had to cut you off because we were on our way into class. Then later, when the phone in the hall started, I went to answer it. You asked to speak to Nash in your very serious, very concerned, little voice. I thought I'd have some fun and told you that he wasn't there."

"Why would you do that? Aren't you Navy? You wouldn't have been in the same barracks using the same laundry room," Danielle said.

"I started off in the Army and then switched. Well, you saw Nash's dress uniform today. It's not really a fashion statement is it, with all that boring brown?"

"You said he was out on bivouac."

"See what I mean? So easy. Officer cadets don't go out on bivouac in March, silly girl."

"You said they did, and he wouldn't be contactable for weeks."

"I did, didn't I? And you believed me," Gillian chuckled.

"I didn't know any different. You knew I was panicking. I needed Nash desperately. I had to speak to him. He was the only one who would understand. He'd be able to tell me what to do. I needed him."

"Ah Diddums...." Nash recognized the tone and the pout that went with it.

"You sounded so lovely when I spoke to you. You promised to get a message to him. You said you had to take supplies out to the team, and you'd see him that day and could give him a message. I thought you were wonderful to do that for me. It's the only reason I confided I was pregnant."

"You don't confide in complete strangers, sweetheart. You are so naïve. I did see Nash that day. He walked down the hall behind me while I was talking to you on the phone." Gillian laughed.

"You bitch. You didn't tell him I was on the phone? I don't confide in strangers. I've spent my entire life keeping people from knowing my business. Do you think I wanted to let other people know before Nash knew? It was a betrayal. I was desperate. You used my fear against me? Against us?"

"My own private reality show." Nash heard the smirk in Gillian's voice.

"Why, Gillian? Why all this?"

"Well, it's like this... I will kill you anyway, so I'll give you the full story, huh?"

"Why do you want to kill *me*? We only met yesterday."

"It's Nash. He has this crazy idea of coming back to this little bit of nowhere to be a farmer. Well, the next step would be for him to realize he really is the kid's daddy and he'll want to play happy families with you. I can't let it happen."

"You said you were engaged, so why would he want to be with me."

"You're clearly not a strategist, are you? One needs to neutralize as many threats as one can to achieve your goal with as little struggle as possible. You're the threat."

"And Brodie?"

"He looks so much like his father, his mother could be anyone, including me."

"He's mine, and he knows it. You said you'd give me the full story. Let's have it." Danielle's voice sounded stronger now. "Did you even give Nash my message?"

"You told me you were pregnant. You didn't say by whom, exactly, but given you were ringing Nash to tell him, it was a fair guess the kid was his and you wanted him to come running home to play house. Have I got it right so far?"

"I told Nash there was a call to the barracks, and you left me to tell him you were pregnant to someone you'd just met. You didn't want to see or hear from Nash ever again. He was such a teenager. You'd found a real man, a fantastic lover."

"Nash wouldn't believe that. He would have rung me back."

"Oh dear. You see, Nash's phone was missing. I don't know how it could happen, I told him. The barracks are so secure, you know. Well, Nash, silly boy, left his phone in the laundry room. I picked it up and kept it till I decided what to do with it. It He was going to search for his phone. Then you rang again, and I said, 'We regret to advise this number is disconnected. Please check the number before dialing again. We regret to advise ...' You made me say it three times before you hung up, you silly bitch. Are you slow?"

Sarcasm dripped through Gillian's voice.

"The phone was never disconnected?" Dee asked.

"I couldn't have you calling Nash day and night trying to convince him of your innocence. It was much better he believed you'd been playing around."

Listening to Gillian was gut-wrenching for Nash. He should have had more faith in Danielle. He should have trusted his own intuition when it told him she wasn't like that. Now he understood why Danielle was so upset when she found he still had the same phone number.

"Brodie is Nash's son. I've never looked at anyone else," Dee said.

He felt Don Hamilton's eyes whip towards him.

"He didn't know that, did he? I gently, so gently, reminded him out of sight was out of mind when it came to young love. I told him you'd rung again to say the daddy had run off. You wanted Nash as a stand-in.”

“You monster. At least now I know why he doesn’t believe Brodie is his. You destroyed our lives, Brodie’s life, to play a power game?”

“Careful, honey. I might lose my patience before I get to the end of the story,” Gillian warned.

The car slowed. “Danielle said they’re in the lounge room, so we should stop about here,” Nash suggested. He took the phone off speaker mode as they arrived at the south-east corner of the house.

“Don, you keep the phone. I’ll go in first, because I know her. When I say, ‘I’m calling the police’, I want you to hit every damn siren you’ve got and call out your usual message when you’re dealing with a hostage situation.”

“Not a good idea, Nash. I should be the one trying to talk her down.”

“She won’t be talked down, Don. We have no time to discuss it. Keep the phone and listen in. If you hear it escalate beyond what you think is reasonable, go straight to the sirens.”

Nash stomped hard, coming up the front steps and in through the front door. He took in the scene in an instant—Dee sitting on the sofa at the far end of the room with a long coffee table in front of her. At her side, Gillian was menacing her with a syringe.

“Gillian? What’s going on?” Nash asked.

Gillian jumped. “What are you doing here? Come to have a cozy afternoon with little Danielle Dawn, eh?” She stood and dragged Danielle with her.

“Caro wants chicken balls from the fridge. What’s with the syringe?”

“It’s like this. Your little goody two shoes has this drug habit, and she desperately needs a fix. I’m here to deliver it.”

“Really? I would never have guessed. I think we can let her go without it, don’t you? Let her suffer? Besides, you need to get on your way back to Canberra, so those papers are back where they belong.” He stepped forward casually, blowing out candles as he went.

"Not without you," Gillian said.

"I'm going back after harvest."

Gillian snorted. "You're only going back to Canberra to resign and then you're coming back to this dump without me."

"Why would you think you would ever have come with me? We're colleagues, that's all."

"But Nash, we could be so much more without this one in the way. I want you to come back to Canberra with me," she whined.

"It's not happening, Gill."

"Yes, it is," Gillian sang. "While I was waiting here, I was perusing those documents you mentioned, these 'Top Secret–AUSTEO' documents, with your handwriting all over them. It seems to me if I go back to Canberra alone, I may have to report I intercepted them being delivered to the Indonesian Embassy—by you. The military takes a dim view of its officers sharing top secret information with another national power, particularly when those documents are marked 'Australian Eyes Only'."

"Mitch knows you brought them here."

Nash maneuvered to wedge himself in the small space between Gillian and Danielle.

"No, he doesn't." Gillian's head swung towards Danielle. "I told you, didn't I? Easy! Mitch would never approve the removal of these papers from the office. They were smuggled out."

Nash pushed his hand against Danielle's body, urging her to move. He felt rather than saw her edge toward the other end of the sofa.

"Not by me," Nash said. "I haven't been there for a few weeks now."

"Then you must have made a quick trip because your signature is next to Friday's date. Look."

Gillian set the syringe on the coffee table as she picked up the document to display it to Nash.

"The joke's gone far enough, Gillian. I'm calling the police."

A blast of sirens erupted in a deafening cacophony. Nash knocked the syringe to the floor and trod on the end of it with his heavy shoe.

Chapter Thirty-seven

"What the fuck?" Gillian screamed. "You brought police? Why? How did you know?" Her horrified gaze darted between them.

"You bitch!" She reeled towards Dee.

Dee spun from her retreat, lunging toward the other woman.

Gillian reared back, caught off guard. She flung the top-secret papers at Dee and sprinted towards the back door with Dee hard on her heels.

Gillian sprang down the few steps to the backyard. She appeared not to notice the long stick-like object till it reared and clung to the back of her leg below where her shorts ended.

"Shit! It's Billy. Nash, make her stay still!" Dee stopped and pivoted to grab her snake handling pole from inside the kitchen door as Don Hamilton careened around the corner of the house with his pistol drawn.

"What is it? Get it off me!" Gillian shrieked.

"Stop!" ordered Nash.

"No. You all want to kill me." Gillian swiveled to see what had attached itself to her. Her hand reached down and encountered the smooth skin over twitching muscles.

She shrieked. "Fuck! It's a fucking snake! Get it off me."

Dee jumped down onto the ground and swung the pole into the triangle formed between Gillian's leg and the snake slashing it upwards, lifting the snake away from the woman. The pole and the snake went flying. The pole hit the protruding television antenna and bounced to the ground. The snake whumped against the side of the guttering, coming to rest on the roof.

Dee screamed as Nash tackled Gillian. "Get hold of her. We have to stop her moving." With both Nash and Dee on top of her, Gillian wouldn't submit and kept struggling.

"Gillian," Dee commanded, "you must be still. Your leg needs to be bandaged to stop the venom. We have to get you to hospital. Don, ring Mal and ask if he has any Eastern Brown antivenom and if it's okay to use on humans. And ring for an ambulance. Nash, you hold her. I'll get a bandage. If we don't get it on now, she won't survive."

Don holstered his gun and pulled out a phone and a pair of handcuffs.

"Got her!" Nash yelled. "We won't need the cuffs, Don. The venom is already slowing her down."

Dee raced into the house and returned as quickly with some broad bandages. "What did Mal say?"

"He used the last lot on Flo Thomas' dog on Friday," Don said. "More on Monday. The ambos are on the phone wanting directions. You talk to them while I handle the pressure bandage."

Don applied the bandage while Nash held Gillian as immobile as he could. "Tell them to look out for us. We'll head up to meet them. Let them know we'll be in an unmarked car. I'll have the red and blue lights on. The way she's been jumping around, well..." He wiped a hand across his face. "Once the venom from an eastern brown reaches the lymph nodes and is released into the bloodstream..." he stuttered to a halt seeming unwilling to finish the sentence to say death could occur within thirty minutes. A pressure bandage applied immediately might slow the process for several hours, but Gillian's early activity would have spiked the venom through her system. Billy was nearly fully grown. He would have injected a full load of venom and the toxin would be powerful.

Gillian was quiet now. Ominously so, Dee thought.

"Let's get her into the car, Nash." Don's somber voice reflected inevitability.

Nash eased Gillian into his arms and strode after Don. Gillian was a sweating rag doll. Her head lolled against his chest and her arm hung listlessly at her side. Nash slid her into the back seat of the police vehicle and strapped her in using all three available seatbelts.

"Should we try to raise her legs?"

"I think the point is moot, Nash. It'll be a miracle if she makes it." The policeman shook his head eyeing Nash's listless cargo. "But I guess we should do everything we can. You coming?"

"I'll get some cushions." Dee sprang back up the steps and returned with the cushions from the couch. Dee's thoughtfulness for someone who threatened her shouldn't have amazed Nash. She was that sort of person.

He turned to her. "We'll talk when I get back." He climbed into the front seat of the car and Don took off as if he could defy the likely outcome.

Dee stumbled back to the yard with no clear focus in mind. She picked up the pole from where it had landed. The snake's tail hung twitching from the guttering. Was he still alive? She wouldn't know until later. Folklore had it a dead snake kept twitching until night fall. If he were alive, she'd take him back to the dam. If he were dead, she'd broken the law by killing a protected reptile. What would Don Hamilton have to say about that?

She'd have to get Billy off the roof. He wouldn't survive up there much longer if he were still alive. She dragged a ladder from the shed, grabbed her welder's gloves from the kitchen and her snake pole.

She edged up the rungs of the ladder until she could reach the snake with her pole. She nudged him. There was no response. Moving up another rung, Dee leaned over and tugged lightly on the body. Still, there was no response. Emboldened, she took a firm grip of his tail and pulled hard. Billy fell to the ground, motionless.

Billy was dead. She shouldn't mourn a snake, should she? But it seemed like one more needless act of violence, and she'd been the one to inflict it.

Dee turned away from the carcass and walked up the steps into the kitchen. She sat down numbly, unable to process what had gone down over the last half hour. She was shaking like a leaf, floating in a waking coma until the sun shifted and the rays glinted off the shards of the syringe lying on the polished wood floor in the next room. She couldn't leave it there for when the children returned. The thought mobilized her.

Television crime shows held only a passing fascination for her but they always surrounded the scene with tape to prevent people coming in. She didn't have that luxury. She'd have the family tromping through the house in the next hour or so. Don was the only police member they had and who knew when he would return.

The only option left was to find some way to record the scene. Her old phone didn't have photo capability.

She dashed to her study, grabbed a clear plastic ruler, a piece of paper from the printer and a disposable film camera lying in her drawer for years. There was no way of knowing if the film would still work. She placed the paper on the floor next to the shattered syringe and the ruler on top of it. The ruler markings were likely to blend with the floorboards, so the white paper was a necessary contrast.

She took some close-up shots of the syringe, trying to amplify all its components using the ruler as a guide for size. Then she moved back to take a wider view of the room for some more shots. She tried to calm her breathing, but it was a lost cause.

'Top Secret' papers scattered everywhere. They might be an issue for photos developed from the film. She gathered them as quickly as her trembling hands would allow and stuffed them into Gillian's briefcase by the fireplace. She took more photos without the incriminating papers in shot. Nash could decide how he wanted to handle them.

Liquid pooled in the top end of the hypodermic. The stopper seemed to have protected a crucial part of the syringe from the onslaught of Nash's boot.

Dee gathered a couple of firm-ish plastic file-sleeves to gather the fragments, so she didn't handle them directly and deposited the pieces into a jam jar. She had sterilized the jar for her last batch of home-made plum conserve. It had been excess to requirements. Dee had stored it with the lid kept closed. It might not be pristine any longer, but it was as good as she had available. She took another photo of the jar in situ, for good measure.

Then there was Billy. She walked outside with the camera and dropped her pole and the ruler beside the dead snake to provide a scale. She snapped off a photo and wound the film on to take another. There were no shots left. What photographs she had would have to do.

Back inside the house, she placed the camera and the jam jar next to Gillian's briefcase. Nash would find them there.

The blood was humming through her veins. It felt like a manic nervousness had overtaken her. She set to and cleaned the room with a vengeance before the phone rang in her pocket. She'd forgotten it was there.

"Hey! Where are you?" Cassie asked. "Brodie's been asking for you and Nash."

"I'm at the house but Nash has had to go to Ballarat with Don. Billy attacked Gillian. Can you come and get me? I'm a wreck—not fit to drive." Her voice was thready to her ears.

"Dee? Are you okay?"

"No," she sobbed.

"I'll tell Rob and I'll be there in five."

Dee glanced down at her filthy frock. "Make it fifteen. I have to change."

"I'll be there in five!"

"Thanks Cassie."

Dee struggled out of her clothes with shaking hands. The dress might never be the same again, but Dee couldn't afford to toss it. She'd clean it up as best she could. It would be fine for in-house family dinners.

She riffled through her wardrobe. Gillian might have labelled her selection as pathetic, but it was all she needed. She pulled out a summery floral dress, leaving it on the bed while she showered. She dressed, brushed her hair, reapplied her makeup and fled the room.

Cassie's car was pulling up as she walked up the hall to the kitchen.

Chapter Thirty-eight

Nash and Don drove in silence as Nash kept swinging to check on Gillian.

"Is she alive?" Don asked.

"I can't tell if she's breathing," Nash said.

"There's the ambulance!" Don's voice betrayed his willingness to let someone else take control of the situation.

"Jemma, Col." Don saluted the paramedics. "Twenty-six-year-old female, around fifty kilos, struck by a two-meter eastern brown approximately twenty minutes ago."

"You sure it was an EB" Jemma asked.

"He's a regular visitor," Nash interjected. "Hi, I'm Nash Broderick."

The ambos nodded. "We'll use a multi-valent anti-venene anyway," Jemma said.

Col deployed a gurney while Jemma went to check on Gillian's condition. She unstrapped the seatbelts and pulled Gillian's shoulders towards the door.

"You guys counterbalance her." She directed Don and Nash where she wanted them and between them, they pulled Gillian onto the gurney, ignoring the cars slowing to see what was happening.

The paramedics worked efficiently, delivering an antivenom injection and a drip. Jemma climbed in beside Gillian and Col strode towards the driver's door.

"We'll take her to Ballarat Base Hospital. You can follow if you like," Jemma said.

"Can I come with you?" Nash asked.

"Nah, mate. Rules. See you there."

"C'mon Nash." Don recognized Nash was finding it difficult to compute the situation.

"You've known the woman a while?" Don asked.

"Yeah. We marched into Officer Training at the same time. She was one of the people who held me together when I found out Danielle dumped me."

"But Dee didn't dump you, did she? She's not a person to cheat behind your back. Did you ever give her the chance to explain?"

Nash hung his head, letting it sway from side to side. "Gillian was so convincing that even when Danielle phoned me, I listened to what she said through the filter of what Gillian had told me. We'd had this big pep talk on relying on our buddies in the service—to trust them to see you right. It primed me to listen to her, I guess.

"I told Danielle flat out I would not be a convenient daddy for her baby. I wouldn't let Grandma or Cassie speak on her behalf either. Fuck! What a waste! What a God-awful mess."

"We all wondered, you know. It didn't seem like what you would do—leave Dee up the creek. It got some people totally riled up. We knew Dee had a dodgy background, but it didn't seem to bother you when you lived at home. Maybe you'd got some high-flying ideas about your self-importance, being an officer in training?"

"I got a taste of Phil Thomson's views at the pub a while ago. What am I going to say to Danielle? How can I possibly explain..."?

"Don't know if you can, Nash. Seven years in the wilderness is a long time. Everyone important in her life seems to run away, poor kid. She's such a lovely person, too. Honest as the day is long. God, I'd hate to think of anything happening to Brodie."

Nash gave a start. He was a father. Brodie was his son! A son he'd ignored for the child's whole life. "He's a great kid. What will he think of his bastard of a father?"

"It depends if you'll do a hit-and-run. Tell him you're his dad and then hightail it again? Yeah. Nah. You'd be dead meat ever after."

"I might have to do that, anyway. I'll have to get Lieutenant Wallis back to Canberra one way or another. It can't wait. If she survives, she'll face consequences. If she dies, there's her father, a senior Army officer, who'll want to know everything." He raked his hands through his hair.

"Were you two ever... you know, involved?"

"We had a bit of a fling all those years ago when I was trying to get over Danielle, but nothing since. I don't know why Danielle thinks Gill and I were engaged."

"You'll get to the bottom of it. Here's the hospital. We'll go into Accident and Emergency with the ambos. They'll want a name, next of kin, all that sort of thing."

"It's Sunday afternoon, not so easy to get those details. I'll see what I can do."

The car pulled into a space next to the ambulance. One look at the clenched faces of the paramedics and Nash knew Gillian was gone.

"Five minutes ago, mate," Jemma said. "Sorry. We usually have time if there's a pressure bandage on straight away." She looked like she was taking the death as a personal failure.

"Don't beat yourself up, Jemma," Don soothed. "She was dancing all over the place and we couldn't get her to stay still until the venom took effect and slowed her down. We put the bandage on anyway, hoping it might help. Yeah. Nah. I sort of figured it was end game." Don rubbed Jemma's back. "Come on. Let's get her inside."

"Don, do you have my phone?" Nash asked.

"Ah. Yeah. In the console. You right to get it?"

Nash jerked his head and turned away, opened the driver's door of the police vehicle, and collected the phone. Everything seemed to be happening in slow motion. He'd handled death before. In a war situation, he dealt with it. This one, though, felt as needless as his parents' deaths and rained in on him the feelings of hopelessness he'd experienced way back then.

He followed the gurney into a side cubicle and took Gillian's still-warm hand as he recited her name, date of birth, address, occupation, and rank. He suggested her father as next of kin but had no contact details for him.

Studying her face, Nash had a hard time believing her treachery. She'd been such a good friend—but the friendship and those feelings of gratitude had been born of villainous deceit. A deceit that cost him the love of his life and six precious years with a son he should have known. He dropped her hand and turned away. Asking first where she would go from the emergency unit, he walked outside to phone Mitch.

"Mate, this is not a secure line, so I'll keep it brief. Gillian is dead—snake bite. We should notify the Navy and the Brigadier. Can you handle that?"

"What? How? What was she doing somewhere a snake could attack her, for fuck's sake?"

"Open line, mate," Nash reminded him. "We are in Ballarat right now. I'll head back to Hamlet Brae when you give me the all clear from whoever is coming to collect her."

"Right. Right. I'll get on it. You'll stay with her? You won't leave her alone?"

"For now." He ended the call.

"Are you coming back with me, Nash?" Don Hamilton walked up to join him.

"I'll wait with Lieutenant Wallis until I know what's happening next." Nash patted his back pocket. Amazingly, his wallet was still in place. "I'll hire a car once I'm free."

"All right. Now listen son, I heard everything she said to Dee, the same as you did. If anything blows up out of this, I'll be there as a witness, right?"

"Thank you, Don. We'll try to hose things down, but if things go pear-shaped, I might have to take you up on your offer."

Don nodded. "If you've got the brass coming, son, you'd better find somewhere to get yourself cleaned up. No hat, no jacket, grubby shirt, and trousers. Things might have changed since my day, but I don't think it would have altered that much."

"Christ! I probably look a sight. I'll get a room where I stayed last time and get cleaned up there."

Don left him at the hotel and headed back to Hamlet Brae.

Nash's phone rang.

"Did you know Ballarat has an airport?" Mitch asked without preamble.

"It doesn't."

"Oh, but it does. They used it in the war apparently and is now available for general aviation."

"I'd forgotten. What does it have to say to anything?"

"Brigadier Wallis will arrive in one hour by chartered light aircraft and will expect you to meet him. He'll need a decent place to stay and you'll be his chauffeur. You can deal?"

Mitch's voice sounded thick, as though he'd developed a cold or he'd been crying.

"I'll make some calls. If needed, he can have the room I've booked, and I'll stay at a pub."

"Right. Right. I'll leave it with you."

"Thanks, Mitch. It looks like I'll be in Canberra sooner than I thought. We can talk then."

One hour! Nash accepted the key from the receptionist at the hotel and walked outside to call the iconic Royal Hotel in town and booked a room for the Brigadier. The next call was to one of the car rental companies. He ordered a car to be delivered to his accommodation stat.

With things in place for the Brigadier, he strode to his room. It was the one he'd had last time. Memories of sharing the same bed with Danielle crashed through his brain.

Danielle Dawn! He had to find a way through this maze and make things right with her. He couldn't blame her if she never wanted to speak to him again.

Chapter Thirty-nine

Nash arrived at the airfield as the chartered plane flew over his head on approach. He was parked and waiting for the Brigadier as he emerged from the aircraft carrying a small overnight bag.

Nash greeted the Brigadier with a salute and handed him a business card.

"This has my private mobile number on the back, sir, should you need me." He led the way to the car.

"Thank you, Captain. Now please explain to me how my daughter comes to be dead in a place she has never visited to my knowledge."

Nash had thought about how to handle what he disclosed to his superior. He wouldn't lie, but he might leave some matters alone, like the transport of top-secret material unsecured across two state lines. He could leave stuff like that in the bag unless it became imperative to mention them.

"Lieutenant Wallis travelled to meet with me to discuss some classified action our unit is engaged in. I am on leave, but she believed my input might throw some light on what was happening, sir."

"What matter was so important?"

"I'm not at liberty to discuss the subject outside of our unit, sir?"

"I am your superior officer, Captain."

"Yes sir, but these matters require specific clearance. My apologies, sir."

"All right. She came to visit you on official business? Here in Ballarat?"

"On official business, yes, sir. My hometown is Hamlet Brae, south of here. This weekend, my family is celebrating the naming of my cousin's daughter We invited Lieutenant Wallis to join the party. This afternoon, she stepped off the verandah of the house and onto a highly venomous eastern brown snake. It struck her leg and held on, delivering a maximum load of venom.

"Lieutenant Wallis didn't realize what had happened, at first, and refused to stay still. I had to tackle her, sir, I'm sorry. The local police sergeant applied a pressure bandage, and we drove to meet the ambulance coming from Ballarat. The paramedics injected her with antivenom and transported her here to the hospital. Unfortunately, sir, she died in transit. You have my most sincere condolences."

"Yes, I see."

"Would you prefer to go straight to the hospital or to your accommodation, sir?"

"To the hospital, Captain."

The rest of the fifteen-minute drive was conducted in silence. Nash directed the man through the hospital labyrinth, introduced him to the attendant and waited outside while the Brigadier approached the gurney where his daughter lay.

Nash walked down the hall away from the doorway and dialed Danielle's number. When she answered, it sounded like the party was in full swing behind her.

"Hang on while I go outside," she shouted into the phone.

"How are you going?" Nash asked.

"I'll be fine. I've stopped shivering anyhow, so a bit better. What about you? Don Hamilton came back to the party to tell me your fiancée didn't make it."

"This afternoon has been a bit of a shocker all round. We were never engaged, Danielle. It was another lie. What did you do about the papers Gillian had with her?"

"I stacked them into her briefcase when you left. I had to clean up. I hope it doesn't cause problems, but I couldn't have the family coming back into the mess. I took photos. I've left the camera with the briefcase. Will you be back tonight?"

It felt odd, but good, to have an almost normal conversation with her.

"Gill's father arrived, so I plan to come back when he leaves in the morning. He's my superior, so he might have other ideas. I'll keep you posted."

"We haven't broadcast Gillian's death. Don thought it best to keep it quiet for the moment. How will you get home?"

"I've got a rental."

"I'll come and get you. The boys can start the harvest, or not, without me. Otherwise, you'll have three cars here to worry about."

"You're right. Look, drive my car. I know you think it's a phallic symbol and not fit to be seen on country roads, but it'll get you to Ballarat more safely than your ute. Can you tell Brodie I'll talk to him about his name, later? You and I need to talk first."

"Yes, we do. I don't plan to be difficult about access for you, but it is something we must work through."

"I've got to go. I'll call you in the morning." Nash's brain was in turmoil. As conciliatory as Danielle's words were, their effect was to sadden him further. It hit home hard and fast how much his stubbornness had cost. Danielle. Brodie. The life they'd planned. There had to be a way back.

He glanced up as his superior approached, his face set in hard angles of grief. "You can take me to my accommodation now, Broderick."

"Yes, sir."

The drive to the hotel was a quiet one. Nash sensed the anguish that Brigadier Wallis was holding in check.

"Would you like to join me for dinner tonight, sir?"

"I doubt I'll be eating, Captain."

"Sir, I wanted to say that Lieutenant Wallis was an outstanding member of our team, an effective strategist and a good friend to many of us. The team will miss her very much."

"Thank you, Broderick. It will comfort my wife. Good night. I'll call you when I need you in the morning."

"Good night, sir."

~ * ~

The phone rang before six the next morning. "Broderick, I'm ready to go. Be here in ten minutes."

"Yes, sir."

Taking another quick swallow of his coffee, Nash snatched his car keys, and headed to the rear of the building. There was no sign of Brigadier Wallis when he arrived at the Royal, so he shot off a quick text to Danielle to let her know he'd be ready to go when she got to Ballarat. He exited the car and walked into reception. The Brigadier turned from the desk and handed his bag to Nash. "I'll be right with you, Captain."

Nash retreated to the car.

The trip to the airfield was quick so early in the morning.

"Gillian's body is in Canberra. The funeral director drove her up overnight. I've had a message to confirm her arrival."

"Yes, sir." Nash masked his shock in formality.

"I shall inform your unit commander of the date and time of her funeral. Perhaps I'll see you then, Captain."

"Sir, yes, sir." Nash got out of the car, retrieved the Brigadier's bag, and carried it to the small plane.

The man climbed the few steps and reached to retrieve the bag from Nash.

Nash saluted. The Brigadier acknowledged the gesture with a brief tilt of his head and disappeared into the aircraft.

Nash returned to his accommodation and checked he'd left nothing behind, made another cup of coffee and ate a bowl of the cereal from one of the breakfast-to-go packs.

The house phone rang, and he was informed that there was someone waiting for him in Reception.

He'd worked out he would have to go back to Canberra immediately to return the military vehicle and the papers that Gillian had brought with her. The duration of the trip back to Hamlet Brae would be his only chance to hash things out with Danielle.

When he turned the corner into Reception, he found Caroline waiting for him.

"Good morning, Nash. Ready?" she asked.

Nash snapped his eyes at her, ready to demand where Danielle was. Caro calmly swiveled her eyes in the direction of the attentive receptionist.

Nash clamped his jaw. "I have to return the rental. Will you follow me?"

Chapter Forty

Dee drove the tractor and catching truck beside the harvester. Her main concern was keeping the correct distance between the two vehicles to avoid collision and ensure as much grain as possible was captured as it came off the elevator.

The family had probably been right to insist it was Caroline who drove to collect Nash this morning. With the children in bed after the party, including Jacob tucked up beside Ciaran, the five adults sat at Dee's dining table with hot drinks.

Cassie and Rob and Caro and Connor sat in shock as Dee relayed the events of the afternoon—finding out what Gillian had done seven years ago, her plan to inject Dee with some unknown substance and then burn the house down, and Gillian's attempt to blackmail Nash into going back to Canberra. Laying it out there, even Dee thought how implausible it would sound to the family, but that's the way it was.

"You mean he never knew about Brodie? Ever?" Cassie's voice was colored with indignation and confusion.

"I told him, but because of Gillian's lies, he didn't believe me. Apparently Nash walked right behind her while she was listening to me telling her how much I needed to speak to him. She told me he was on bivouac and wouldn't be contactable."

"Surely Nash knew better than to take what she said at face value?" Connor frowned.

"She was there with him and very convincing and I was two states away supposedly having a fling with some randy guy passing through town. Who would he believe?"

"You're still defending him, Dee. You've done that for seven years. It's time to stop. He should have followed up with you directly. He should have trusted you. He's my brother and I don't know how he could be so gullible." Cassie was firm.

Dee huffed a laugh. "What does Anna always say? 'Coulda, shoulda, woulda won't move a hill of beans?' Now we know what the baseline damage is, we can move on. We can focus on 'can' and 'will' and see where we go from there."

"You'd forgive him, just like that?" Caro demanded.

"It's not a matter of forgiving him. If he acknowledges Brodie as his son, I won't stand in the way of Brodie getting to know his dad. He already has a hero-worship thing happening. It doesn't mean I roll over and pretend it's all happy families. I'll collect him from Ballarat in the morning. We can talk about it on the way home."

"No!" The chorus around the table was definite.

Robbie ventured, "I don't think it's a good idea, Dee. You're vulnerable and so is he. You could do untold damage to each other right now, even when you're trying not to."

"He's right, Dee," Cassie said. "You'll say, 'I'll let you see Brodie,' and he'll translate your comment as meaning 'but you can forget about mending your own broken heart or for us to ever have a relationship again'. It's probably what he wants a chance to do, now he knows the truth. Or he'll say something about what he might do on the farm when he comes home, and you'll take it as 'You think I've been doing a lousy job running the place for the past six years!' You know it." Cassie always put the teacher's spin on things.

"We have to talk sometime."

"You know, Dee," Connor sat back in his seat. "We need you out on the harvest tomorrow, especially since we'll be a person short, even with your mates Tom and Fred helping. My guess is Nash will return to Canberra to explain to the brass how one of their people ended up dead. He'll be gone, but your harvest must go on so we can get to ours. Caro can't work the machinery. You can.

"Logically, it makes more sense for you to do your own job and let Nash Broderick stew in his juice for a little while longer. Don't get me wrong. I love the guy, but he has been something of a shithead, putting it mildly. Give him time to understand what his blind arrogance and ignorance have done to you, to Brodie, to Grandma, to all of us on some level."

Caroline beamed at her husband. "Exactly! You are so wise, my darling. The harvest is the priority. It's settled then. I'll go to Ballarat. He won't bite my head off, even if he wants to, because I'll hit back and then he'll have to answer to you as well. Stroke. Of. Genius. Now everything's settled, I'm for bed."

"But..." Dee ventured. Caro ploughed on.

"We all have an early start tomorrow. Leave Jacob where he is, Cassie. I'll bring him in to you in the morning with Brodie after I see these guys off." With that, Caro effectively dispersed the group, ending any further discussion.

Dee dragged her attention from her mental replay of last night's discussion and glanced into the rear-view mirror of the tractor. Frank's harvester wasn't positioned where it should be. Smoko was long gone, and lunch was still a way off, so it wasn't a scheduled stop. She eased her foot on the brake to bring her rig to a halt, climbed down and went back to see what was happening. Frank exited his cabin and joined her.

"What's up?"

"I'm okay but the Mount Mercer crew seem to have a problem." He jerked his head toward the team working on the offside. Together, Frank and Dee walked to the other group.

Connor glanced up at their approach. "We've got a bearing gone on the clean grain elevator. The boys probably got a bit carried away with the grease. The lubricant expanded, and the bearing failed. Doesn't take long to fix, but I don't have a part with me."

"Josh carries all sorts of odd parts at his place in town. I can head in and pick it up if you tell me what you need."

"Right. I'll put Bruce on your tractor, and we'll keep moving as much as we can. I'll remove the grease fitting here while you're away, so it's cleaned and ready to repair when you get back. Ryan can drive you over in the other truck to pick up a car."

Connor's authority went unquestioned, and everyone headed in the directions he had assigned them.

Dee thanked Ryan for the lift, climbed into the ute and glanced across at the ubiquitous calico bag. She heaved it up to check her purse, driver's license and credit card were where there. Satisfied, she pulled out her mobile and let Robbie know she'd call in to collect her new phone on her way to the mechanic. She rang Josh and told him the bearing she needed. He'd have one waiting.

She sighed in relief. The pickups needed to be quick so she could get back to the paddock. She dropped the bag onto the floor and started the motor.

The text from Nash arrived around six this morning as she and Connor were eating breakfast.

"Hmm," Caro pursed her lips. "It's too early for the kids. I'll ring Grandma. You guys get going. Grandma can keep watch here. I'll be back in time to get them into town."

Dee had opened her mouth to speak when Connor thrust a flask into her hand. "Right to go?" Dee was being maneuvered, yet again, but she let it ride. There was work to be done on the farm.

The turnoff into town from the harvest site was five hundred meters from Anna's place. Dee glanced towards it but could see no sign of the military car. It could still be at her place. Nash's car was where he left it the previous day.

She was no wiser about whether Nash had gone.

Robbie had the phone on the counter with a new sim sitting beside it. "I know you're in a hurry, but I couldn't port your number onto the new sim until you got here. The one that's in the phone you're using is the wrong size so I can't just swap it over. I'll be as quick as I can."

"Ta, Rob. Everything seems to be in a hurry now."

"Nash gone?"

"I don't know. His car is still at Anna's. I don't know about Gillian's. He'll be back, though, so I must find somewhere to live. If you get any 'for rent' ads for the window of the shop, could you tell me?"

Robbie's hands kept moving. "Your old place in Dutton Street is available."

Dee could not have measured the feelings rolling through her soul at the mention of the house. Shock, sadness, disappointment, night-terrors, embarrassment, worthlessness, abandonment. They all took hold. "I think I'll wait till something else comes up or I could try in Meredith or Elaine. If need be, I guess we could go to Geelong or Buninyong."

"There you go. All done. Try not to annihilate this one, huh?" Rob handed over the phone. "I'll keep an eye out for you, Dee, but I could talk to Nash instead."

Dee shook her head. "I don't want any favors from Nash Broderick until this mess is sorted. That won't happen in the few weeks between now and Christmas." She handed over her credit card. "I'll pick up some boxes from the supermarket and get started on packing when I get time. Thanks Robbie. And thanks for having Brodie this week."

"He's never a problem. You take care, Dee."

"See ya!"

Dee went straight to the supermarket while the thought of packing was fresh in her mind. Margaret Ranley was exiting through the sliding doors.

"Danielle? Is that you under all that dust and dirt?"

"Hi Margaret. Yes. It's harvest!"

"Of course. Listen," she pulled Dee to one side and checked around for potential eavesdroppers. "I had a letter from the department this morning. At this point, they don't think our school qualifies to have a nominated Graduate Teacher. I'm sorry, Dee. You can apply for the position through normal channels, but there'll be some competition. I don't know what to say. I'm disappointed for me and I'm disappointed for you. I'm so sorry."

It felt as if the bottom dropped out of her stomach. She hadn't counted on the job being a shoo-in. Of course, she hadn't, but it was another boulder crashing into her piling on top of all the others wrought by the last week or so.

"Thanks for letting me know, Margaret. I'll keep a lookout for the ad. I'll put in an application and see how I go."

"Put me down as a referee, Danielle."

"I will. Thanks for your support."

Margaret patted her arm and walked away.

A young supermarket assistant helped Dee load some broken down boxes into the ute. If she got the packing done, she could be ready to go wherever she got a job.

She drove the short distance to the garage. Josh passed over the part and took her credit card. "It's amazing so small a part can bring the harvest to a screaming halt."

"Happens all the time, Dee. Someone gets a bit grease-happy and bingo—no bearing, no clean grain elevator, no harvest," he said.

"Thanks Josh. I'll see you later."

She steered the car towards home. The intersection between the garage and the school was Dutton Street. She turned left and crawled by in front of her childhood home. Cleaner than it had been when she lived there, it had been painted and someone had tried to grow a lawn. It looked like any other respectable bungalow along the street, but there was no way this side of hellfire she would put Brodie in there.

She kept driving.

She glanced across at Anna's house out of habit before she turned onto the road towards the harvest. A strange car was bouncing over the track from Anna's house to her own. *'What the...? Anna!'*

Thoughts of iced up drug addicts rushed through her head. She swung the car violently towards Anna's place and gunned the motor. The car came to a screaming halt with clouds of dust all around. She flung herself out of the car and into the house.

"Anna?" Her voice bounced off the walls.

"Yes, dear? What's got you all in a panic? Has something happened out in the paddock?"

"You're okay!" Dee felt her body deflate. Her heart kept racing. "I saw a car..."

"Yes, well..." Anna's face closed into a frown. "My grandson sent along these surveyors. This lot were building surveyors. The ones to-morrow will be land surveyors. He's got some bee in his bonnet and he's not telling me. I told them the best way to get to your place was over the track." She cackled.

"Oh Anna," Dee grinned. "Nash has gone then?"

"Uh huh. Breezed in here, grabbed a few things—not everything mind—and Caro dropped him back to your place to get whatever Gillian had left there and he took off."

"Where's Caroline?"

"She's gone into town to check out the community hall. She reckons since you and Cassie are both working, she can deal with the stuff for the kids' party on the weekend. I reminded her it's a pirate theme."

"Oh Lord. She's amazing. You know she vetoed me going to get Nash this morning?"

"I gathered. What are you doing here, now?"

"I've been into town to pick up a part. On the way back, I saw the dust and car along the track, and panicked a bit."

"A bit? They could have heard you in town the way you yelled." Anna chuckled. "Since you're here, you can take this sultana cake with you. I made it for tomorrow, but I can do another one. If they've had a frustrating morning out in the paddock, they could probably use a bit of home-baked TLC. Give me a sec, I'll slice it up for you."

"Thanks Anna, they'll love it. They might even forgive me for taking so long. Mwah. I'll give you a hug when I'm clean!"

"You take care, darling girl."

"I will."

Panic pummeled Dee. Adrenaline raced through her body as her mind considered Nash's reasons for the surveyors. Clearly, he'd decided to make some changes when he came back. She hoped he'd factored Brodie into whatever he planned. She'd fight tooth and nail to make sure he didn't abandon her son once Brodie was aware of his father's identity. She knew all about abandonment.

The trouble was, she might be the one to create a geographical distance between them. She needed to work and if there were no teaching jobs close by, she'd have to move farther afield. There was no question Brodie would go with her.

Could nothing ever be simple in her life?

Chapter Forty-one

The drive home with Caroline on Monday morning was tense. Nash wanted to sort things through with Danielle, but she wasn't there. He thought she'd chickened out, until Caro made it quite clear they had maneuvered Danielle the same as they had with him. The family was keeping them in opposite corners till they both came to terms with the facts.

It made sense on one level, but his frustration boiled over a couple of times during Caro's oh-so-sensible explanation. He needed to talk to Danielle, but he didn't have time to go haring into the paddocks to find her.

Caro waited at Grandma's while Nash gathered up the few things he chose to take with him and dropped him back to Danielle's place to collect the military vehicle Gillian had driven.

Stepping onto the verandah, he recalled the conversation with his grandmother about having the buildings checked over. He'd get a building surveyor in immediately if he could, and a land surveyor to mark out a significant area of land around this house and apply to have it subdivided from the property. There would be no doubt, in the future, who had access to which house.

One phone call to a bleary-sounding person at the end of a mobile number set his desired actions in motion. Apparently with the harvest in full swing, the surveyors' work was slow. The man promised Nash a building surveyor would be on site before lunch. The land surveyor might take longer, but not more than a day or two.

He strode into the lounge room. Atop Gillian's briefcase lay a disposable camera and a glass jar with the remains of the syringe. He wasn't sure what was on the camera, but the syringe was obvious. He'd have it analyzed back at base. There'd be issues of chain of custody for the evidence if they brought a case to court, but he'd worry about it later.

The camera was another matter. He couldn't have it developed at a civilian camera shop in case top secret materials were on there. If he asked the lab to do it and they found something incriminating, he'd be in deep water there too.

He riffled through the briefcase and found the documents Gillian waved around on Sunday afternoon. It seemed such a long time ago, but it was only yesterday afternoon for chrissake. He dug further into the bag and found the keys to the car.

He allowed Caro to give him a hug of farewell and got on the road. He forced himself to take the recommended break every two hours at Ballan, Seymour, Albury and Jugiong. Fortunately, peak hour traffic had settled by the time he rolled into the nation's capital.

Although dressed in civvies, Nash had no trouble accessing the building where he worked. He'd been worried about getting the documents through security, but he was waved through after the briefcase went through the scanner.

He went straight to his office and refiled the papers in his secure storage. Collecting the folder they had been in along with the glass jar, he headed down a level to the forensic laboratory.

The team's resident forensic guru, Mikey, had bluetooth earbuds in and his large body was jerking in what Nash determined was some response to the music only the big man could hear. Mikey's hands, though, were engaged in a task on the bench top.

Nash banged on the window. The man's face lit up as he ambled to the security door to let Nash in.

"Nash, brah. Whatcha doin' man?"

"Hey Mikey. Got a couple of rush jobs for you if you can handle it."

"Not much on right now, so she'll be apples. What is it?"

"I'd like you to check for prints on this syringe," Nash said as he handed over the jar with the syringe. "And I want to know what it contained."

"Cool. You usually bring me more of a challenge. This is playground stuff."

"Well, there is one other thing. It's more sensitive, though. You got some paper and a pen? This is my signature, right? You saw me write it."

"Yeah...?"

"Now, this is my signature too, yes?" Nash handed over the folder.

"Trick question?"

"That's for you to work out, my friend. If it is the same, no problems. If it's not, I'd like you to give me your best guess who signed on my behalf."

"You'd know if you'd signed it, man." Mikey's face fell into a confused frown.

"Imagine I had a memory loss or something, I don't know. Just see if they match, okay?"

"Sure, it'll take longer than the syringe job."

"I figured. Think you can have it done by Wednesday morning?"

"Should do, unless there's an outbreak of espionage happenings."

"Thanks, Mikey. I'll owe you one. Say, these are great photos," Nash peered at several unframed black and white landscapes dotted along the wall. "Did you do these yourself?"

"Yep. Pet hobby."

"Where do you get them developed?"

"Do that myself, too."

"You use the lab?"

"Nah. I've got a darkroom at home."

"Do you lend it out? What I mean is, what would it cost me to borrow your dark room for a couple of hours?"

"You know what you're doing in there?"

"I started doing photos as a project in high school and kept it going when I could. You might need to give me a five-minute refresher."

"You don't seem the type of bloke who needs to develop his own sex-kitten pics, brah." Mikey's eyes narrowed.

"Why would I have those type of photos?"

"They're what my mates use it for. They don't use digital, cos the wife might find them when they automatically upload to the cloud. They can't take them to a public processor, so they come to my place. I don't take payment for the room, but I do barter. For you, I'd say one of your Brumbies tickets for an hour in the room."

"It's not rugby season for another couple of months."

"They've already sent out their season tickets to the top members, yes?"

"My rugby tickets are precious."

"I wouldn't want them if they weren't. No fun in that. Besides, you Victorians don't understand the nuances of a fine game like rugby union. I don't know why you bother."

"Let's not go through the rugby versus Australian football argument again. My tickets, eh? Well," Nash scratched the side of his neck. "Two tickets for two hours in the room?"

"Yep."

"I'll make it three if we can do it tonight."

Mikey's eyes widened. "You're on! My place in an hour. I'll buy the pizza."

An hour later, Mikey stepped Nash through the process of developing negatives from the film as he mixed three different lots of solution to go into the developing trays. As soon as Nash was inside the dark room, and inhaled the smell of the chemicals, he remembered the process in detail.

"I'll give you half an hour to develop your negatives. While they're drying, we can have pizza. Then you can go back and make your photographs. I should have charged you extra for the photo paper. The third ticket will cover that."

"Thanks Mikey. I'll get started."

Nash had never attacked one of the disposable cameras before and it was trickier than he expected, especially in the red-light glow of the dark room. Once he got the film out, he was set. He worked the film through the developer, onto the stop bath and into the clearing agent to fix the film and a final water wash. He hung the film to dry, flipped on the light and opened the door.

"How did it go, brah?"

"They look okay, though I was concentrating on getting the negatives. I'll know more of what's on there when I make the photos."

"Okay then. There's the pizza!" Mikey's smile broke out as he headed to answer the summons of the doorbell. "Grab a beer from the fridge!"

Mikey returned to the sitting room with three large pizza boxes. "I wasn't sure what you'd like. I got a variety. We've got plenty of time to eat. You can't go back to your negatives for two hours. We might have enough time for me to find out why someone from Victoria thinks he knows anything about the game they play in Heaven."

The two hours passed quickly, and Nash headed back to the dark room, flicked the red light on and turned off the overhead light.

He worked through the film, exposing each negative and setting the print aside to develop. Once he had the entire roll done, he began processing them.

The first photo vindicated his decision to develop the pictures himself. 'Top Secret – AUSTEO' was visible on the papers in the shot.

The development process became robotic. Dip, submerge, shake out, move to the next tray, hang to dry. Dee had taken some good clean shots here, and she'd had the understanding to take some without the damning papers. The snake was huge. Much bigger than he had realized.

Then his heart nearly stopped as the submerged paper slowly changed to reveal an image of Dee, holding a young child, as she leaned over to blow out the candle on a cake with a big 21 on it. Her twenty-first birthday! He should have been there. He was in Afghanistan for his own twenty-first and it passed without acknowledgement. He should have been there for hers, and for the birth of their son and every other damn thing happening in her life over the past seven years. If the camera was so old, he was lucky any of the photos were turning out and luckier still they were clear. He set the photo aside and carried on with his task.

With the photos hung to dry, he went back to the sitting room. Mikey had left a note. "Gone to bed. Beer, coffee, and leftover pizza in the kitchen. Take your time. See you tomorrow."

There was no surprise. It was already after midnight. Nash made an instant coffee and slumped over the kitchen table. It had already been a long day, but he couldn't leave until the photos were dry enough to handle. He drank the coffee slowly. Back in the dark room he emptied the processing trays and tidied the room.

Finally, he could stack the photos and gather the negatives. With one last look around the room to check that he'd left nothing behind, he slipped a wallet-sized copy of the photo of Danielle and Brodie into the pocket of his shirt, letting it nestle close to his heart.

He let himself out of Mikey's home and headed for his own bed.

Chapter Forty-two

Nash was still on leave, technically, so he could do what he wanted. He chose not to go to the office on Tuesday. He'd wait until Mikey had some information for him on Wednesday.

Being in his apartment made him antsy. Gillian had helped him to find it. It had been a refuge for him mostly, but now it felt like it was part of the whole betrayal thing because of its association with her.

He spent the rest of the morning packing a suitcase. He didn't expect to be here again once he left after Gillian's funeral. There'd been no word on the arrangements so far.

He wanted to be back in Hamlet Brae in time for Brodie's birthday party on Saturday afternoon. He should find a gift, but what? He'd seen the kid playing with a computer. Something techy? And there was Jacob's birthday to think about too.

He rang Danielle and got an out-of-range message. He phoned Robbie.

"Nash! Good to hear from you. Are you okay?" Robbie asked.

"Hanging in there. Listen, I need some ideas on what to get the boys for their birthdays. I know Brodie likes computers and Jacob likes fire trucks, but I don't know what they've got and what they'd like."

"You're right about Brodie and his computer. He's way beyond his age in what he does with that thing. What he'd really like is a gaming keyboard, but they're expensive."

"No problem."

"Well there is, actually. If you're trying to make things right with Dee, it won't work in your favor to swan into town playing Santa Claus with expensive gifts making her look bad."

"I should have thought. It makes sense."

"What you could do, is get a really basic one, a cheapie. Tell Brodie it's so he can give it a go. Then, if everything with Dee turns out okay, you're in the box seat for you and Dee, together, to get him a better one for Christmas or next year or whenever."

"When did you get to be so wise?"

"Handling your woman and mine has honed my skills over the years, mate. I listen to the way they do things and it seems to work."

"What about Jacob?" Nash ignored the implied criticism of his absence from Danielle's life.

"Anything fireman related would be great. He can't get enough of the stuff. Nothing more expensive than what you get for your own boy. Let me tell you, it's great to acknowledge that to you directly after all this time. You have a son, Nash, and he needs a dad."

"I still can't believe it myself. I've spent seven years believing Danielle went behind my back."

"You'll get it sorted—if you handle it properly. Gotta go, mate. Customer."

"Thanks, Rob. I'll probably see you on the weekend. Three o'clock, Community Hall, right?"

"Yep. See ya."

Nash knew where to purchase all kinds of technology gear around Canberra, but toys for a four-year-old were another matter. He'd start there. Find something for Jacob and then concentrate on Brodie.

Some hours later, he'd accomplished the toy-buying mission, including a colorful hanging animal mobile for Catherine and a police car for Ciaran. There was also a little something for Danielle if she'd accept it.

He was back in his apartment when a text came through from Mitch to advise him Gillian's funeral would be held on Thursday morning.

A timeline meant a plan. He could be out of Canberra by the weekend, depending on what Mikey found and what action Nash needed to take. He headed back to his packing. His minimalist crockery and cutlery were expendable. He'd leave them behind. The few novels he'd bothered to keep could stay where they were. He whittled his possessions to personal stuff to go with him. Anything else could stay for the next tenant or the cleaning crew. It didn't matter to him.

He'd buy a backpack for the gifts. Everything else would fit in his suitcase. His pillow, sheets and towels could go into the duffle at the last minute.

Pulling a beer from the fridge, he sat down and spread the stack of photos on the table. The candles, the papers, the syringe all pointed to a level of premeditation and strategy admirable in a conflict situation but used against Danielle? It made his blood turn to ice.

What would drive Gillian so far? He and Gillian were never engaged. They weren't even romantically connected. Sure, they had a brief, very brief, relationship when he was grieving over Danielle, but it was done and dusted nearly seven years ago. She'd gone out with other people in the time since, hadn't she? Hadn't she?

He paused. He couldn't put a face or a name to anyone he'd seen her with outside the office. He was no better, he guessed. He hadn't had the will to go looking for romance. Looking back, he realized his head might have shut the door on Danielle, but his heart never did.

He gathered the photos and dialed the Indian restaurant downstairs to have a meal sent up. He'd have dinner and an early night.

~ * ~

Nash went straight to Mikey's lab the next morning.

"Yo, brah!"

"Good morning to you too, Mikey. What is it with this 'brah' stuff, anyway? You sound like you're channeling an American sitcom."

The big man's eyes lit up. "Yeah, brah. It's cool, dude!"

"We trust you with the nation's secrets?" Nash rolled his eyes.

"You can't live without me, brah!"

"What have you got for me?"

"The glass jar had your prints on it and that's all."

Dee must have had the foresight to wipe down the jar.

"The syringe was easy. I could only get a print and a half off it and they matched Lieutenant Wallis." He frowned. "The contents were an intensive dose of heroin. I couldn't gauge how much was in there, but even a small amount in such concentration would be lethal. Someone would have had a good time for about five minutes then passed out cold, never to awaken. Whose was that?"

"I'm still trying to work things out. And the signature?"

"The surface scribe was a good match, but the indents on the paper were all wrong. For example, your capital B... you stroke from the bottom to the top on the leg of the letter, but your doppelganger stroked top to bottom, same with your 'k'. The first letter of your signature is a capital I, right? Is that a trick? Anyway, the leg is an upstroke, then you stroke right to left across the top and left to right across the bottom. The fake is top to bottom then left to right top and bottom. It's definitely not your signature on the folder."

"Then whose? Gillian Wallis?"

"Nah, brah. I don't know how you're gunna take this. The nearest match is Captain Hepworth."

"Mitch?" Nash slumped back against a cold steel bench. "You sure?"

"Well, it could be someone from outside, but they're not going to have access to files stamped, 'TS-AUSTEO'. I limited my search to people who work in this building and have access–there are a lot of them. He was the one whose formations were consistent with the signature across the board. I'm sorry, brah. I don't know what this means. It's not my job. Here are my reports and the folder for you to replace the files."

Several seconds passed before Nash reached out a hand to accept the documents. His mind was in turmoil.

"Thanks, Mikey... I think." Nash searched the other man's face, looking for clues he would never find there. Mitch was the only one who could give him answers to the questions he had.

He pivoted towards the door.

"Don't forget those tickets, brah!"

Nash gave a back-handed wave and went upstairs to his office, shut the door, and closed the blinds to the interior workspace. He tried to puzzle through the implications of Mitch signing out a report as if he were Nash. There was no way of looking at the issue that it made sense.

He thrust his chair back so hard it rammed against the wall behind him. He grabbed the photos, the file with his counterfeit signature and Mikey's reports and strode to Mitch's office further along the corridor. His door was closed, and his were blinds drawn in much the same way as Nash's— the 'do not disturb' sign of the office.

Nash ignored it. He turned the handle and walked in. Mitch had a photo of Gillian on the desk in front of him and tears streaming down his face.

He looked up as if to dismiss any peon stupid enough to disturb him. He saw Nash and stormed to his feet.

"What's the meaning of this?" Nash hurled the file down on the desk at the same time Mitch yelled. "You killed her, you bastard. You fucking killed her."

Nash pitched the photo of the snake at his colleague. "This killed her, you moron. What I want to know is why you tried to set me up."

Mitch rounded the desk and raised his blazing eyes at Nash. "She wouldn't have been there if not for you, asshole. I should knock your fucking block off."

"You! You want to take a shot at me? You're on. Not here and not in uniform. Upstairs in the gym. Five minutes."

Nash swiped the folder and the photos from the desk and thundered back to his own office. He jammed the material in his filing cabinet and locked the drawer, before bounding up six flights of stairs to the gym.

There was no sign of Mitch. He slammed open his locker and pulled out the gear he kept there. He ripped off his tie, toed off his shoes and had unbuttoned his shirt by the time Mitch appeared.

Nash ignored him as they both changed. When he was dressed, Nash moved to the rack of boxing gloves, threw one set at Mitch, and pulled a pair onto his own hands. This would be no friendly sparring match as the many fights before it had been.

"Explain yourself, goddammit! Why did you sign the file as if it were me?"

"It was you," Mitch declared silkily. "Your signature, perfectly. No one will understand why you came back from your holiday to sign out a file until they realize how inflammatory the material is and that you were on your way to a foreign embassy with it."

Nash jabbed at him, not intending to connect, warming up his muscles.

"Not so perfect, mate," he spat. "How do you think I knew it was you? Mikey matched the strokes to your handwriting."

Mitch threw a punch that Nash dodged.

"You bastard," Mitch ranted.

"For what? Doing my job to ferret out treacherous mongrels like yourself?"

Mitch attacked again. Nash blocked with his left arm.

"I wouldn't have had to do it if you'd left her alone."

"What do you mean? Left who alone?"

"You know, you arsehole. Gill! You kept her on a string for seven years." He threw himself at Nash and connected a fist with Nash's chest.

Nash stepped back to regroup. "Gillian Wallis was a colleague, nothing more." It was Nash's turn to take a shot and he connected with Mitch's jaw. Mitch's head swayed at an angle, but he brought it back to scream at Nash.

"How can you say that? You slept with her, you fucktard, and then you kept her dangling." He rammed Nash's midriff again.

"Seven years ago, when I thought—I thought!—Danielle betrayed me. Your friend Gillian made it up. Did you know?" Nash kept bouncing on his toes as Mitch did.

"Not right away."

"But you've known—for how long? And you didn't tell me? What sort of mate were you?"

Nash landed a double punch. "You colluded with her? To make sure I didn't know about my son? Why?"

Mitch swayed but pulled himself upright. "Because she wanted you." He punched hard and hit Nash on the side of the face.

"What did it matter to you who she wanted?"

"I loved her!" Mitch thundered into Nash's body, pummeling his midriff.

Nash staggered back. "I don't get it," he spoke through gritted teeth.

Mitch shook his head in disgust. "Classic love triangle or square or whatever. I loved her, she wanted you, you were still pining over some bitch back home."

"You do not get to speak about Danielle ever again." Nash landed a left-hand uppercut that sent Mitch sprawling. "Then what, you sent Gill to my home, to incriminate me, so I'd be locked away for a very long time. Huh? Then she would turn to you? I thought you needed my help. I thought you sent her."

Mitch staggered to his feet. "I didn't send her. I just signed out the papers. I knew what she would do, and I knew what you would do. She would make any excuse to go to you and your big head would be flattered she'd come running. I don't need your help any more than I need the help of your prissy little minions.

"If Gill wanted to see you, I'd let her, but it would be the last damned time. You'd be languishing in Holsworthy Barracks for quite a while if my plan came off. With her family connections, she couldn't afford to acknowledge she even knew someone who was a security risk, let alone have anything to do with him.”

“Did she realize it was a set-up?”

“She bought the excuse same as you did, fuckwit.”

Nash hit him again.

“She used the same line of blackmail to get me to come back.”

“Did she? I’m impressed. Great minds, as they say...” Nash hit him again.

“How did she happen to have a syringe full of heroin ready to attack Danielle?”

Mitch turned his head away as if giving himself time to assess the damage to his body before he stood straight, fists ramrod straight at his side and bellowed at Nash. “She’s been using for years because you, you bastard, took no notice of her.” He moved, a heavy blow sent Nash reeling and Mitch dropped to his knees with an anguished cry. “I loved her. I always loved her. She didn’t see me. She wanted you.”

Nash was torn. This was his friend who held him together when the world was so black. He was also the mongrel who kept the most important secret from him. He’d destroyed six damn years of him knowing his son.

“I’ll see you at the funeral tomorrow, Hepworth. I’ve submitted my resignation and I’ve written a report on Lieutenant Wallis’ behavior, with accompanying photographic evidence. It’s not pleasant reading for someone who was a trusted member of the nation’s strategy team. If you ever come near me or my family again, I’ll make sure her daddy gets to read it.”

Nash left him huddled on the floor.

Chapter Forty-three

Nash sat aboard a bus travelling along the route from Ballarat to Geelong on Saturday, letting his mind go blank. He felt like shit and probably looked worse. It was enough for other passengers to steer clear of the spare seat next to him.

He'd gone to the funeral and he'd stood shoulder to shoulder with Captain Hepworth without speaking.

Brigadier Wallis circulated amongst the mourners. When he approached Nash and Mitch, his disapproval was clear.

"What makes you men think you can show up to my daughter's funeral looking like you've been brawling in some back alley?"

Nash swung his head in Mitch's direction. Mitch was barely holding it together, by the look of him. Nash took a small step forward. "Sir. The senseless loss of Lieutenant Wallis left both of us with the need to punch something. We took it out on each other."

The Brigadier's features softened a little. "Queensberry rules?"

"Sir, yes sir."

The Brigadier jerked a nod and moved on. Nash had enough. It certainly was because of Gillian they'd battered each other. If it suited a father to take their actions as a mark of respect, he'd allow him that comfort. The whole idea of Gillian Wallis left him feeling sickened, disgusted, and abused. His feelings for Mitch were no better. He turned on his heel, and without speaking to another soul, he left.

In the two days since, he'd tried to reason through how he'd gotten into a position where he was at the mercy of two people he'd trusted so completely. When he'd arrived in Canberra, the mantra of the Army was, 'This is your new family.' Anyone you'd left behind was secondary. He'd been predisposed to accept Gillian's lies, because she represented his new family. Depending on your comrades was a big deal.

God, he must have been an impressionable idiot. A soft touch.

And Mitch.... He'd had no reason to doubt Mitch's friendship. How could he have been so blind? If Mitch had been in love with Gillian all these years, he could understand why a man would do things normally out of character. Didn't he do the same by not going home because he'd believed their lies that Danielle betrayed him?

On Friday morning, he went to the lab.

"Hey, Mikey! Here's what I owe you for the dark room." He took a sheet of paper from his breast pocket and held it out.

Mikey face split into a wide grin. He pounced on the paper. "Come to mama!" He quickly scanned the sheet and looked in puzzlement at Nash. "This is for the entire season!"

"Nope. Just the home games. I think it's time for me to quit while I'm ahead on the rugby stuff and concentrate on Aussie Rules again. At least I understand the game plans there."

"Yeah. What did I tell you? Victorians! Huh!" he dismissed the state with one flick of his wrist.

Nash's grin came through. He hadn't thought he'd be able to smile again. "Thanks for all you did for me, brah," he exaggerated the word as he took the man's hand. "I'll see you round."

Nash moved on the seat, trying to ease the pain of his battered body.

"Hamlet Brae," the driver announced. "The next stop is Hamlet Brae."

The bus slowed. Nash pulled himself to his feet, grabbed the backpack of gifts and stomped down the steps. The driver already had the luggage compartment door open for Nash to indicate the bags he wanted. In moments, the bus moved off.

Nash winced as he donned his slouch hat and hooked the backpack onto his shoulder. He bent to grasp a bag in each hand, pausing as a car cruising towards town stopped in front of him.

"Brodo! You should have said you were coming! Get in," Tom invited. "You going out to the farm or down to the party?"

"I was going to the party. I'm worried now I'll scare the kids."

"Kids round these parts don't scare so easily. I'll come with you for moral support."

"Thanks, Tom. I'd appreciate it. I'm feeling unaccountably nervous."

"Well, you do look worse for wear. Not the shining hero who drove away from here having rescued our beloved Dee from a scheming assassin."

Nash grinned. "You know, Tom. You should get back into writing. You'd do well with fiction."

"Hah! I might do it someday boyo."

"You're looking better than I've seen you in years. Something happening?"

"Too early to say. I took a good long look in the mirror and it's time to set things right."

"I have no idea what you're talking about, mate. I can't think of a damned thing you've ever done wrong."

"Yeah, well. We all have a history, boyo, and sometimes it comes back to bite you on the bum. I can't fix it, but I can apologize."

"You've got me intrigued."

"Ah, don't you worry about it. It's a long-term goal. You'll know if I bring it off."

"Okay. If you need a hand with anything, just say so."

"Thanks. She'll be jake. Here we are."

Nash's legs shook like jelly. He'd never felt nerves like this, even wandering behind enemy lines in the desert. Here was his whole life laid out before him. If he got it wrong now, there was no way back. Dammit, he had no idea how to prepare for it. He couldn't write a strategic plan for this.

"Brodo! You okay?"

"Scared witless, mate."

"Yep. I know what it feels like. Best to face it head on. Let's go." Tom's words were such an echo of the 'face your demons' mantra of his early army training, he stiffened his spine in a conditioned response.

Hauling himself out of the car, he waited till the blood returned to his legs, used both hands to straighten his jacket, and finally turned to pick up his bags.

"I'll be right with this one, boyo. You go on ahead." Tom snatched the suitcase.

Nash flung the backpack onto his left shoulder, carrying the duffle in his right, squared his shoulders and kept his eyes fixed on the open doorway.

He stepped inside, sliding his duffle to one side of the door, vaguely aware of Tom rolling his suitcase in to join it. He dropped his hat onto the bags.

Nash stood in the archway, taking stock of what seemed like hordes of giggling, screaming boy and girl pirates, running frantically around a circle of chairs in the middle of the hall with a vast pirate ship along one wall. He recognized Caroline's artistry.

The music stopped, and the children scrambled to find a seat. Except one.

Brodie stood stock still, wearing an eye patch and a black Akubra turned up with a kilt pin and a long black feather. It looked like the same style of hat Nash had dropped on his duffle, the Australian Army slouch with the rising sun emblem as the pin. Brodie's gaze was trained firmly on the new arrival. He hurtled towards Nash.

"Captain! You came!" It seemed to Nash the world fell silent as he focused on the glowing face of his son. His. Son!

"You invited me."

"Mum said you had to go back to Canberra to sort stuff out. I didn't think you'd make it. It's my birthday today. I'm six. Jacob turns four tomorrow. Did you know that? That's why there are little kids and big kids here. You want to play musical chairs with us? It's cool. There's always one seat short so you have to race to make sure you don't miss out."

Nash crouched down to be at eye level with the child.

"I'm too big to sit on those chairs. I can watch while you play."

"No. I've missed out already cos I came over here. My best surprise is you're here. Thank you, Captain."

"Brodie," he hesitated and glanced across the room to where his Danielle Dawn was watching the reunion. His heart stopped. She looked so beautiful standing there with a host of emotions skipping across her features.

He turned back to his son. "Do you think you could stop calling me Captain, now?"

"What will I call you? I'm too little to call you Nash. Anna Nana would say it was rude."

"How about 'Dad'?"

The color drained from the boy's face. "You're my dad? Does Mum know? Does Mum know you're my dad?"

"Let's ask her," he recommended as Danielle's concerned face came into view.

"Mum," Brodie whispered as though speaking aloud would shatter the dream. "Is the captain really my dad?"

Danielle, too, came down to join the huddle close to the floor. "Yes, Brodie, he is. It took him a long time to work it out. He thought you belonged to someone else. Is it okay for him to be your dad?"

The boy's face bloomed brighter. "It's excellent! I got a dad for my birthday!"

Tears welled behind Nash's eyes. He cleared his throat. "Brodie, could you take care of this, please?" He passed over the backpack with a wince against the twinges in his shoulder. "There's a birthday present in there for you and for Jacob and a gift for Catherine and Ciaran. Think you can handle it?"

"Thank you, Capt... Dad!" Brodie threw his arms around his father's neck and kissed him hard on the cheek. "Wait till I tell Anna Nana!" He tore off across the room as fast as the heavy backpack would let him.

Nash and Danielle rose to their feet together.

"You're hurt. How did that happen?" One of her hands wavered in the air is though wanting to touch but wary of its reception. It fell to her side.

Nash shook his head. "Don't worry about it." He couldn't take his gaze from her face. Tears welled in his eyes again. He blinked them away.

"Everyone here thinks you're a hero for saving me from the wicked witch." Danielle cracked a smile.

"Does the hero win the princess?"

Danielle's smile faded. "Only in fairy tales, Nash," she whispered. "You were such a bastard. You'd not even waited till you'd evicted me before you brought in the surveyors."

"About that..." Nash scratched the side of his neck. "I can't make it up to you for the trash I've loaded onto you for the past seven years. It breaks my heart to think of it. You were my world, Danielle. *Are* my world. I realized this week the reason there has been no one serious in my life is because, although my head locked you out, my heart never could. I still love you, Danielle Dawn."

He felt her stare bore into his soul. "You were prepared to throw us into the street."

"No," he groaned. "The opposite! The surveyors were there to carve out a share of land around the house so I can put it into your name, whether or not you forgive me. I couldn't bear the thought of you not having somewhere to call home ever again. I want you to be safe. Whatever happens, the house and the land are yours."

"You had no trouble believing I was a cheat."

"I should have got on a bus and come home to sort it out. I was a coward. I couldn't bear to see you pregnant with another man's child. I couldn't." He closed his eyes.

"You called me a thief. You thought I'd steal from Anna?"

"No! It was an excuse, a God-given opportunity to keep you at arm's length. Every time I saw you, I wanted to hold you and never let you go. I called myself every kind of sick masochistic bastard to still want someone who treated me the way I thought you did. I would willingly have killed Michael the night he proposed."

"Hey!" Michael's indignation cut across Nash's explanation. Nash flicked an apologetic glance at his cousin and realized all the adults' attention was on the duo.

He lowered his voice. "Can we go out back?"

Taking her hand, he led her to the steps outside the open double doors. Danielle sat on the top step and Nash one tread lower. Reaching out he tore a stalk of grass from the clump beside him and ran it through his fingers. It gave him something to focus on and avoid the condemnation in Danielle's eyes.

"I've been an absolute mongrel to you since I've been back. I know it."

"Not to mention the last seven years..."

"That too. It was a defense mechanism. I should have come home years ago, but you were here. Having you near and seeing you loving someone else? I couldn't do it. I hatched the plan to send you away. You couldn't have felt worse than I did."

"Right. I take that as an apology for the last seven years? Thank you. Apology accepted." Danielle propelled herself to her feet.

Nash grasped her hand, staying her retreat and tugged her back down. He stared into her sunburnt face.

"Let me explain. I had plenty of time on the bus to work out where I went AWOL with you. When I went into the army, it was tough leaving here, but I had you behind me and you to come home to. Then when the shit hit the fan and I got the message you wanted nothing to do with me until you discovered you were pregnant with someone else's baby, I totally lost it." He lowered his head to hide the quick spurt of tears in his eyes.

Clearing his throat, he went on. "You go into the military understanding their job is to break you down and rebuild you into the person they want and need you to be. They didn't have to break me down. What I thought was your betrayal did that. I couldn't function." He tossed aside the piece of grass he'd crumpled in his spare hand.

"Ironically, the ones who orchestrated my downfall, were the ones who held me together. I was numb. Over time, I pulled out of it but I couldn't bear your name to be mentioned. It destroyed me all over again, every damn time."

"And what about me, Nash?" She snatched her hand from his and hugged her arms around her body. "Pregnant. With no one to turn to except your family. I became another stupid teenage pregnancy statistic. How do you think I felt, knowing you'd thrown me over because the army had a stronger pull? You'd had your fun and then you were free to do whatever the hell you wanted. My plans to become a teacher and make something of myself were all gone to dust. There was no career for me to look forward to—just the same damned poverty cycle my parents had. Then I had our son to consider."

Nash dragged a hand through his hair. "I don't know how you did it, Danielle. I really don't. I've thought about it a lot and it makes me sick to my stomach I was the one to leave you high and dry. I'll probably never be able to make it up to you."

He took her hands in his. "All I can say now is, I love you, Danielle. I want to go back to where we were seven years ago. I want to see if we can work it out. It'll take a lot of work from me, you don't have to tell me."

Standing, he pulled her to her feet one step above him. "This is your time, Danielle Dawn. You can make or break me. You can have your revenge. You can walk away. You can abandon me the way I abandoned you and Brodie. I hope you won't. Can we try again? Can we see if we can still be the team we used to plan?"

"I waited for you for so long, Nash. You never came."

"I'm here now and I'll never leave again, I swear. Please, please, forgive my stupidity for listening to others ahead of you. From this moment on, I will listen to you always—first, last and every moment in between—if you will give me one chance. Can you ever love me again?"

"I never stopped loving you, Nash. It wasn't a safe space to be, so I've hidden it away. I don't know if I can bring it out into the light again." Her face looked so sad.

"Let me help you, please," he begged.

He pulled a small box from his breast pocket.

"Danielle Dawn, please forgive me. Please, please love me enough to try again. If you're prepared to give it a go, accept this ring and wear it on your right hand until you're ready to change it over. It's a let's-see-how-we-go ring. I want it to be more, and maybe it can be when the mending is done."

She glanced over her shoulder through the open doorway. "Everybody's watching!"

Her gaze scanned his face, the minute movements focusing on one of his eyes and then the other.

"Yep. Make or break time, Danielle Dawn."

He waited.

She put a hand to his battered face.

He felt his heart cracking further apart the longer he waited for her answer.

Finally, she nodded.

Her smile was tentative, his was not.

He slid the ring from the box and onto her right hand.

"Let's see how it goes," Danielle agreed.

Danielle's face streamed with tears. Nash hauled her into his arms. "I love you Danielle Dawn," he whispered into her hair. "Now and forever."

He pulled back to tuck an errant strand of hair behind her ear and lowered his mouth to hers in full view of their family, friends and their precious son.